I0777314

Published by: Cinnabar Moth Publishing LLC
Santa Fe, New Mexico

Cover Design by: Ira Geneve

ISBN-13: 978-1-962308-06-9

Library of Congress Control Number: 2023949907

Latency

NATHANIEL KOSZER

Chapter 1

In the basement of a skyscraper hundreds of stories high, a constant shaking and groaning accompanied the cacophony of breaking glass and falling bricks from the street above. A man and a woman had spent the night here, fearing those sounds meant their building was on the verge of collapse. Finally, the sun rose and the sounds gave way to stillness. The death of the noises gave life to new fears, in that now the man and woman had to take action.

"Are there any sort of supplies on the cycles?" the man asked. He was bleary-eyed, his face was flush, and even the simple task of standing up seemed to be a struggle.

"I doubt it," the woman replied, her expression as beleaguered as his. "And you're sure there was nothing in these boxes?" she continued, glancing around the small storage room.

The man shook his head. "Just lots of cleaning supplies. And we can't risk going back upstairs," he replied. "I can't even hear the big one lumbering around, that has to mean they're searching another building. We need to move now. We'll worry about supplies after we get out of New Orleans, and after it feels safe."

The woman nodded and walked over to one smaller pile of

boxes. She pulled them away and the room lit up in an orange glow. The boxes had been covering a young girl, no more than six years old, whose skin had trails of orange light swirling across her arms, legs, and face.

"We need to leave, sweetie. We're going to find our cycles in the garage, Ok?"

The little girl nodded.

"Do you remember that woman? Alison?" she asked the girl. "Do you remember where she and her friends live?"

The little girl nodded slowly, while the man's face furrowed with skepticism.

"If anything happens to us, you go straight to her. Do you understand?"

"She can't go to them!" the man exclaimed in an elevated whisper. "They're a bunch of fanatics!"

"They are, but they will keep her safe!" the woman responded.

Tears welled up in the man's eye as he nodded in agreement. The three of them left the storage room and walked down to the end of the hall. They swung open the heavy metal door that connected the hallway to the building's garage. On the other side of the structure, the man and woman could see that the garage's front door had been completely torn off and thrown into the street. Most of the vehicles were huge electric motorcycles, and many of them were in pieces. The man and woman found two that looked functional in the corner closest to the hole where the front door used to be. The woman straddled one cycle and the man sat the little girl behind her. He then walked over to the other cycle, threw his leg over, and sat down. They grabbed the handlebars at the same time, and the instant their palms made contact with the grips, the engines revved to life and they shot out of the garage.

They were on the road for about ten seconds before a dark shadow briefly covered them and passed over. Two-hundred feet down the street, a metallic grey humanoid figure descended out of the sky and landed with enough force to form snaking cracks around its feet. Even further away, the side of a building erupted outwards, and a far larger and bulkier figure covered in heavy grey armor barreled out to join its comrade. This new giant was flanked closely by a much smaller and skinnier bipedal robotic figure.

"Fly, Sera! Now!" the woman yelled as the lead figure raised its machine-gun-equipped arms and took aim at the cycles. Upon hearing the scream of her name, Sera was no longer seated on the back of the cycle, but was instead flying upwards as if some invisible jet engine had turned on. She was terrified, but remembered what she had to do. She turned to fly away as fast as she could, towards the outskirts of New Orleans, just as the machine guns opened fire on her parents.

Chapter 2

For the first time in what seemed like an eternity, a cool breeze swept through the streets of downtown New Orleans. Entering out onto these streets from the main doors of a small building was a man in a blue military uniform. By this time of the day, a little more than an hour before sunset, most soldiers would have been at least slightly disheveled. Having worked a full day, they would have a sweat stain, some hair out of place, maybe an untucked shirt or two. Not this man. Perfectly laced and polished boots led to pants that somehow seemed freshly pressed, which led to a fully zipped-up tunic with various patches across the breast. The whole ensemble framed up a six-foot-tall athletic build, and perched on top was a clean-shaven, blemish-free face and perfectly slicked-back hair.

As the man took a few steps from the door, he felt a vibration in his inner pocket and unzipped his coat to reach inside. He pulled out a military issue mobile that projected the word "Can" into the air. He slid a small earbud out of the top of the mobile and stuck it in his ear while slipping the mobile back into his pocket.

"Investigator," a cold, deep, mechanical voice said through the earbud.

"What do you need, Can?" the investigator asked.

"What are your coordinates?" Can replied.

"I just left headquarters," he said.

"You are required to update me on the progress of the investigation prior to you exiting the facility."

"You were not at the facility, how am I supposed to update you if… wait, are you serious?"

The investigators initial thought was interrupted by the sight of a humanoid shape flying high above the city and stopping directly above him.

"Androids are always serious," Can said.

"You sent Russ to confirm my location?" the investigator asked. "Are you going to send Tank barreling through a building next to provide backup? Don't you all have better things to do?"

"You should have waited for me to return before exiting the facility," Can replied, ignoring the investigator's questions.

"For all I knew, that could have been days from now! I am not just going to sit around waiting for you!"

"You will do exactly that. If you disobey an order again, I will have Russ follow proper protocols for insubordination."

The investigator stopped walking. He knew what that threat really meant.

"Ok, Can, I guess it's long overdue that we had this conversation. I am here because you fucked up. I'm here because you let some person or people steal from right under your nose multiple times, and they didn't even do it quietly. You have holes in the sides and roofs of your buildings and all sorts of equipment gone. And most importantly, I'm here because despite you being the most advanced AI in the world, unrivaled by any human, you can't figure out who did this or how to stop them. You, the mighty android, asked for help for the first time, and I answered your call. You need me to succeed, because if I fail and Spidre gets word of these thefts, and you know he will, that will be the end of your free rein in this city. So stop being a prick, do not threaten to kill me, and if you aren't around when I am leaving for the day, I will update you via mobile instead."

The investigator started walking again. Can stayed silent for only a moment, but it was a moment longer than usual.

"Androids cannot be pricks. A daily update through your mobile is acceptable. Your assessment of the current situation is correct. However, if your investigation is not a success, and is not a success soon, then Spidre may become aware of the situation regardless. That would be unfortunate for us, and for you."

"Still threatening to kill me," the investigator replied. "And it's a threat that isn't needed at that. I'll get your guy. I spent today looking through more records of supplies that went missing during transport."

"I have already looked through those. It is a waste of time," Can replied.

"You have already looked through everything, you're an android. I'm here because you missed something. How or why, I don't know, but I intend to find it."

"Find it soon. I will consider this your update for today. We will discuss again tomorrow, investigator."

The investigator ripped the earbud out and jammed it into the mobile so hard he thought the pocket might rip.

God, I hate that thing! the investigator thought to himself as Russ slowly flew out of sight.

But he's right. If I don't close this investigation soon then everything will be lost. I have one more night, maybe two at most before they start thinking that I'm delaying the investigation purposefully. The investigator arrived at the megaskyscraper he and the rest of the military called home, along with hundreds of thousands of other people in the smaller apartments below the top floor. He stepped inside and into an empty elevator waiting in the lobby.

"303," he said aloud. The doors of the elevator shut and a few seconds later he was on the top floor. He walked down the long hall to his apartment, stepped inside, and sprang into action. He went to the window to check for Russ, and not seeing it, he closed the blinds. He stripped down to his boxers and carefully hung his military uniform up on a hanger, then put the hanger on a post on the backside of his closet door. He opened a drawer at the bottom of the same closet and pulled out an old but well-kept t-shirt and jeans. Next to his bed were a second pair of boots that he slid on. Lastly, he pulled out the drawer of his nightstand, reached into the back, and pulled out a small box with a second, slightly larger earbud inside. He put that one in his ear, placed the mobile on his nightstand, and heard the earbud say "receiver connected."

After one last peek through the blinds, the investigator went back to the elevator and back out of the building. He walked in the opposite direction of headquarters, away from downtown and away from the inhabited area of the city. The massive glass buildings gave way to the crumbled stone and rusting steel of structures long abandoned.

He walked in this way for another forty minutes, into an area that centuries earlier had been used for industry. Tall fences and warehouses dotted the area, all in various states of disrepair. One building among them looked quite a bit newer than the rest, but still very much not in use. It was this building that the investigator set his sights on. He approached the fence that surrounded the building and put his hands on a sign that read "Property of UN Peacekeeping forces. No Trespassing."With the slightest effort, the investigator pulled the sign down and took a section of the rusty fence with it. He stepped through the hole and found a busted-out window big enough to squeeze through. Inside was a multilevel warehouse filled with all sorts of old machinery. A metal staircase was in the corner, and the investigator climbed it until he reached the roof access door, which he opened and stepped through. He looked out towards the west. The sun was just starting to set. Despite the distractions provided by Can and Russ, he had made it in time.

"Please be the right spot," the investigator thought to himself. "And please be the right night."Less than five minutes later, the investigator heard a new sound. It was similar to a gust of wind, but the air was still only filled with the cool breeze he had felt all afternoon. He peered over the roof's edge and down the street, where he saw an orange glow hurdling down the roadway at incredible speed. The glow was nearly the same color as the sunset. Had the investigator been lower down and observing the glow against the sky, he might not have been able to make it out. But against the cracked black street, it could not be clearer.

In mere moments, the glow was at the fence line of the building. It shot up in the air and started to approach the roof but stopped dead at the sight of the investigator. Only then did the investigator see that the orange glow was a person, a woman about a foot shorter than him, wearing a dark-colored sleeveless kung fu uniform. Her hair was cut very short. The orange glow swirled and twisted across her otherwise dark skin, constantly moving and changing shape all over her face and extremities.

"Holy shit!" they both exclaimed at the same time.

The woman turned and flew away just as swiftly as she had approached.

"Wait!" the investigator yelled, but it was too late. She'd already made up her mind to flee.

The investigator sighed and took a quick look around. No one in sight. No androids, no people, just him and this glowing woman. He crouched and jumped in the air. As he did so, the boots on his feet evaporated, replaced by a clear blue aura coming out of his toes. He took off flying, just like the woman did, except he was just a touch faster. Gradually, she came back into view, seemingly oblivious to the fact that another person was flying directly behind her. He descended about two feet, turned over so he was facing away from the street, and boosted his speed even more to put himself directly into her view.

"I think we should talk," he said with a smile.

The woman responded with a blood-curdling scream. Startled, the investigator instinctually descended even further and put some distance between him and the woman. It was a good thing he did so, because as her scream began, the swirls of light in her skin moved faster and faster and became brighter and brighter until a burst of energy exploded outwards from her body. The shockwave roared through the streets, rattled the nearby buildings, and threw the investigator down towards the roadway. He landed hard but refused to take his eyes off of the woman, who was now falling out of the sky about fifty feet from him. When she crashed down, the investigator forced himself to his feet and ran barefoot to her landing site. As the dust cleared, the woman, now no longer glowing, rolled over and leapt to her feet at the sight of the investigator approaching. The investigator noticed her wince as she landed, an ankle injury from the hard landing, he suspected.

"You're hurt," he said.

"Back the fuck up or I will teach you what hurt means!" she

responded, bringing fists up in front of her face.

The investigator stopped and put his hands up.

"I promise, I'm not a threat. Far from it. My name is Naren. I'm a LO-EC, just like you."

At the mention of the word "LO-EC," the woman softened. Her fighting stance became less rigid. They stood there for several seconds, looking each other up and down. While they studied one another, the glow in the woman's skin returned. The woman eventually gazed at Naren's feet. His toes were spread out in an odd manner, and in between several of them on either foot were ragged, metallic circles with black holes at the center. She dropped her fighting stance, turned so her right side was facing Naren, and pulled back the cloth on her right shoulder, revealing her own, much larger metallic circle with a hole in the middle.

"I'm Sera," she responded as her eyes filled with tears.

Chapter 3

"You're not from here," Sera said as they continued to stand in the roadway. "If you were, my followers would have known about you."

"Followers?" Naren asked.

"Long story," Sera replied.

"Well you're right in any event. I transferred from Los Angeles about two weeks ago," Naren said.

"Transferred?" Sera asked.

"Long story," Naren said back with a smirk. Sera smiled.

"We should go somewhere else. Whatever you just did to make that explosion, it made a lot of noise," Naren said.

"I think I know a spot. Can you still fly?" Sera asked.

"Yes. Can you? Naren said while looking at Sera's ankle.

"I can manage. I've had worse," Sera responded.

"I can only imagine. I'll follow you," Naren said.

The two of them took off into the air and headed North for another forty minutes. By that point, there weren't even abandoned buildings anymore, just an endless barren wasteland where farmland once was. Then in the middle of that nothingness, a giant crater appeared over the horizon. As they got closer, Naren noticed that the crater was full of even smaller craters, as if multiple explosions had taken out chunks of the land one by one.

"You… you did this? With those explosions of energy? Why?" Naren asked, looking around as they landed.

"I call them my blasts, 'explosions of energy' is a mouthful," Sera responded with a chuckle. "But I have to do this. At least twice a day, sometimes three. If I don't, the energy builds up too much and it starts to hurt."

"Hurt?!" Naren was shocked.

"Yeah. It feels like my insides are burning," Sera answered with a grimace.

"Holy hell…" Naren said, looking around again before training his eyes back on Sera.

"How uhh, how do your clothes stay on?" Naren glanced away as he asked.

"These uniforms are made of a high-quality silk. It's light enough that most of the energy passes right through it, but sturdy enough that it can take the remaining hit. But it doesn't last forever, three or four uses at most. Usually when I let out a blast, I disrobe first."

Naren looked around again.

"What did you mean earlier? When you said you transferred here?" Sera asked.

Naren took a deep breath and turned to face her again.

"You aren't going to like my answer," Naren replied.

"You're military," Sera said.

"I am. Special investigator," Naren replied.

The two of them stayed silent for several moments. His admission created palpable tension.

"You're going to need to explain before we go any further. Don't hide anything." Sera said.

"Okay. Well first things first," Naren replied as he took the earbud out of his ear and threw it to Sera.

"That is the only piece of technology I have on me. It's a long-range receiver that I connected to my military issue mobile in case they call. The mobile, I leave at home so they can't track my whereabouts. If you feel the need to crush that for your own safety, do it," Naren said.

Sera thought for a moment.

"I'll hold onto it for now, but the fact that you were upfront about it definitely helps your cause," Sera said.

"Good, I need all the help I can get," Naren replied, getting another smile out of Sera.

"The basics of the story aren't so complicated. I was able to alter my father's old military ID, and thanks to it and LA's horrible record-keeping, I was able to be hired as an investigator there. I took the investigator position in Los Angeles to find more of us and more about who we are. When the androids put out a memo asking for help with an investigation, I read the details of the thefts and assumed a LO-EC had to be behind it, so I jumped at the opportunity."

Sera noticeably winced at the mention of the androids.

"So that's it? You came here to find me?" Sera asked.

"Well, not you specifically. If I knew I would find someone as incredible as you, I would've come sooner," Naren said, feeling the blood rush to his face as he uttered the words. Sera felt the same sensation.

"That was cheesy. But it gets you back this," Sera said as she tossed the receiver back to Naren.

"I appreciate it. It was kind of expensive," Naren said.

"I figured out what you would steal next after looking through the records of transport goods that went missing over the years," he continued. "The androids must have missed it, because it was all labeled as lost due to faulty equipment rather than as theft."

Sera winced again.

"Are you ok?" Naren asked this time.

"I… have a history with them," Sera said, her voice more hushed.

"Then I won't mention them again unless I absolutely have to. I guess whoever wrote up the stuff you stole over the years couldn't imagine someone ripping a transport door open while the thing was moving, so they just assumed it was a faulty lock and that the food and seeds simply fell out of the back. Combine the seed theft with the lights, wiring, and battery that you took, and you could only be making a hydroponic garden. Which means the only thing left to steal was equipment to dig a well, which is only stored in the warehouse where we met tonight."

"And you never told… them… that you discovered these thefts?" Sera asked.

"No. But I think if I don't get them something soon, they will start getting suspicious." Naren replied.

"I'm impressed. You figured almost everything out exactly correct and still somehow managed to hide it all," Sera said.

"Wait, almost everything?" Naren asked.

"The only thing I have ever stolen from a transport is the seeds, nothing else." Sera said with a smirk on her face. Naren was perplexed.

"You haven't been stealing UN food supplies for the last 20 years?" he asked.

"20 years?!" Sera exclaimed. "I'm only 26!"

Naren stayed silent for a few more moments.

"And you're sure there are no other LO-ECs in New Orleans?"

"Positive. My followers would have known about them and

probably tried to bring them in."

Naren began looking around, eventually setting his gaze off to the west.

"There is another one of us out there somewhere," he finally said.

"What?!" Sera responded.

"They're fast, too, at least as fast as you and me. Or maybe they can also fly."

"Couldn't it just actually be the transport doors malfunctioning?" Sera asked.

Naren shook his head. "If it were a malfunction, it would happen on all types of transports, not just ones carrying food."

They fell into silence again, and Sera looked in the same direction as Naren.

"There is so much open area between all the major cities. We're never going to find them," Sera said.

"It would take months, years even. I can't take that much time away from work, and I assume you have a lot of work to do with the garden."

Sera nodded.

"We'll think of another way," Naren said. Sera nodded again as she took a seat in the middle of the crater, still facing west. Naren sat down beside her.

"Can you tell me more about your followers?" Naren asked.

"Oh, sure," Sera replied. "Well, the quick and dirty version is that they consider me like a messiah, or a god having come back to earth. Because of that, they have cared for me since I was little. I wanted to use my power to finally help them, and some of them are amazing scientists and engineers, so together we designed a hydroponic system that I can power." Sera pointed at the metallic circle on her shoulder as she finished talking.

Naren understood the story, and also the sub-story hidden underneath. There could only be one reason why she hated mention of the androids, and why someone other than her parents would have cared for her since she was little.

"I have another question, but it may be a difficult one for you to answer," Naren said.

Sera clenched her jaw, took a sharp inhale through her nose and nodded.

"You're the most powerful person I've ever met, probably the strongest person on this planet. And I gather you have a great deal of motivation to destroy… them… for good. Why haven't you?"

Sera curled her legs up into her chest and laid her forehead on her knees.

"Because I can't," she replied.

"You're telling me an explosion like these is not enough to take them down?" Naren asked, looking around at the earth carved out around him.

"Yes, that is what I am telling you!" Sera exploded. "I could blow up Can but not before it gave an order to Russ to fucking eviscerate me! And if I went for Russ first, I could probably take it down, but then I'd be powerless while Tank crushed me or tore me in half! And no matter how much energy I save up, my explosion would not be enough to take down Tank. It's too big and its armor is too thick. To do any damage, I'd have to somehow get inside of it and explode it outwards, but how the fuck could I do that?! And even if I somehow did, then I'd be powerless with Russ still fully functional and ready to riddle me with holes! I have thought about this nonstop for twenty fucking years! If there was a way for me to take them down, they'd be fucking gone!"

Sera started sobbing. Tears started to well up in Naren's eyes as well.

"I'm sorry," Naren said.

"It's ok," Sera said after a few sniffles.

"What else could destroy Tank?" Naren asked.

Sera sniffled again, wiped her face with the back of her hand, and looked at Naren.

"What?" she asked.

"The two biggest problems are Tank's durability and the fact that all three of the androids never stray far from each other. But I'd be willing to bet there are specific situations where they are forced to separate from one another. And Tank is tough, but it has to have limits. You said that you could explode Tank if you got inside it. What else could do enough damage?" Naren asked.

"I guess if a building fell on it or something with that kind of force hit it, it might work," Sera responded. "Or if it got dropped from a high enough place."

"Could you lift Tank on your own? Could you and I do it together?" Naren asked.

"Maybe together, but we'd never get a chance. Russ would shoot us dead, and even if it was somehow already dealt with, Tank has huge electric blades on each forearm. I can't break those, and I don't think you can either."

Naren smiled.

"You're right, I doubt I can break his blades. But I know somebody who could."

Sera raised an eyebrow.

"I have a twin sister," Naren said.

Chapter 4

"The trap looks fully set up," Naren said aloud.

"Affirmative, the strategy we have is sound," Can responded. Naren tensed his jaw to keep from smirking. Can seemed to have no idea that the trap Naren referenced was not the one set for Sera.

The two of them stood on the street outside of the building where Naren had met Sera two days earlier. Can's wiry metal frame stood about as tall as Naren, but it did not have a head. Instead, it had about a dozen red sensory inputs forming a circle around where a neck would normally be. At the end of its right arm was a small laser cannon that popped out just above its hand. Currently, Can's sensory inputs were trained on the roof. Up there were four peacekeepers, soldiers in sky-blue armor, each facing a cardinal direction and pointing one laser-cannon-clad arm in from of them. Meanwhile, Naren's sights were trained on Tank, who was standing further down the street at the opposite end of the building. Tank had the same headless feature and sensory input layout as Can, but that was all they had in common. Tank's forearms were giant blades that ended in hands instead of a blade tip, and they were glowing white hot and sparking from electricity flowing through them. Its eight-foot tall, heavily armored frame was facing towards the building and awaiting its next voiceless remote command from Can. Finally, high above the building was Russ, a tiny grey dot against the cloudless sky.

After a few minutes of silence, Naren noticed that the orange glow of sunset had come, and his heart began to pound. Every second that passed seemed like an eternity. Finally, the silence was broken by machine-gun fire coming from far overhead.

"The target is here," Can said at the exact moment Russ's machine guns came to life. The peacekeepers on the roof scrambled to the northern edge and fired their laser cannons indiscriminately down the street. Tank turned to face the same direction and threw its right arm out to the side, ready to strike if it found the opportunity. Between Tank's arm and body, Naren got his first glimpse that day of Sera's orange glow barreling towards all of them.

Sera had only one thought in her head: "Keep pushing! Stay ahead of the machine-gun fire!" The laser blasts were easy enough to dodge. The soldiers were slow to fire and slow to adjust. They had never encountered anything as fast as her before. That didn't matter to Russ, though. With the androids' shared ability to remotely communicate, and Can making constant adjustments and recalculations, it took all Sera could muster to stay ahead of Russ's bullets. She was heading straight for Tank, and in a few moments was right on top of it. Tank brought its arm around for a mighty swing, but Sera angled up and towards the building, her feet just clearing Tank's arm. Her new position put the building between her and Russ's machine gun, and her new trajectory put her on a collision course with the wall directly under the peacekeepers. She curled her hands into fist and slammed into the wall at speed. The wall disintegrated, and the roof supporting the soldiers began to collapse. As the soldiers fell in front of her, she grabbed one of them out of the air with her left arm and as he screamed. She glanced towards the building's south side. The well-drilling equipment was exactly where she and Naren had left it, on the top floor near the southern wall. She flew towards it. As she did so, a terrifying rumble echoed from below as Tank plowed into the building with the intent of bringing it down on top of her. As the rest of the roof, floors, and walls sank around her, Sera scooped the equipment up. slung it over her right shoulder, and barreled through the collapsing southern wall. The impact either killed the soldier in her grasp or knocked him unconscious. Either way, he stopped screaming. As she exited the building, she looked to the left and saw Naren for the first time, with Can standing right next to him and aiming its laser cannon up at her. She threw the lifeless soldier at Can as its laser let loose, and the shot burned into the soldier instead of the intended target. The body continued towards Can and after a few more unsuccessful laser shots, Can was forced to step out of the way as the body approached its legs. Sera continued flying south. Even with the equipment on her shoulder, she was able to steadily increase the gap between her and Russ as it pursued her. After another five minutes or so of occasionally dodging machine-gun fire, Russ reached the edge of its communication range with Can and was forced to give it up. A smile beamed across Sera's face as she looked back at Russ turning away from her and flying in the opposite direction.

"Yes!" she screamed out loud. The smile didn't leave her face for the rest of her flight. After continuing south for a couple more minutes to be sure she wasn't followed, Sera turned towards the northeast and flew for another fifteen minutes before landing outside of a row of short buildings that appeared long-abandoned from the outside. She strolled inside of one and went down to a basement door. She opened it and entered a room that seemed to stretch the entire length of the building complex above. Rows of lights hung down from the ceiling, and large boxes of supplies lined the walls, along with a grey battery that was about the same size as the boxes. In the center of the room, about fifty people were sat together in a loose circle and quietly chanting in harmony. When Sera walked in, an older woman in the center stopped and stood up. The rest of the group followed suit.

"I did it, Alison!" Sera cried as tears streamed down her face.

"You must be exhausted!" Alison yelled back. She then directed some in the group to bring Sera food and others to unload the equipment Sera was carrying. As Sera sat on the floor to eat, a group of people began assembling the drilling equipment.

"The plan worked?" Alison asked.

"Flawlessly," Sera replied. "Every move I made, every prediction Naren had. It was all spot on."

"Good, I'm glad we can trust him," Alison replied. Sera raised an eyebrow.

"You are a terrible liar. You still don't trust him? Even after this?" Sera asked.

Alison pressed her lips together a drew a breath through her nose.

"I don't think he's working with 'them'. But…" Alison replied. Sera glared in response.

"…I just don't understand why you had to risk getting caught. Why couldn't he have just kept his mouth shut and let you…"

"Because then he would have died, Alison!" Sera snapped. "If I had just gone back and stolen what I needed, they would have said Naren failed to do his job and would have killed him the second they found out! The only way for all of us to get through this was for him to tell them everything and be right, and then for them to still fail to catch me. Hell, even with doing all this, I wouldn't be surprised if they still kill him just for good measure!"

They sat in silence for a while as Sera tore into her food. Finally, Alison broke the silence.

"So what happens now?" Alison asked.

"Now, Naren convinces them that the investigation should end. That the thefts will stop now that I have everything I need, that trying to catch me or find me will be impossible, and that they're better off closing the investigation to avoid further attention from Spidre. If that works, he'll come here when the investigation is closed for certain. He suspects that will be in about two weeks. If he doesn't show up, then either they are continuing the investigation or…" Sera trailed off as she neared the end of sentence. Alison understood the missing piece.

"You care a lot about this man, don't you?" Alison asked.

"He figured out this whole plan less than forty-eight hours after meeting me. If anyone can figure out how I can destroy the androids for good, it's him," Sera replied.

"Is that the only reason you want him around?" Alison asked with a smirk creeping into her face. Sera began to smile back but then turned her head down towards the ground.

"Let's see if he returns. Then I'll let you know if there is more to it," Sera responded.

The day after the conversation with Alison, Sera went to her crater to let off a blast, and when she returned, she went to the roof of the building hoping to see the blue aura of Naren's feet on the horizon. She felt disappointed when he didn't show, but then immediately felt silly for feeling that way. One day was nowhere near enough time to close an android-led investigation. Still, every day after that, she continued the same pattern, and every day felt more and more worried when Naren didn't show. On day fourteen, Naren still didn't show, and Sera sobbed while Alison held her close. Bleary-eyed and exhausted the next day, she returned to her spot on the roof and had to rub her eyes several times before believing what she saw, a blue aura heading towards her just under the roof line of the buildings.

Naren landed, and the bags under his eyes showed he had been going through a similar struggle. He had known Sera survived the heist but had had no idea what happened to her after that.

"I'm sorry I took so long. I…" Naren began to speak but was cut off when Sera rushed towards him, wrapped her arms around him, and planted her lips firmly on his. He draped his arms around her shoulders and pulled her in even closer. They stayed in this embrace for over a minute, neither wanting this moment to end.

"Is it stupid of me to say that I think I love you?" Naren asked.

"Yes, it is," Sera replied. "I love you, too," she continued with a coy smile. Naren smiled back.

"So, what now?" Sera asked.

"Well, I have good news. I found a procedure that separates Tank from the rest of the androids. It's risky, but I think it's our best shot."

Sera's heart jumped.

"What do we have to do?" Sera asked

"You have to get captured," Naren replied. Sera initially went wide eyed but then slowly figured out what Naren must mean.

"And we'll have to find a way to get my sister here that doesn't attract Can's attention. So I can't send money to her or purchase a ticket on the TCT or anything like that, but I can send a message through the underground net access when the right opportunity arises," Naren continued.

"How long do you think that will be?" Sera asked.

"I don't know," Naren replied. "But when the time comes, we will be ready."

27

Chapter 5

It was only the end of April, yet the mid-day sun was making the streets of Los Angeles swelter. Through the heat and humidity rose another uncommon occurrence, a commotion out at the old Dodger Stadium. A crowd of people were filing in at both of the entrances. Among those at the east entrance was a woman who stood about 5'7". Her outfit was meant to make her look as intimidating as possible, and it was working. A sports bra and baggy khaki pants framed a perfect set of six-pack abs and showed off arms and shoulders chiseled out of marble. Her feet bore a heavy pair of black boots, and her hands were wrapped in white cloth. It was that cloth that drew the majority of her attention at the moment. She wanted to make certain they would not unwrap during the upcoming fights. The last thing she needed was for her secret to be revealed in front of the whole Los Angeles battalion.

She followed the flow of the crowd through the threshold and inside. She was taken aback—the stadium's state of disrepair was even worse on the inside. It was a stark contrast to the 300-story apartment buildings surrounding the area, with their all-black, all-glass, 25th-century facades. As the woman descended further into the bowels of the stadium, the crowd around her formed into several single-file lines. In front of her stood a man who looked to be at least 70 years old and was having some trouble walking.

This guy is entering a fighting tournament? she thought. *No, he must be in the wrong place.* The old man got to the front of a line and was indeed, not where he intended to be.

"The entrance to the market is on the other side of the stadium, sir," a skinny man sitting behind a table said. "You need to go out the way you came and go in the west entrance."

The woman heard their interaction and scowled. The last thing she needed were little things like this slowing her down. The older man walked away from the table, and she stepped up.

"Do you have ID, miss?" the skinny man asked.

"No," the woman replied bluntly. Her abrasiveness made the skinny man jump.

"Ok uhh, name?" he blurted out.

"Nadine," she replied.

"Age?"

"Twenty-six."

"Any disabilities or medical complications that would cause you excess risk of serious injury or death while fighting in the tournament?"

"Who cares?"

"It's uhh, a lot of paperwork if someone dies at one of these things," the man's voice cracked as he replied.

"Ah. No, no medical issues."

"Stand still for a moment," the skinny man said as he fumbled with a tiny military issued mobile and snapped a photo.

"Okay. You're in the fourth free-for-all round. Listen to the ring announcer for further instruction," he said as he held out an orange piece of paper with a big number "4" on it. Nadine took it and moved to where the rest of the crowd was. Her new waiting area was on the steps between two sections of seating. The seats themselves were filled entirely with soldiers, all dressed head to toe in sky-blue armor. All with the exception of one. A man in the front row, undoubtedly the largest man Nadine had ever seen, was wearing bright red armor. The armor plates on his forearms looked off, almost like they were bloated. Nadine had never seen the man in person before but knew exactly who he was. She also knew that despite her fighting skills, he was a man best avoided.

God damnit I hate this, she thought to herself. *Spend my whole life avoiding these assholes and now I'm right in the thick of it. I knew that whenever he made contact again it would be madness. I didn't know it would be this. Naren, what the hell have you gotten yourself into?*As Nadine pondered the events since Naren's message two days ago, and anxiously thought about the events she suspected might be coming, more tournament entrants filed in behind her. Eventually, enough had congregated that the entire row was filled, as was the area behind the seating where concessions used to be. As the line at the registration tables dwindled, Nadine grew impatient.

How long are they going to let people keep coming in!? she thought as a man ran up to the table in a t-shirt and black jeans. She normally wouldn't have even taken note of his appearance, except for the fact that he was wearing a pair of fingerless gloves. She had tried to find a pair all over the city, to no avail. When it was time for the new guy's picture to be taken, he tensed up a noticeable amount.

"Huh. Looks like I'm not the only one hiding something today," she thought. Despite the man's reaction, he was let through and disappeared among the crowd. A few minutes later, the workers at the registration table stepped away, and a soldier ran onto the field.

"My fellow peacekeepers! It is with great pleasure that I announce the start of the first round of Captain Byron's farewell tournament!"

Raucous applause filled the stands in response. Byron himself cheered and pumped his right fist, the red, bloated armor on his forearm gleaming in the sun.

"Yes, my friends! As you know, our beloved captain is leaving us, moving on to bigger and better things, commanding the notorious Brooklyn Battalion. As a token of his appreciation for our service, he has organized this tournament for our entertainment. And earlier this week, all the possessions that won't be accompanying him to New York were sold at auction as prize money to attract the best fighters!"

Another round of cheering ensued.

"There will be four free-for-all rounds! The winners of those will face each other one on one! Competitors get eliminated by ringout or knockout only! Gotta keep it civilized right?!"

The crowd booed.

"Will the fighters assigned to the first free-for-all round please enter the arena!"

Several people shuffled past Nadine and hopped the fence onto the field. The arena looked similar to a boxing ring, only about three times the size. The floor was unelevated and made of hard rubber padding. Three uncolored ropes marked the edge. About 100 feet past them was another set of ropes that stretched across the ballpark's outfield. On the other side of those was the market the old man had intended to go to. Several people were lined up against the outfield ropes, hoping to get a good look at the action.

The first round passed by with Nadine only somewhat paying attention. At the end of it, the announcer ran over from the registration table and declared the winner's name to be William. He seemed to be young and in shape. Despite that, he was leaning on his knees, gasping for breath, and sweating profusely. Nadine was not surprised. There was no roof on the stadium. Fighting under a sun this hot was a brutal trial for any normal person. It almost made Nadine glad she wasn't normal.

The second round looked to be passing just as uneventfully, until Nadine saw a flash of sky blue among the mass of fighters.

"What the hell?" she thought.

As more fighters fell to the mat or out of the ring, the view became clearer. He didn't have a gun or a helmet, but there was, in fact, a lone soldier fighting in armor amongst the other competitors. The entrants in the waiting area noticed him, and a sense of uneasiness spread throughout.

"Not a complication I needed right now," Nadine muttered to herself through gritted teeth.

The round ended and the soldier stood victorious. He did not look as tired as the first winner, but Nadine surmised a lot of fighters avoided him during the skirmish. It wasn't the best idea to strike a soldier in front of his fellows. Nadine did a quick survey of the other fighters around her. There were no other soldiers in the tournament, or at least none identifying themselves so obviously. Raucous cheering rolled through the stands as the soldier stood beaming with pride, and the announcer bolted back into the arena once again.

"Didn't need to go to the registration table to find out who this guy was. I'll never forget a man who shares the same first name as our beloved world leader! Give it up for the winner of round two, Private Bart!"

The stands cheered once again.

"Trying to prove yourself to your fellow soldiers, eh Bart?!" the announcer asked.

"God damn right!" Bart replied, drawing laughter and even

more cheering from his onlookers.

As Bart exited the arena, the round-three contestants started making their way down the steps towards the field. Again, Nadine found herself loosely paying attention. When the round was down to five remaining competitors, she was surprised to see that one of them was the man with fingerless gloves. She was even more surprised when he won a few moments later.

"And we have another semifinalist!" the announcer shouted. "My fellow peacekeepers, give it up for Edgar, the winner of round three!"

Nadine thought Edgar's behavior was strange. He looked to be out of breath, but there was not a bead of sweat on his brow.

"Is he faking being tired?" she thought. "What point would that serve?"

Edgar went to stand with the fellow round winners on the left-hand side of the arena. Nadine and the rest of the round-four contestants started making their way down the steps towards the field. She entered the ring and took a position near the right corner furthest from the stands. Only three competitors were in the corner behind her while she faced the rest of the arena. She glanced over her right shoulder at Edgar, who happened to be looking at her at the same time. He looked away and started blushing.

The feeling is mutual, Edgar, she thought, surveying his muscular, six-foot-tall, broad-shouldered frame. She almost felt bad that she would have to level him in one of the upcoming rounds. As the last fighters filed into the arena, she glanced at him once more. This time, he was staring into the market in the outfield, at something she could not see from where she was standing. She made a mental note of it and refocused; the round was about to begin. This was her chance to make up some time. She needed to finish up this fight as fast as possible.

"Round four begins now!" the announcer shouted.

Nadine threw herself backwards, smashing the fighter behind her into the corner post. The man crumpled to the ground as Nadine grabbed the two competitors next to her by their shoulders and effortlessly tossed them out of the ring. She charged into the center of the arena and a woman ran at her with a left hook. Nadine ducked under it and flung her over the ropes. Two more people came at her, and she ducked down and thrust her arms into their stomachs. As they doubled over in pain, she grabbed them by their shirt collars and flung them out of the ring behind her.

This is still taking too long, she thought.

As if she had kicked herself into another gear, Nadine became a blur of blows and throws. Screams erupted from all around the arena as she quickly but methodically made her way through the fighters. Two minutes had just passed when the round was over. Every competitor lay flat in and around the arena, save the woman in the center who had put many of them there.

The announcer rushed over from the registration table. "What a performance! I was told that this young lady, who just dominated our final free for all round, goes by the name Nadine! Well done, miss!"

Nadine exited the arena and took another glance at Edgar as she lined up on his left. He was looking at her again, but this time it was nervousness, not attraction. She stared forward until she remembered Edgar eyeing the market earlier. She turned and saw that for the most part, people who had been up against the ropes watching Nadine's round were turning back toward the stalls. All except one man, who was staring in her direction with a quizzical look on his face. He looked like an older man, someone in his early- to mid-50s. Despite the heat, he was wearing a matte-black faux-leather jacket over a white shirt, black pants, and fingerless gloves similar to Edgar's.

Where is everyone finding these gloves!? she thought. The man's stare remained unbrroken. It creeped Nadine out.

"Without further ado, let's start the semifinals!" the announcer bellowed, drawing Nadine's attention back to the arena. "First up are the winners of round one and round three, William and Edgar!"

Nadine was not surprised that she was the one tasked with fighting Private Bart. That was the luck she'd had over the past few days. She wasn't worried about losing to him, just concerned about how the other soldiers would react to him getting floored.

The announcer commenced the first semifinal fight, and Edgar and William started dancing around each other. Nadine was closer now, and there were less people in the arena. She could observe Edgar's fighting style with full clarity, and everything about it seemed off. It might not have been so obvious to the soldiers in the stands, but to Nadine it was clear as day. Edgar was holding back, and significantly so.

"Why on earth is he dragging this out!?" Nadine thought. She did not have time for some fool who wanted to play around with a far weaker opponent. Only when William looked like he was on the verge of collapsing did Edgar deliver the finishing blow, a powerful right hook to his opponent's jaw. William was laid out flat, and the audience roared.

He was trying to make the soldiers think he's weaker than he is, and it worked. But why? Is he afraid of getting recruited or something? She couldn't dwell on the thought too long, though. The announcer beckoned her and Private Bart into the arena.

"I can't do the same thing Edgar did. Whatever reason he has for making himself look weaker, I don't have that luxury. This needs to end ASAP, soldier or not."

Private Bart took his place across from Nadine and squared up.

"The fight begins now!" the announcer yelled. He had barely finished talking before Nadine unleashed a left cross between Bart's eyes. She was too fast. He stood no chance. One punch and he was flat on the floor. Nadine looked to the stands to see their reaction. Most of the soldiers seemed shocked, a select few were angry. Byron had his hand over his face and was shaking his head. He was disappointed in Bart, not angry at Nadine, and his opinion was the one that mattered.

"Well, that was fast!" the announcer shouted as he jumped back in the ring. "Nadine, do you have to be somewhere after this or something?!"

Scattered chuckles could be heard in the stands as Nadine turned and stared Edgar down. He looked even more nervous than before. He had shed the fingerless gloves and balled his hands into fists. He took several deep breaths as the announcer called for him to enter the arena. It was obvious he wasn't going to hold back this time. As soon as Edgar entered, the announcer dove out of the ring.

"The finals begin now!" he bellowed.

A reflexive lean to the right was all that saved Edgar from having his head taken clean off by Nadine's vicious cross. Every time a punch or kick came his way, his arms moved to block with no time to spare. He was doing better against Nadine than anyone else that day, but still could do nothing but back up and circle right.

As Nadine threw a left hook, Edgar ducked to the right instead of blocking. He came at her with a hard left, but she was already leaning left to dodge, as if she knew what he was about to do. She stepped forward and threw a right jab, landing a shot squarely on Edgar's chin. Edgar took a step back towards the far-right corner of the arena. He was dazed but only for a moment, surprising Nadine. Edgar saw her expression and came forward to launch an offensive again. Before his left arm was even fully extended, Nadine was around it and lighting up Edgar's face with punches. Edgar ducked out to his right and retreated to the spot where he had started the fight.

Edgar screamed in frustration. As Nadine came sprinting forward, he raised his right arm to his face while curling his left arm next to him, so that his body blocked his fist from the view of the stands. He moved his index finger ever so slightly away from his middle finger and his hand became encircled by a brilliant, bright blue aura.

"Nooooo," Nadine cried out to herself, feeling her body reflexively act before she could get it under control. Her enormous boots evaporated and were replaced by the same blue glow of Edgar's fist. Before Edgar could even comprehend what was happening, Nadine jumped forward while her body arced into a backflip. A distinct boom echoed throughout the stadium as her foot made contact with Edgar's chin and sent him flying. She landed back on the mat the same time Edgar landed outside of it.

"Seize her!" Byron roared as he leapt over the railing and onto the field, his soldiers mere microseconds behind.

It was Nadine's nightmare scenario. The thing that her grandmother had told her to never do, she had just done in front of the most dangerous man on the west coast and his entire battalion. Her usually calm, thoughtful mind descended into a state of panic. She turned for the exit by the market and took off as fast as she could. Soldiers were closing in from either side as the panicked market-goers scattered. Out of the corner of her eye, Nadine thought she saw the creepy old man punch Edgar as he stumbled to his feet, but the thought instantly left her mind as she ran. She made it into the entrance tunnel before the soldiers could trap her on the field, but now soldiers from outside the arena were funneling in. She charged at them head on and for an inexplicable reason, they didn't shoot. Instead, soldiers wearing electric blades on their arms ran to the front and attempted to attack her. She ducked under and around their swings before getting in close and landing hits of her own. Even with armor and helmets, her blows were too much for them. One or two punches each and they were down.

"Let me through!" she heard Byron roar behind her. She battled her way through the sea of sky-blue armor and ran for it. With every step, she could hear Byron's footsteps getting closer and closer. She lit up the blue auras in her feet again and bounded eastward through the barren field that surrounded the stadium, the energy acting as a boost to her movements. She reached the old I-5 Highway and jumped off a twenty-foot cliff overlooking it. The energy coming from her feet carried her over the highway and among a series of abandoned buildings to the north. She ducked into one of them and hid behind a wall, hoping she had put enough distance between herself and Byron. About four seconds later, Byron crashed through the same wall Nadine was pressed against, sending her tumbling across the ground. She lay perched on her elbows as a shotgun barrel raised out of Byron's bulbous forearm and pointed at her. She closed her eyes.

"Surrender! You are under arrest!" Byron bellowed.

Nadine was dumbfounded. Her panicked mind couldn't make sense of it. Her grandmother had always said that revealing her powers was a death sentence. She stood up and turned, putting her hands behind her back.

Byron tackled her again and pinned her down as he pulled out a pair of cuffs that looked comically small in his hands.

Other soldiers caught up with Byron and he handed her over to them. They led her onto the highway, throwing a bag over her head as they walked. Finally, they loaded her into the back of a transport vehicle and locked the door. She felt the vehicle start moving forward. As she sat there, her mind started slowing down. She began to think more clearly, starting with the fact that she was alive and following the logical progression from there. She thought about what was going to happen next. She was alive, which meant hope was not lost yet. Her chances were not good, but she still had a shot.

I'm still coming, Naren, she thought to herself. *It just may take me a little longer.*

Chapter 6

Edgar woke up with a pounding head and eyes that refused to focus. As he stumbled to his feet, he could only make out that he was in a large room, with a dirt or gravel floor, collapsing walls, and what looked like blankets scattered all around. As his eyes glanced to the far end of the room, he saw the orange glow of late-day sun coming in through a gap in the walls. He realized he must have been unconscious for at least a couple hours. He started taking slow, dizzy steps towards the gap. As he got closer, he noticed the gap was much larger than he thought, and about four feet off the ground, with a thick wooden board set up to get outside. He put a foot on the makeshift ramp just as a figure appeared in the doorway. It rushed towards him and pinned him to the wall. Edgar's adrenaline kicked in and his eyesight returned, revealing the figure to be the same older man he'd seen at the tournament. The man was in incredible shape for his age, yet still seemed much stronger than he should be. No sooner had Edgar balled his hand into a fist than the man jumped back.

"Sorry, sorry! You just can't go outside!" the old man yelled.

"The hell I can't."

The man let out a frustrated sigh. "It's dying down out there but it's not safe yet, another half hour we may be okay."

"You're the one that punched me, aren't you?" Edgar said after some moments of contemplation.

"I'm the one that saved you! What the fuck were you thinking doing that in a public place?!"

Edgar moved his arms out to the side and straightened his fingers. He stretched the index finger on his right hand out away from the rest of them, revealing a small, circular, metallic opening where his index and middle finger met. And as his finger moved away from the rest of his hand, the blue glow returned. This time however, the glow didn't stop at his fist, but shot out to his side until a four-foot-long beam of pale blue light jutted from his hand.

"We aren't in public now. Move," Edgar replied.

"Jesus Christ!" the old man yelled as he put his hands out in front of him. "Put that thing away now!"

"Get out of my wa—" Edgar started to yell, but stopped when he noticed the old man's palms. He had taken off his fingerless gloves and the center of his hand was a metallic circle similar to Edgar's.

Edgar withdrew the blue beam of light coming from his hand and walked over to the old man. He grabbed one hand and held it out to the side in such a way that he could get a good look but also prevent anything that might come out of it from hitting him. Up close, the old man's hole looked a little different from Edgar's. Less ragged, more perfect, but still obviously of similar origin.

"You're like me?" Edgar said.

"Well, yeah," the old man replied. "I mean you have far more power than I do. I can't do any of those fancy tricks with my hands, but we are both LO-ECs."

"I'm sorry," Edgar said. "I am not whatever it is you just said.

I've never heard of a LO-EC."

The old man seemed stunned at first, but then a wave of understanding fell across his face.

"No one ever explained it to you. You have no idea what you are, do you?"

Edgar's mind raced back through his childhood. All the times that he asked his aunt and uncle what it was that made him different, and all the times they told him to stop asking those questions and to never use his powers, especially in public.

"Now it all makes sense! No wonder you use your powers so recklessly. I bet no one even told you to keep it a secret?"

Edgar suddenly felt offended, like this old man was accusing his family of not raising him right.

"Hey, my Aunt and Uncle told me that every time I ever asked about it. But if I had won the tournament I wouldn't have had to worry about money for a while, wouldn't have to worry about bugging them maybe for forever. It was worth it."

"No, it wasn't," the old man said. "What that woman did had a lot of Byron's men distracted, but if I was able to see your fist glow like that, then there's a possibility some of his more observant men might've seen it too. You're lucky she hit you before it formed into that long energy beam. And if that woman had been anyone else, literally anyone else, you would've killed her and faced the wrath of Byron in her place."

Edgar frowned, frustrated by how correct this old man sounded.

"Being one of us is supposed to be a death sentence," the old man said. "Every other LO-EC was supposed to have been killed off twenty years ago. Up until today I thought I was the only one left. Well, only one besides our world leader anyways."

Edgar was confused. "Spidre. Bartholemew Spidre. High Ruler

of Earth Spidre… is a LO-EC?"

"That is correct," the old man said. "His powers are actually similar to yours."

Edgar's head was spinning. He was taking in far too much new information at once.

"How do you know all this?" he asked the old man as he massaged his own temples.

"Because I used to work with him. My name is Symon. I was a professor doing research under Spidre before he became High Ruler, before he became one of us, and before he made being one of us a killable offense."

Edgar nodded as he began to understand.

"And there used to be more LO-ECs? More people like us?" Edgar asked.

"Not like us. Like me," Symon replied. "You are an exceptional rarity, far more powerful than the LO-ECs that were hunted down. We were stronger and faster than normal humans, but that's it. Far from a match for the world's army."

"But that woman in the tournament, Nadine. She was an 'exceptional rarity' too, right?" Edgar asked.

"No doubt in my mind," Symon responded.

"You knew her?"

"Never saw her before in my life. I know as much as you. I can assume she was at the tournament for similar reasons to yours, though. She must have needed the money for some reason or another and thought there was no person entering who could pose her a threat."

"Except she ran into me," Edgar said as his head sank. "And I forced her to use her powers in front of the military. Figures. First person like me I've met since my parents, and I got her killed."

Tears welled up in his eyes.

"She isn't dead," Symon said with a smirk.

Edgar's head jerked up. "What?! You're telling me she fought off Byron!? I mean she was a great fighter but—"

"She did not defeat Byron. She did give the peacekeepers hell before Byron himself caught her, and they still didn't kill her. I, for the life of me, cannot figure out why."

"So what did they do?"

"They just put her on a transport. And it wasn't even a prison transport. The prison city in San Antonio is to our east. They were taking her north, meaning there's only one place they could be heading."

Edgar had a blank stare on his face.

"Spidre's compound," Symon said with a sigh. "It's in San Francisco. You really don't know much about this area, do you?"

Edgar shook his head. "I do know San Francisco is not that far. Is your vehicle fast enough to catch up to the transport before it gets there?"

Symon was stunned. "What?"

"Your vehicle. If Spidre wants you dead and knows who you are, then there is no way you're living this close to him, and no way you took the Trans-Continental Transport."

"You're right, San Diego is my usual home. I'm impressed you figured that out. And I'm even more impressed that you're risking taking on a military convoy for someone you don't know. You're going to go save the damsel in distress?"

"You saw the same as I did, that is one damsel that doesn't need saving," Edgar replied, "but I imagine after she's done kicking ass, she'll need some help escaping. And she's in trouble because of me. There's no way I'm letting that go," Edgar responded. His past mistakes and what they'd cost him and his family stabbed at the back of his mind.

"So, are you going to let me borrow your ride or not?" Edgar asked.

"I'll do you one better, I'm coming with you." Symon replied.

Edgar squinted.

"You look surprised," Symon said.

"You spent the last twenty years hiding from Spidre, and now you're going to head straight at him?"

"Whatever Spidre has planned for that woman can't be good. And I've allowed Spidre to do far too much to the rest of the LO-ECs in the world. If we three are the last alive besides him, we need to keep it that way, and stay out of his grasp at all costs."

Edgar nodded.

Symon began walking across the room. It was then that Edgar realized what he'd thought were blankets when his eyesight was blurry were blue tarps covering debris piles. Symon walked over to the largest tarp and pulled it off, revealing two enormous, tan-colored motorcycles. They looked like they would be at home on a racetrack, except they were electric, the tires were partially covered, and one of them looked considerably more beat up than the other. Edgar could not believe his eyes.

"What's your name?" Symon asked.

"I'm Edgar."

"Edgar, do you know what these are?" Symon asked.

"Elcycles," he said. One of the few memories he had of his childhood was his dad pridefully showing off his own, trying to help Edgar's four-year-old mind understand just how much faster they were than every other commercial vehicle. "Like a cheetah racing a turtle," was his father's approximate comparison.

"That's the reason I'm here. I've been hiding out in San Diego with my one cycle, but it could stand to be replaced. I knew some folks were collectors of old LO-EC stuff, and I knew people would take advantage of the commotion caused by Byron's exit to sell said stuff."

"Wait, you bought that at the stadium?!"

"God no! Two days ago, from some guy in the hills. I was at the stadium for asparagus."

Edgar wasn't sure what to make of that sentence. "I'm sorry, what?"

"Asparagus. Can't find any anymore, and I've been craving it for ages! Byron's food stores were massive, and not exactly ideal for being part of the tournament prize. I thought there was a chance they'd have asparagus among the stuff they were selling at the stadium."

"Oh. Well, did they have any?"

"Nope, still asparagus-less," he said with a sigh. "I think the coast is clear now. Ready to go pay our High Ruler a visit?"

"I'm sure he'll be happy to see us," Edgar said with a smirk "but uh, how do you start this thing?"

"Does only your right hand produce that energy beam?" Symon asked.

"I uh, I call them my blades, because they can cut through pretty much anything," he said as he squinted and looked away from bashfulness. "I can make them come out of either hand, but not at the same time. If I try to do both at once neither works."

"Makes sense, given how infrequently you must've used it," said Symon. "See the hole in the middle of either handlebar? Keep your fist closed and hold the hole between your fingers up to it. When they touch, activate your uh 'blades', and the cycle will convert the energy."

Edgar wasn't sure what to make of the 'infrequently', comment but was too distracted by Symon's instructions to question it further. He did as he was told and sure enough, the cycle lit up. The gentle hum of the electric engine brought on feelings of nostalgia for his childhood.

"We should get on the road ASAP if we're going to catch the convoy before it gets behind Spidre's force field," Symon said. Edgar eyes narrowed and his mouth fell open.

"I'm sorry, did you say force field?"

"Uh, yeah," Symon replied. "Wait, you didn't even know that Spidre has a force field surrounding his entire compound? You really don't know much about the west coast."

Edgar shrugged.

Chapter 7

Edgar was impressed with how easy the elcycle was to drive. Point the handlebars in a direction, and the cycle went that way. You could even flip them around and it would do a full U-turn. With the autonav programmed to go to San Francisco, Edgar picked up on driving with little effort. Edgar and Symon agreed that if they took to the highway and pushed hard, they could catch up with the convoy before it got to the San Francisco compound. They figured any soldiers lingering in their path in LA would be left in the dust. They were correct. To their right and left was nothing but long-abandoned buildings eventually giving way to arid abandoned farms. To their front and rear was nothing but the old highway. They hoped that further along, the convoy transporting Nadine had not yet reached its destination.

Once again, they were correct. Down the highway, a convoy of fifteen transport vehicles drove along at a steady pace. Inside the middle car, Nadine was blindfolded, sat on a bench, and handcuffed to the floor by her hands and feet. Two armed guards sat across from her, machine guns connected to the armor on their forearms. She had stayed silent for most of the ride, thinking, listening. Finally, she gathered enough information to speak.

"The two of you are going to die within the hour. You know that, right?" Nadine asked. The two guards snickered.

"No, I guess you don't know. You wouldn't have reacted that way if you had figured it out," she said. "You haven't even questioned how I know it's just the two of you."

The soldiers' faces dropped.

"Honestly, I figured that out pretty easily. You two breathe so loud it's like I have fucking sonar all of a sudden. It didn't even take me long to figure out that Byron is not with the convoy. If I'm still alive, it would be on Spidre's orders. Taking me alive was a chore all on its own, and Byron is a lazy fuck. He's not going to go the extra mile for someone else's motivations."

The soldiers started looking worried.

"So that means there is no one person on this convoy who can take me on. And when Byron captured me, we were right next to the highway. He marched me onto the road, cuffed and blindfolded me, and put me on this truck. Then this truck went straight north. Never turned. So, we aren't going to the prison, that's east. We're going to Spidre's compound. Not sure why, but that's where we're going."

The soldiers were looking more and more concerned by the second.

"So, I know where we're going, and I know I can take on everyone here. The question is, do I wreck the convoy now, or when we get to the compound? Waiting does have its merits. See, I need a fast vehicle. I have somewhere else to be. And this convoy is nothing but slow transports. But the compound might have something faster. Then I remembered the mistake I made earlier. Letting my instinctual reactions take over and hitting that guy when he revealed his powers. I bet he feels guilty about that. I doubt he has ever met another LO-EC in his life, and he got me arrested immediately. He's not from Los Angeles. I would've run into him before if he was. That means he has a ride. So, I may need to fight my way out of Spidre's compound with a fast vehicle, but there is also a good chance I will be provided an opportunity to make my escape earlier…"

Outside the transport vehicle and just down the highway, Edgar and Symon saw a faint orange glow creep up on the horizon. It was an unmistakable sight amongst the monotony of dilapidated buildings surrounding it, and bright enough to compete with the setting sun to the West.

"That's Spidre's compound!" Symon shouted over the wind howling in their ears. "Get ready!"

No sooner had Symon finished his sentence than the convoy appeared on the road in front of them. With the top of the force field just peeking over the horizon, the two bikes split ways around either side of the convoy. They swung around and stopped as they reached the front, blocking the first car and bringing the line of vehicles to a dead halt.

Nadine smiled as the transport lurched forward and ceased moving. She effortlessly shattered her constraints and, relying on hearing only, grabbed the faces of the two soldiers and slammed their heads against the inner wall. She ripped off her blindfold. Less than a second later, the rear doors came flying off the truck and Nadine strolled out, a smile still on her face. The soldiers in the seven cars behind hers piled out and rushed her, while the seven in front split their individual attentions between Nadine, Edgar, and Symon.

Edgar and Symon heard the commotion from the middle car and looked at each other.

"Did she figure out we were coming?" Edgar asked. Symon shrugged and thought for a moment. Edgar could not operate his blade and the elcycle at the same time, so barreling through the soldiers to grab Nadine and run was far too risky. That meant the best plan of action was for her to come to them while Edgar cleared a path.

"Get to the front!" Symon yelled as loud as he could.

"On my way!" Nadine replied.

Nadine turned towards the front of the convoy and was met with the faces and guns of the peacekeepers. Her feet lit up and she flipped away from the road. The soldiers, who had all been advancing together, chased her at full speed. Since some were faster than others, they split up, exactly what Nadine was counting on. The first one arrived and threw a punch. She threw his fist aside and thrust her palm into his exposed chin. The second arrived, another punch thrown. She leaned back to dodge, then grabbed his hand and pulled his face down onto her raised knee. A third soldier arrived but before she could even react, Nadine back flipped and landed a nasty kick to her chin, leveling her.

One of the soldiers could be heard transmitting over a comm in her uniform "Convoy to compound, prisoner has escaped and we are under attack. I repeat, we are under attack!"

Edgar could hear the commotion and was amazed. He was right: in no way did she need their help fighting. His only purpose at the moment was to help her escape. And with the soldiers now approaching him, it was high time he lived up to his purpose. He flung his right arm out and unleashed the energy from his hand. He charged at the soldiers and swung at them with all he had. One by one, they tried to grab him or hit him, and one by one he passed them, taking off whatever limbs they offered and leaving them in his wake. At the same time, Nadine had taken out enough soldiers that she did not need to keep running and picking them off one by one. Her movements were just short of a blur now, blue auras arcing through the air and landing on skulls. The sounds alternated between the crunch of bone and screams of pain. While this was going on, Symon was holding position by the elcycles, dispatching any soldiers who strayed away from the two super powers in front of him.

The amount of noise coming from the sudden battlefield was baffling, and Symon was finding it hard to concentrate on any one thing. After a couple minutes though, he started to hear something new, something not coming from Nadine, Edgar, or the soldiers falling at their feet. It was the sound of powerful electric motors revving. He turned around to look towards the compound and saw dust being kicked up.

Impossible! How could the backup have gotten here already!? he thought.

Something was coming up on the convoy at a ridiculous speed. As it got closer, Symon realized he wasn't hearing multiple electric motors, but one powerful engine revving insanely fast. Only one vehicle could rev like that, an elcycle being operated by a LO-EC.

"Spidre is coming!" Symon yelled.

He had just finished his sentence before a black elcycle stopped twenty-five feet away. The rider, however, continued flying towards Symon and tackled him. The two of them tumbled over each other, and when they came to a stop, Symon was being pinned down by a man about the same age, but a hundred pounds heavier, five inches taller, and wearing a dark-blue military uniform with black stripes on both arms. He had a head of thick grey hair and a well-manicured beard that framed a scowl which looked like it had been there for decades. It was Spidre.

"No. You're dead. You're dead!" Spidre shouted.

Through clenched teeth and struggling to breathe under Spidre's weight, Symon managed to utter "You're really shitty… at getting rid… of your enemies."

Spidre's eyes burned with anger. He raised his hand and flung his wrist back as far as it could go. As he did that, an energy beam similar to Edgar's sprung out of his palm. For Symon, everything seemed to start moving in slow motion. It took less than a second for Spidre to turn his wrist, but to Symon it felt like a century. It took a few more moments for Spidre to start bringing his blade down, but to Symon, it felt like an eternity.

For Edgar, everything was moving far too fast. He disengaged with the soldiers as Spidre and Symon were tumbling. He started running towards them as they exchanged words. He leapt forward as Spidre raised his arm. And as Spidre started swinging down, Edgar just got his blade in under Spidre's before it fell on Symon's neck. Edgar swung upwards with all the power he could muster, throwing Spidre off of his prey. Spidre and Edgar scrambled to their feet and found themselves staring at each other eye to eye.

Spidre threw his left arm to his side and as he threw that hand back, a second blade came out. He charged at Edgar and their blades of energy met and rebounded off each other. They both bounced back from the force and quickly jumped back in. Edgar couldn't even think. His reflexes were the only thing keeping his blade in between Spidre's onslaught and his flesh. There was no chance of him getting on offense. Fortunately, Nadine was just finished throwing the last standing soldier out of her way. She looked over and couldn't believe her eyes.

Holy shit, Spidre's a LO-EC!? she thought. Suddenly, Spidre jumped backwards, getting as much space between himself and Edgar as he could.

"Why the hell did he do that?" Nadine thought. "Only

reason to get that kind of distance would be if he planned on shooting—oh shit!"

Nadine sprinted as hard as she could as Spidre raised his right hand and pointed it at Edgar. She boosted into the air as Spidre's energy beam separated from his hand and launched forward. For the second time in one day, Edgar was faced with a blow he stood no chance of dodging. This time however, Nadine's fighting knowledge was working in his favor. She flipped over Edgar and landed on top of Spidre's beam, her feet protected by her own aura. The beam diverted and cut deep into the ground inches from Edgar's feet. The two of them rushed Spidre and attempted to mount an offensive, but Spidre was impenetrable. Every blow from Edgar's blade was met in kind, every kick from Nadine deflected. The stalemate continued until Nadine went for a drop kick with both feet. Spidre brought both his blades up to block it, but the force from the blow sent him stumbling backwards.

Nadine was getting exhausted, and she knew Symon and Edgar could not be faring any better. Spidre on the other hand, did not look the least bit tired. This fight had to end soon. She thought of a plan.

"His elcycle!" she yelled, hoping Edgar understood. He did. Nadine and Symon ran over to Spidre to continue their bout while Edgar ran past. Spidre figured out the plan and tried to shoot off another energy beam as he scrambled to his feet. His shot was wild and missed, ten feet above Edgar's shoulder. Before he could get another shot off Nadine was on him, once again putting him on the defensive. Edgar raised his blade over his head and brought it down just behind the black elcycle's handlebars. The metal frame groaned and collapsed, rendering it useless. He ran for Symon's elcycles as Nadine roundhouse-kicked Spidre's blades away from his face. Symon seized the opportunity and threw a punch as hard as he could while Spidre's defense was down. Spidre was only dazed for a moment, but it was enough for him to stumble to one knee. Edgar was already on the farther elcycle.Nadine ran and jumped on behind Edgar while Symon swung on to the nearer cycle. Spidre took one last shot as they sped east, away from the compound, away from the highway, and away from any sign of civilization. His shot buried itself in the dirt where the cycles had just been. He looked over at his own elcycle. It was cut clean in two. They had escaped, and he had no way of catching them. He let out a blood-curdling scream that Edgar, Symon, and Nadine could still hear as the elcycles took them away from danger.

An hour later, and the speed of the elcycles had brought them far out of view of any highway. Despite the elcycles' size, the tracks they left in the arid landscape were surprisingly light and disappeared within minutes. The trio felt comfortable enough to stop.

"I'm sorry, for earlier," Edgar blurted out to Nadine.

"Yeah, you're a big dummy," Nadine replied. "Give me one of the elcycles and we'll call it even."

"Not his to give away," Symon said. "Where do you need to go?"

"New Orleans.

"Someone's in trouble?"

"Another one of us."

Symon paused, stunned for a moment by this new revelation. Then, a realization.

"That's why you entered the tournament."

"Needed money to buy one of those," Nadine pointed at the elcycles. "Had a seller lined up and everything."

"Probably the same guy I bought this one from," the professor pointed at the newer cycle.

Edgar was baffled. Symon and Nadine were so smart that in

one ten-second conversation they'd figured out everything they needed to about each other.

"I uh, I don't think I should go to New Orleans with you." Symon said. "I'm a little ashamed to admit it, but I was a liability in the fight with Spidre. I only got one lucky shot in, and I know what's waiting in New Orleans. I won't be any help in that battle."

"Agreed," Nadine replied, taking Symon aback. She turned to face Edgar.

"You—" she began to talk.

"Yes, I'll come." Edgar agreed without hesitation. Nadine was surprised and impressed.

"I… may or may not still feel bad about getting you captured," he continued.

"I'll take it," Nadine replied.

You're going to need somewhere to lay low after," Symon said.

"I don't foresee any circumstance where that isn't true."

"And I'm assuming you can power one of these? The elcycles are fast but it would still take a full night driving non-stop to get to New Orleans, and Edgar doesn't have the energy for that."

Edgar winced from feelings of offense but had to admit to himself that Symon was right. He was starting to feel drained. Nadine unwrapped her hands and held up her palms. The center of each contained a metallic circle very similar to Symons', but not as perfectly round.

"They aren't like my feet, I can't force energy out of them," Nadine said of her palms. "But they were able to rev up my parents' elcycle when I was a kid."

"Good," Symon said. "Take the older elcycle. When you're done in New Orleans activate the autonav's home setting and it'll bring you right to my front door. I'll take a wide berth around Los

Angeles to get back to San Diego without being spotted."

"I'll need some food too, if you have any."

"Well aren't you demanding," Symon said as he reached into his jacket. He grabbed two rectangular objects wrapped in paper and tossed them to Nadine. She peeled back the corner to reveal a greyish bar. She looked up at Symon with a raised eyebrow.

"It's soy-based. I made it. Tastes bland but keeps the calories up," Symon said.

"I appreciate it," Nadine said.

"You better get moving," he replied. Nadine nodded, mounted the elcycle and turned back to look at Edgar.

"You coming, you big dummy?"

Edgar hopped on the back of the cycle without hesitation.

"People usually call me Edgar, but dummy is ok, too."

"I'm Nadine." Nadine replied. "And I'm glad you're coming, Edgar. You may be a dummy, but you're a dummy who can fight, and I'll need all the help I can get in New Orleans."

"Why, who's there?"

From somewhere in the corners of his mind, Edgar realized the answer just as Nadine replied.

"The androids," she said as she and Symon kicked off and the elcycles went their separate ways.

A shiver ran down Edgar's spine. *The androids,* he thought to himself. *What have I gotten myself into?*

Chapter 8

Nadine revved the engine of the elcycle and with Edgar sitting behind her, they took off away from Symon, who gave a quick wave before heading in his own direction. As they parted, Nadine and Edgar were both filled with a sense of disappointment, although neither of them voiced it. Symon was the best chance either of them ever had at finding out what they were, what history had led them to this moment, and they were driving away before learning any of it. They hoped that when this was all said and done, they could sit down with Symon and learn everything.

21 Years Earlier

"What's your name, buddy?" Symon asked as he bent down to get eye to eye with a child of about five years. However, as he kneeled over, Symon's white lab coat got caught in the back of his knee, causing him to lose his balance and fall straight onto his backside. The child burst out laughing at the sight of this and his giggle fit put a smile on Symon's face and the face of the child's mother, who before this had her lips pursed with nervous energy.

"Do it again!" the child screamed out.

"I don't think I could do that again if I tried," Symon replied. "My name is Symon. I'm the head of LO-EC research here at the Salt Lake City labs. I'll be observing you today and asking you and your mom some questions. Is that okay?"

The little boy nodded in reply.

"What is your name?" Symon asked again.

"I'm Shaun," the boy said.

"Shaun, do you like playing games on your mom's mobile?" Symon inquired. The boy nodded and smiled wide.

"Can he play now, mommy?" Symon asked the boy's mom.

"Yes, of course!" she replied and handed the phone to Shaun. Shaun sat down at a nearby low table that had been set up next to various lab equipment. The phone's holo projection lit up with a large purple ball, and Shaun started manipulating a smaller red dot that flew anywhere he touched in the projection. As he did this, Symon got off the floor and turned to Shaun's mother.

"If it's okay, I'd like to go over the medical evaluation that my technicians performed." Symon said.

"Yes, please," mom replied. Symon nodded and pulled his own mobile out of his coat pocket. A holo image of an adult human popped up in front of him.

"What you're looking at here is a normal LO-EC user. You, me, anyone else in Salt Lake City, or any other LO-EC user in the world."

"Isn't it just LO-EC? Not LO-EC user?" the mom replied.

"That's the colloquial term for us, yes. But LO-EC also refers to the source of our power, the Latent Organic Energy Converter. I'll be talking about both a lot so to avoid confusion, I'll be saying LO-EC user and LO-EC device," Symon said.

"Got it," mom replied.

"That's the LO-EC device right there, just a two-inch square box of paradigm-shifting biotechnology," Symon said as he pointed to a cube shape in the holo image's stomach cavity.

"And all these squiggly lines you see are the network that the LO-EC device grows in our bodies after it is surgically implanted," Symon said as he pointed widely to dozens of lines that extended out from the cube to the rest of the body like a circulatory system.

"That's what the LO-EC devices grow using our excess body heat that would have otherwise escaped into the atmosphere," mom replied. "And it stops growing when these pop out," she continued as she held up her palm, which had the same grey circle with a hole in the center that Symon's hands had.

"The microtransformers. Exactly!" Symon exclaimed. "I'm glad you know the basics, that will make this easier."

"Do you get parents who don't know this?" mom asked.

"All the time," Symon said. "They get their LO-EC device implanted, only knowing that in nine months, it will convert all their excess body heat into useable bio-energy stored in their palms. They're just excited to leave conventional electricity behind. They have no idea how the technology actually works."

"Wow," mom replied.

"Some of them didn't even realize that normal adult humans sweat and have to take breaks from physical activity to keep from overheating or getting dehydrated. They have no idea that the LO-EC device is the key to them never overheating, continually producing more and more energy, and being so much stronger and faster than non-LO-EC users."

"I'm surprised, but I guess that makes sense if they grew up in Salt Lake City. When was the last time you saw a normal human here?" mom asked.

"It has been a long, long time," Symon replied. "But I digress. Here is Shaun's internal map to compare to a normal LO-EC."

A new holo image popped up. It was another cut away image similar to the previous one, but the body had the proportions of a child, and the network inside was far more chaotic.

"Oh, my god," mom exclaimed and put her hands over her mouth. Tears began to well up in her eyes.

"It is not as scary as it looks," Symon said. "I have seen far worse."

"Worse… than this?" mom asked in reply.

Symon nodded. "Well, to be completely honest, all of this research is still relatively new. LO-EC tech has been around for 200 years. But the first born LO-EC user was only reported on April 27, 2511. So we only have eight-and-a-half years' worth of research to go by. Still, in that time I have seen dozens of children who were born with LO-EC systems in place. And compared to all of them, your son's case is fairly standard."

Mom lowered her hands and wiped her eyes.

"Should I explain what we're looking at a little more?" Symon asked. Mom nodded in reply.

"When the LO-EC network crossed the placental barrier for Shaun, it looks like it grew two LO-EC devices: one you can see here, just behind his belly button; the other is back here, under his right kidney." As Symon said this, he pointed to two irregularly shaped lumps in the image.

"They're not cubes," mom replied.

"Correct. LO-EC devices and microtransfomers that grow as a result of LO-EC networks crossing the placental barrier are rarely in the correct spot or in the shape we are accustomed to seeing. They also don't always function normally, or at all. That appears to be the case for this LO-EC device," Symon said as he pointed to the lump near the kidneys.

"Is that bad? Will Shaun…" mom couldn't finish her sentence.

"No," Symon said firmly. "I know that's what all of us are worried about. How could you not, with so many born LO-EC users dying before they can even walk? But that usually happens due to their system having one or more functional LO-EC devices but not enough functional microtransformers. Their body produces more and more energy with nowhere for it to go until…"

"And that's not the case for Shaun?" mom interrupted.

"Fortunately, no," Symon replied. "The three microtransformers you can see on his right forearm may be irregularly shaped, but they seem to work fine."

"So any child born without microtransformers will die?" mom asked.

"Many, but not all," Symon said. "Some are born with an entire LO-EC system that doesn't work. And I even had a couple children who had no microtransformers, but their bodies were just constantly twitching, almost bordering on vibrating, and in doing so they were constantly burning off the excess energy. They could move so fast and with such force that their limbs could displace air and knock down objects across the room."

"Jeez," mom replied.

"But those cases are exceptionally rare, and Shaun is not one of them. The jets of blue energy that you've seen him force out of the microtransformers can be very dangerous for other people and things around him, though, so you'll have to teach him to be responsible with that."

"But he can't hurt himself with them?" mom inquired.

"The beams themselves would be harmless to Shaun. However, they could possess enough force to propel him unexpectedly. But as long as he doesn't force out the energy while in close proximity to a wall or floor, he should be fine."

Mom breathed a sigh of relief.

"Do you have any other questions for me?" Symon asked.

"Not that I can think of right now. Can I call if I think of anything?"

"Absolutely! You two are vital to helping us figure out why this born LO-EC plague started so suddenly, and how it can be curbed. Any question you have may be the breakthrough we've been looking for. So please call if you think of something."

Mom nodded, and as they all exchanged farewells, Symon closed the holo-image on his mobile and pulled up his missed-call log. He never took calls while interviewing study participants. He was surprised to see multiple missed calls from several people, and the most recent missed call was the most surprising of all.

"Bartholemew Spidre? Now that's a name I haven't seen in years!" he said to himself as he pointed his finger to the 'call back' option. Spidre's name displayed in the air. After a few seconds, the person on the other end picked up, but the holo image remained the same.

"Symon," a gruff, deep voice said.

"Bart! It's been a long time! How are…"

"We need to get a handle on this situation, Symon," Spidre interrupted. "We need to act fast, and I'll need your help if we're going to…"

"Whoa, whoa, slow down," Symon interrupted in response. "What's going on?"

"Don't tell me you haven't heard!" Spidre yelled.

"Heard what? I've been in my lab all day!" Symon yelled back, as he swiped the holo image of Spidre's name away and pulled up another image that displayed breaking news. On screen was video of a giant, churning, blue burst of energy exploding outwards and leveling about five square blocks of a city.

"Boston, the non-LO-EC quarter," Spidre replied. "A born LO-EC user leveled the whole fucking place,"

"Oh my god," Symon said as a shiver ran through his body. He couldn't believe what he was seeing, but Spidre's description was the only thing that made sense. Only born LO-EC users could produce energy that behaved like that, but he had never seen anything even close to that level of power before.

"Suspects?" Symon asked.

"They have no fucking clue who did it, or why," Spidre replied. "The UN just appointed me to oversee a worldwide LO-EC compliance response.

"You? They're trusting a LO-EC to respond to a LO-EC created problem?"

"They reasoned that having a LO-EC in charge of the operation will convince other LO-ECs to comply peacefully. I hope they do. I want to be ready if they don't. Preparing for the latter is what I need your help with."

Upon hearing this, Symon went cold. A sense of dread crept up inside of him.

"What do you need, and where do you need me to report?" Symon replied.

Chapter 9

A sudden bump in the road, and Edgar was jolted awake. All he saw were stars and the crescent moon lighting a desert landscape. His lower back was stiff from sitting in the same position on the elcycle. He must've been asleep for hours.

"Ugh. Sorry, I can't believe I just knocked out like that," Edgar yelled, competing with the sound of the electric motor.

"You practically fell asleep mid-sentence. One minute you were telling me about when you met Symon, the next you were gone. You were leaning on me the whole time too, felt great," Nadine said, her words dripping with sarcasm.

"Ugh. I'm so sorry!"

"Don't worry about it. You don't use your power much do you?" she asked.

"Power?" Edgar asked. "Is that what you call what we can do?"

"Well yeah, what else would you call it?"

"I guess I never thought about it before. No, I've almost never used my 'power'. I was always told not to. Why did you ask that?"

"That's why you fell asleep. I'm not quite sure how our anatomy works, but I do know that using your power wipes you out."

"That explains why I'm so hungry, too. So, what, you've used your power enough that it doesn't affect you?"

"Yeah, I'll be ok. I've never used my power in public before today. In private though, during my martial arts training, I try to utilize it in any way I can."

Nadine let go of the cycle with one hand and reached into her right pocket. She grabbed one of the soy bars that Symon had given her and handed it to Edgar. As he tore away the wrapper, he continued the conversation.

"So that's how you figured it out? Through martial arts training?"

"Sort of. Technically, it was my brother who figured it out."

"Your brother?"

"My twin brother, Naren. We used to learn and practice Kung Fu together. He noticed that when I used my power it took a greater toll on me."

"Sounds like your brother was just as smart as you."

"Not was. He's still alive, as far as I know."

Edgar thought for a moment. "He's the reason we're going to New Orleans."

"Ooh, I'm impressed. Maybe you aren't such a dummy after all," she said with a mirk. Edgar smiled as well.

"But you're correct," Nadine continued. "He's been working there as an investigator for the past 18 months. Before that he was working investigations for the UN peacekeepers under Byron."

"That uh, that doesn't sound safe," Edgar said.

"There was a lot that we did that wasn't safe. He worked investigations while I remained off the radar. That allowed me to set up an underground net access point not far from where we lived."

"But why? What's the point of taking such huge risks?"

"Because we wanted to find you," she said as she slowed down the cycle and came to a stop.

"Take over," she said. "I haven't eaten yet either." They switched places on the cycle and their journey continued.

"We wanted to find out if there were more of us out there, and maybe find out more about what we are, as well. The two best sources for that info are from other people on the net and from military intel. Go figure that after all that hard work, I found you through sheer luck. Well no, that's not true. There was some probability there, too. We both did need money and felt we would be unchallenged by other fighters. Made the tournament an attractive choice to the both of us. Still, had nothing to do with our net access or his military research."

"So, you guys did all that hard work for nothing?"

"Well, no, we had some success there on occasion. The big break came when a call came to the UN from the androids, asking for help investigating robberies at their facilities. The details of the case sounded… strange… unlikely for a normal human to accomplish. It was a good lead, and we knew he couldn't pass up the opportunity, so he left for New Orleans."

"Why didn't you go with him?"

"It would've risked exposing both of us. Byron might be a strong, experienced fighter, but he's a fucking idiot. He's careless, or lazy. Either way, he doesn't check into things very deeply. The androids are different. They're cold, calculating, and paranoid. They wouldn't have trusted an outsider and would've followed his every move, inevitably leading them back to me. So, I stayed in LA and he went to New Orleans, and for 18 months I didn't hear a word from him. New Orleans has an underground access point, so I would occasionally hear things through the net about him. I knew he was alive, but never heard from him directly until two days ago, when he sent a message telling me to win the tournament and meet up with him along old highway ten between Houston and New Orleans."

"But why does he want you to meet him? Why now?"

"Well, he went to New Orleans to find another LO-EC. I can only assume this means he found one, and he needs my help to escape. I'm the better fighter of the two of us."

"Is he not a LO-EC?"

"He is, and he is amazing, but don't tell him I said that. His power isn't ideal for fighting, though."

"What makes it amazing, then?"

"He can fly," Nadine said, her lips pressing together out of jealousy. Edgar didn't know what answer he was expecting, but it wasn't that.

"That's… fuck that's so fucking cool. Ok, so he can fly, and you're a good fighter. But how can you possibly take on a whole army of androids?"

"Huh?" Nadine replied.

"The force in New Orleans. It's an army of androids isn't it?"

"What the fuck are you talking about? It isn't an army, they're three android prototypes."

Edgar turned bright red. "Seriously?" he asked.

Nadine burst out laughing. "Back to being a dummy, I see!" she spat out before continuing to laugh some more. Edgar turned even redder.

"No, they aren't an army. Thank god they aren't, or we'd be fucked. Where did you hear something so ridiculous?"

"I just figured it had to be. I mean, how could just three androids police an entire city?"

"That's how powerful they are. They have the bare minimum number of soldiers to do their grunt work, and that's it. The population is just terrified into submission there. From what Naren found out about them before he left, they're three prototypes that were just too expensive, too complicated, and too dangerous to replicate. Russ is an offensive specialist but is fairly tough-skinned, Tank is defensive, but still has some offensive capability, and Can is the strategic brain, the only one capable of the complex thought and strategy that controls them all. Individually they're all formidable, especially Tank, the defense prototype. Together though, they are just completely overwhelming. But they do have certain weaknesses built in to keep them from being a threat on a global scale. They're wired to only use short range comms to communicate with each other, and they're programmed to be unable to build more of themselves."

Edgar thought for a moment. "You said one of them is a strategist. Doesn't that mean we could be walking into a trap?"

"It's possible, but then that would mean Naren is definitely in trouble, all the more reason for us to get there. Besides, Naren's quite smart. If he could figure out how to trick the peacekeepers into hiring him, I don't think he'll get caught now, let alone give away information about our net access points and my existence."

"Yeah, I was wondering about that. How was he able to become an investigator?"

"A little mix of genius and luck. Our dad was an investigator, and a serious computer nerd. He taught us a lot about the net, and the basics of reprogramming IDs. Naren had my dad's ID when he died, and after years of trial and error, we were able to change the year of birth and slightly change the name. Byron and his crew had a reputation for being careless with their paperwork, so Naren took a shot and pretended to be a newly recruited investigator in LA. It worked."

Edgar was impressed. "You two are something else. I'm really looking forward to meeting your brother," Edgar said.

"I'm sure he'd say the same about you if, you know, he knew you existed," Nadine said with a smile.

A few minutes passed in silence, and Edgar's focus turned towards the road. He didn't notice at first that Nadine was pressing up against his body and wrapping her arms around his waist. Then it hit him: she had fallen asleep. In that moment of realization, Edgar forgot about everything that had happened and everything that what was about to happen. All he could think about was how warm her skin felt pressed against his body and how amazing her embrace felt wrapped around him.

Chapter 10

It was the dead of night in New Orleans, and Naren hadn't slept since the evening before. He was pacing at the foot of his bed with the lights off, wearing a pair of blue boxers and a white t-shirt. In comparison to his usual well-maintained appearance, he looked like a nervous wreck. He sighed and sat on the end of his bed.

As if on cue, the moment Naren sat down, his mobile started ringing, the 2" x 3" matte-finish screen lit up and filled the room with a holo-image of the word CAN.

"Finally!" he thought and snapped a tiny earbud out of the back of the device. The headset, sensing it was now in Naren's fingers, auto-answered and turned the holo-image off as he swung it to his ear.

"What do you want, Can?" he asked.

"You do not sound like you were sleeping," Can's deep, cold, electronic voice answered on the other end.

"Jesus Christ. You say that every single time you call me late at night. Let it go, already," Naren snapped back, despite his insides being tied in knots.

"That is fair," Can replied. "The thief has been subdued and captured. The thief was a LO-EC. The thief was trying to steal the replacement lighting you specified in your investigation summary."

"You're welcome," Naren replied dryly.

"Please meet us at headquarters to complete your report," Can said after a long pause and before hanging up.

"God, I hate that prick," Naren muttered as he took his light blue uniform off its hangar and slipped it on. He grabbed an old watch from the post of his bed, put his wrist through it, and exited his apartment. Right across the hall was a lift. He got inside and three seconds later had descended 100 floors to ground level.

He walked through the city, lost in his own thoughts about the events he was certain would soon come. He arrived at the military headquarters and was greeted by a ten-foot tall, fifteen-foot long black oval sitting in the center of the street. He knew what it was, but until now had only seen it in storage. It was a high-priority prisoner transport vessel, one of a very select few in the world that had not been disassembled for parts yet. They served little purpose in this LO-EC-free world. Four-foot-thick carbon-fiber walls on every side, enough room on the inside for one, very important, very powerful prisoner. One end of the oval screwed off to access the interior, and Tank was in the process of sealing it up when Naren arrived. The interior, normally dark, was lit up with a bright orange glow, which was cut off from the world as Tank placed the cover on the access port and screwed it in. A look of worry fell across Naren's face.

"Why do you appear so concerned?" Can said as it walked over from headquarters' front entrance. Its appearance still gave Naren the creeps, no matter how many times he had seen it.

"He… Is he really that powerful that you need such a container?" Naren replied.

Nice recovery. Now, don't fuck up again, he thought to himself.

"The thief is a female. And it is procedure to use the high-priority containment vessel when available to transport LO-EC subjects in the event of their capture. It is surprising you did not know that."

"I guess I'm surprised you're following procedure. You usually just do what you want. Hell, I'm surprised Russ left her alive. Where is that creepy psychopath anyway?"

"Androids cannot be psychopathic. Russ is airborne, surveying the city while we prepare for the prisoner's transport. As for why she was left alive, it turned out your 'hunch' was correct. A few months after you told us Spidre would want the subject captured alive, an official transmission came in from San Francisco instructing all Commanders to do just that. We are to transport her to San Antonio by sunset tomorrow. They will transport her the remainder of the way to Spidre's compound."

What the fuck? Naren thought. *I didn't know about that. When did such a high-level transmission come in? And what could Spidre want with a LO-EC?* "Good, so I guess you understand how important this is to Spidre," Naren said aloud. "Therefore, you won't have any objection to me joining Tank on the escort team."

"I have several objections to that. Perhaps you have forgotten, but Russ lacks a vocal processor. Tank is proficient at delivering a report. You are also a detective. You are no longer needed for this case. A soldier is the more logical asset to accompany Tank."

"I'm sorry, but since when did Tank need soldiers for backup?" Naren snapped back. "Is it getting weak in its old age or something?"

Tank stopped rolling the vessel towards its transport vehicle and turned its heavily armored, 8-foot-tall humanoid frame to face Naren. It lit up the two massive electric swords in its forearms to threaten Naren with, bathing its gunmetal grey body in blue light.

"Oh, enough with the dramatics Can, I know you're telling Tank to do that. Trying to scare me into submission is not going to work, and you know it."

Tank remained in the same position. Naren sighed. "Look, the fact is that Tank only needs soldiers around to notice threats it may not. It doesn't need offensive or defensive back up. So, putting me on the transport in place of one soldier is not going to make a difference. Furthermore, I'm asking to do this to help you. For whatever reason, Spidre thinks this LO-EC is something he needs to deal with himself, and you needed my help to find her. He is going to need convincing that I am all you need to keep this city under control. If you think Tank will do a better job than me at convincing Spidre to keep his peacekeepers out of your city, then, by all means, have me stay here."

Can and Tank remained silent. After a few moments, Tank shut down his electric swords and resumed work on the transport vehicle.

"Your argument seems valid. Very well, you will accompany Tank to San Antonio." Can said. "However, I would recommend you stem your arrogant nature. It will get you killed one day," it threatened.

"I could say the same for you," Naren responded.

"Androids cannot die. The transport leaves in one hour and thirteen minutes. Take this time to go back to your apartment and gather what you need to make the trip."

Chapter 11

At dawn, the transport left New Orleans for San Antonio. It was a huge truck, with an electric engine that ran across the entire bottom of the vehicle. The engine was covered by a metal platform that extended out from either side of the prison containment vessel in the center. The extensions were where armed guards were meant to line up. It could hold up to 20 on either side, but at the moment, it held only six. Tank was so massive that it had to stand sideways on the front-left side of the vehicle, with one soldier between him and Naren at the back left. On the right side were three general peacekeeping infantry. The containment vessel they all surrounded was held a few inches in the air by a dozen metal beams and its own independent suspension system, meaning the vessel's occupant would have no idea what was going on outside unless the entire thing toppled over. The vessel's sealed access port butted against a large metal wind guard at the front of the transport, making it impossible for the seal to be removed from the inside. Tank, now far out of communication range from Can, was relying on its own rudimentary strategic programming. This proved to be quite an annoyance to the four soldiers and Naren.

"It has now been ten minutes since our last status reports," Tank boomed in an electronic voice slightly deeper than Can's. "Please provide updated status reports one by one. Front left of transport reports no change in status."

"Center left reporting no change in status," the soldier in front of Naren said, frustrated.

"Rear left reporting no change in status." Naren said.

"Rear right reporting no change in status."

"Center right reporting no change in status."

"Front right reporting no change in status."

"Reports received. No changes in status reported. Situation continues to be nominal. Please provide new status report in ten minutes."

Naren had, in fact, noticed something. To the south, dust had been kicked up in a way that seemed off. Maybe it was the wind acting weird, maybe it was something else. Either way, he knew it was nothing he should let Tank know about. He noticed it a couple more times over the course of an hour. He always observed it in the south, and always kept the observation to himself.

Without warning, the transport came to an abrupt halt. Naren knew that could only mean one thing. Tank jumped off the car, and the vehicle swayed back and forth. Naren followed suit, and before Tank turned and blocked his sight, he saw an elcycle approaching from the east.

"It's Nadine!" he thought. But who's the other… holy shit did she meet another LO-EC?"

Nadine leapt from the cycle with energy blazing from her feet and hurdled towards Tank. Edgar ran after, close in tow, blade sticking out of his right hand. Naren started to lean back, preparing to launch at Tank full force when he felt a rush of air, and the soldier in front of him was thrown into the side of the prison transport, seemingly by nothing. As the soldier fell lifeless to the ground, Naren looked south, across the sprawling arid plain, to see another man standing there with his left hand crossing his body.

"Got one!" the mystery person cheered out loud. He stood about 5'9" and was stick skinny. His hair was long and unkept, he had no shoes, and his once white t-shirt and khakis looked to have years' worth of stains on them. Even more strangely, the man's entire body seemed to be constantly twitching, almost vibrating. In an instant, his right arm went from his side to above his head. The movement was accompanied by a loud snapping sound, akin to the crack of a whip. It was so fast that the air in front of him displaced and sent a shockwave rolling away from him and towards Naren. Naren reflexively jumped back and rolled out of the way. The man took off running at Naren, his feet carrying him even faster than the shockwave he had just unleashed. He lunged to try and tackle Naren, who managed to get into position just in time to throw the man over his shoulder and send him flying. The man landed on his back about 30 feet behind the transport and immediately popped back up.

"How the fuck did he do that!? Doesn't matter, just recover and go at him again," the mystery man thought. Right before he took off running again, he caught a glimpse in between Tank and the transport and saw the other three soldiers coming around the front of the truck. The man took off running towards Naren and flung his right arm up while doing so. The shockwave passed in between Tank and the transport and careened into the unsuspecting soldiers. Nadine and Edgar, protected by Tank's massive body, were unphased. The soldiers were decimated.

The mystery man unleashed a barrage of punches and kicks at Naren as soon as he was in range. The shots came so fast that

Naren had no chance to counter, only dodge. And dodge he did. The mystery man was growing frustrated. He could tell he had a huge speed advantage, yet he couldn't land a single blow on Naren.

As the fight progressed, the mystery man turned so that his back was to Tank. And Tank was now right behind him, bringing his massive forearm down for a blow. The man realized just in time and dodged left as Naren dodged right.

"Hey asshole! We're not done yet!" Nadine yelled as she drilled a kick to the back of Tank's head. The blow sent the android's right knee and left hand to the ground. Nadine jumped over the android while Edgar ran around to Tank's left and thrust his blade into the center of its massive grey hand, pinning it to the ground. Nadine whirled around and threw a kick at Tank's forearm, smashing his left electric blade. Simultaneously, Tank swung hard with his right hand, landing a direct blow on Nadine that sent her flying over Edgar's head. Naren turned just in time to see Edgar jump back and Nadine bounce off the side of the transport and slump to the ground.

Naren turned to face Tank. His eyes welled up, his face turned red, his fists clenched tight.

Tank was facing in Nadine's direction and flexing his left hand. The blade was broken but his fingers still functioned. "Yes, we are done," Tank boomed in his loud, low, robotic voice.

Naren lost it. The leather boots bound around his feet evaporated and were replaced by a brilliant blue glow. He launched forward with reckless abandon and slammed into Tank fists first. Tank was laid out flat, while Naren was brought out of his rage by the searing pain in his fingers.

The mystery man was stunned stiff. "He's one of us. But then what…" his thought was cut off as Naren turned to him and Edgar, who were now standing side by side.

"Handle it," Naren said to them with menace in his voice, as he took off into the air and came down at Nadine's side, nearly toppling over as he came to an awkward, running stop.

Edgar and the mystery man turned to one another.

"Edgar," Edgar said.

"Victor," the mystery man replied.

Tank was starting to sit up and roll over to his right side.

"Keep him on the ground!" Edgar yelled as he ran towards Tank.

Victor darted forward and threw up his left arm as he did so. The air he displaced hurdled towards Tank and knocked its shoulder back, forcing it to lean on both of its elbows. The android tried rolling over again, and again was put back on its elbows by another blast.

"Its head is exposed, I'm never going to have another shot like this," Victor thought as he jumped in the air and landed a drop kick to Tank's face.

"You all right?" Naren said to Nadine, a few meters away.

"No, you fuck, my arm's broken!" Nadine sputtered out as she stumbled to her feet holding her right arm against her body. "What the fuck are we doing, Naren?"

"Luring him out, among other things," Naren replied, and looked over at Victor as his drop kick landed.

Except the kick didn't work. Instead of getting laid flat out, Tank used the momentum of the hit to somersault over and get back on its feet. By now, Edgar had caught up, and he and Victor took turns trying to land blows and throw the massive android off balance while avoiding its heavy hits.

"Your fingers!" Nadine yelled. By now Naren's hands had swollen to three times their normal size.

"We can't worry about that now. We might take Tank down here, but we need to topple this transport to do it. Can you—"

Before he could even finish the sentence, Nadine swung around and threw a heavy kick at the first support beam of the vessel, splitting it in two.

"We topple it, then we run," Naren said.

Edgar darted in and swung his blade at Tank's chest. It landed, but only made the slightest of cuts in the android's thick armor. Victor noticed Edgar breathing very heavily, and he was starting to get winded himself, a weakness Tank did not share. He knew he had to try and end this fight soon.

When Edgar jumped back, Victor rushed in and slid into Tank's right leg. The blow knocked Tank to one knee, but it maintained its balance enough to bring its damaged left arm around. Victor scrambled to get back to his feet and turned to run but couldn't get away before Tank's massive hand was crushing his shoulder. He screamed in pain as Tank lifted its right hand and swung its functional electric blade down towards him. Edgar rushed in and threw his blade over his head, taking the full force of Tank's blow as it crashed down. Edgar had stopped the blow before it hit his newfound fighting partner, but now a searing pain radiated through his entire forearm. He wrapped his other hand around his wrist to fight against the force Tank was still bringing down. Tank's other hand was still wrapped around Victor's shoulder, holding him there so he couldn't fight back. Edgar could barely see straight he was so exhausted, but he could feel his blade slowly sinking into Tank's. It sank deeper and deeper until the electricity in the blade shorted out and Tank's forearm was sliced clean through.

Tank's severed hand hit the ground just as Naren and Nadine dove off the transport and the containment vessel toppled over. It hit the ground and a massive explosion erupted from inside, sending everyone tumbling.

"What the fuck!?" Victor and Nadine yelled at once.

The explosion caused a dust cloud to envelope the entire area. Victor couldn't see more than a couple feet in front of him. After about 20 seconds, a streak of blue light careened towards him and Naren appeared.

"Is Tank handled!?" Naren yelled.

"Uh, its blades are gone," Victor replied, clenching his injured shoulder.

"Good enough. Let's find him, Sera!" Naren yelled. He took off straight in the air. Behind him, Victor noticed another streak of light take off. This one was larger, and bright orange. He heard a loud crash, and then what seemed like an eternity of silence. The dust had just started to clear when Tank fell out of the sky and smashed into the ground a few feet from where Victor was standing. The mighty android now lay on the ground in pieces. Victor looked up to see Naren careening back down to the ground and the orange streak taking off back towards New Orleans.

Naren pulled up at the last minute and tumbled over himself as he landed. The dust had cleared now, and Victor saw Edgar struggling to his feet while Nadine was limping over and shaking the ringing out of her ears. They were both holding their arms.

"What. The fuck. Just happened?" Victor inquired.

Naren stared down at Tank's decimated body and started tearing all the badges and medals off his uniform. It was agony for his broken fingers, but he felt it had to be done. When he had nothing left to tear at, he looked up at Victor. "I know I owe everyone an explanation, especially you," he said. "And I will give it. But first, we need to get somewhere safe, and get these two some food," Naren said, glancing over at Nadine and Edgar. "You have a hideout, right?"

"I'm sorry, what?" Victor replied.

"All the raids you did over the years circled around one large swath of land between the highways here. So, wherever you've been hiding out must be relatively close by. Can we please go there to talk? It's not safe out here on the road."

"How the fuck did you know all of that?" Victor said.

"Well, it was kind of my job to figure these things out," Naren said, pointing to his investigator badge on the ground. "But not anymore. I needed this title to get certain things done. Two things, specifically. And they got done today."

"And those things being?"

"Wiping this piece of shit and the other androids off the face of the earth," Naren said, glancing over at the remains of Tank. "Although to be fair, doing that was someone else's dream to achieve, I was just helping out."

"And the other thing?"

Naren smiled. "Finding you."

Victor was stunned. *Why? Why the fuck does he care about me? How did he even know about me?* he thought.

"Look, I promise you, I will explain everything, absolutely everything," Naren said. "But we need to get out of here first. It is a long story, the complex at San Antonio is going to send people to investigate when the transport doesn't arrive, and we're in no shape to handle them. All four of us are injured, and these two are in dire need of some food. So, can we please get a move on?"

By this point, Edgar and Nadine were sitting on the ground, waiting for the conversation to finish. Nadine was looking a little shaky, more in pain than anything. Edgar looked like he was about to pass out.

"You look awful." Victor said to Edgar.

"Thanks, asshole," Edgar replied.

"Shit. Fuck. Sorry. I uh, haven't had to talk to anyone in a while. When was the last time you ate?"

"We had a little bit of food on the road, some soy bar thing. The last full meal was yesterday morning, before I left for the tournament in Los Angeles."

"Christ. No wonder you look like shit."

"Seriously?"

"Fuck! Sorry! But if I went that long without eating, I'd already be passed out. And that's without traveling across the country or fighting an android."

Victor turned back to Naren.

"Fine. Let's get out of here and get patched up. I'll hear your story and we'll see where to take it from there."

Naren smiled and turned to Nadine. "Can you still drive the cycle?"

"I can manage."

"Ok. Let's get your guy on the back and get moving. When we get to the hideout, I promise everything will be made clear."

They helped Edgar onto the cycle and Nadine revved up the engine. They took off and followed Victor as he ran North.

Naren followed from the air and alternated between wincing from the pain in his hands and looking down at the three people who had just helped him stop the unstoppable.

Chapter 12

"So umm, I can only give you stuff I found in the forest, like berries and dried meats and stuff. The food from the UN is better, but it also lasts longer. And I don't think I can stay here anymore, so I'll need it."

Nadine and Edgar barely acknowledged Victor, they just grabbed a strip of meat off a string hanging from a tree and tore into it.

Edgar, Nadine, and Naren had followed Victor miles off-road to an old campground. The area was a small dirt clearing surrounded by low trees that covered the sky with their canopy. The clearing was on a slight incline, at the top of which Victor had constructed a large lean-to. All his supplies and the food he had foraged were now pushed to the back wall to make room for everyone as they sat and set their wounds as best they could.

"How did you find this place?" Naren asked after swallowing a huge mouthful of food.

"My parents used to take me camping here all the time, taught me how to find food and build houses and all that. The area is called 'Kisatchie National Forest'. It's too big and I keep too low a profile to ever get noticed by the peacekeepers. Well, kept a low profile till today, I guess."

"How did you get UN supplies?" Edgar asked

"There's a bunch of big cities near this park, and the old highways are used for government supply runs. If I go out looking for food, I try to stay near the highway, and if a truck goes by that's lacking on security, especially if I'm low on supplies, I run up, pop open the back, grab what I can, and get out before they even see me. I was looking for food near I-10 when I noticed the transport Tank was with, and when I saw you two on the elcycle, I knew something big had to be going down."

"Isn't robbing military convoys a little risky?" Edgar asked.

Victor shook his head. "I'm too fast, so I figured I'd never get caught. Guess that wasn't true."

He looked over at Naren.

"No that's a spot-on assessment," Naren replied. "Everyone just thought the trucks were old and the latches were breaking. No one noticed that the missing supplies were the result of theft until I came around. Well, no one in New Orleans. But don't worry, the whole time I was there I had them believing someone else was doing it."

"And who is that?"

"Her name is Serafina, Sera for short. She is the reason I came here, and the reason I figured out that you existed."

"You're wrong," Victor said. "I don't know a Sera. I don't know anyone, and no one knows me."

Something about the way Victor said that made Nadine curious. "Victor," she said. "How long have you been here by yourself?"

"Shit, I have no fucking idea," he replied.

"Well, what caused you to come here?" she asked.

"My parents told me to run when the peacekeepers invaded Chicago, so I ran here."

Naren and Nadine both went slack jawed. Edgar and Victor looked confused.

"What's the big deal?" Victor asked.

"That… was twenty years ago Victor. You're telling me you've lived in the forest, alone, since you were a child?"

"Jesus Christ," Edgar said.

"I… didn't realize it was that long," Victor replied, half embarrassed and half amazed.

"I'm… I'm astounded, Victor," Naren said. "I knew you had been out here that long, but by yourself? I mean as a kid how did you even…"

"You still haven't told me how you knew that," Victor interrupted.

"Fair enough, we'll hear your story later. Sera doesn't know you, but she is the reason I knew about you. Let me start at the beginning to be as clear as possible."

Victor nodded.

Naren told the whole tale from beginning to end: How he was able to join the military, why he came to New Orleans and Nadine didn't, how he met Sera, what Sera's powers were, and how they hatched a plan destroy the androids, reunite with Nadine and, hopefully, lure Victor out of hiding.

"Your girlfriend sounds pretty incredible, Naren," Nadine said, with a smirk as Naren finished his story.

Naren turned bright red and stroked the back of his head, embarrassed. "I guess I was laying on the complimentary lingo a little thick, huh?"

"You are terrifying," Victor said.

Naren chuckled. "What does that mean?"

"You designed this whole plan, and it worked exactly as you wanted it to. Are you some kind of genius or something?"

"My plan was far from genius," Naren said. "While I did want to stay and help Sera, the fact remained that I was, in essence, a prisoner in New Orleans. I couldn't leave without the androids getting suspicious, and communicating with or sending money to Nadine was out of the question. My plan caused me to be separated from my sister for a year and a half. That's not genius, that's fucking stupid."

Tears started to well up in Naren and Nadine's eyes.

"I could go on," Naren continued. "Even with the plan, all of us are injured and exhausted. And had you attacked me first instead of the soldier in front of me, I'd be a goner right now. And most importantly, it took all four of us combined to end Tank. Nadine was able to bust one sword, so I was correct in assessing her abilities, but even still he had all four of us on the ropes. If Edgar hadn't been there to disable the other sword, I don't know that we would've succeeded."

"Yeah, I noticed he wasn't in any of your plans," Victor said, turning to Edgar. "You don't know each other?"

"I entered the tournament yesterday, same as Nadine. I was sick of scraping by, and Byron's fortune would have had me set for a while. We met in the final and I, uh, sort of forced Nadine to use her powers and got her arrested."

A look of anger flashed in Naren's eyes as they trained on Nadine.

"You used your powers in broad daylight?! In front of hundreds of people!? What the fuck were you thinking!?"

"It was my fault!" Edgar exclaimed. Naren's angry eyes trained on Edgar.

"She was overwhelming me, and I wanted to win so bad! I

needed that money, Naren."

Naren remained silent.

"I, uh, I did help her escape though. Well, Symon and I."

"Symon?" Naren asked.

"That elcycle there? That's Symons. He's another one of us. Well, sort of like us. He can't fly or blow up or anything, but he's strong and has the holes in his hands just like Nadine. He was in LA buying another elcycle to replace this one. He was at the tournament and saw the whole thing, pulled me out before the guards could grab me. Then he and I ambushed the convoy just outside of San Francisco."

"San Francisco?" Naren asked as he turned to Nadine. "Why were they taking you to Spidre's compound?"

"I still haven't figured that out myself," Nadine replied.

Naren's look changed to concern. "Something is going on here that we don't know about."

"How do you mean?" Nadine asked.

"When I first met Sera, and she robbed the warehouse while the androids were guarding it, I was worried that if she did happen to get caught, they would kill her. So, I made up a lie that Spidre would want someone that unique taken alive. Then last night when they caught her, Can told me that it and the other Commanders received orders a few months ago to take any criminals suspected of being LO-ECs alive."

"What the fuck?" Nadine said.

"Yeah, it's been bothering me all day."

"Well, I don't know what this has to do with it, but Spidre isn't the man you thought he was. He's a LO-EC, like us. A powerful one. He came out of the compound to fight us himself. I suspect he thought it was just me and that he could handle a one-on-one fight."

Naren's look changed to one of astonishment. "I, uh. Ok. So what can he do?"

"Blades can come out of his hands," Nadine said. "It looks sort of similar to Edgar's but they come out of his palms, and they're a little more ragged looking. But he can do both hands at once, and he can shoot them off like an energy beam."

Edgar was impressed. He had seen Spidre's blades up close, and hadn't noticed their raggedness, or that they came out of his palms. He couldn't help but feel a little jealous at Nadine's perceptual ability.

"Ugh, this is frustrating." Naren said. "All of this was meant to help us find out more about who we are, and now there are even more questions than before."

"I had an idea about that," Nadine said. "Edgar, you talked to Symon more than anyone here. How much do you think he knows about LO-ECs?"

"Uhm, a lot I think," Edgar replied. "More than we do, at the very least."

"And we need to go back to him anyway, to return the elcycle," Nadine said. "I suggest we all go there and ask if he can fill in some blanks for us. He said he would let us hide out. If nothing else, it'll be a destination, and we need to get on the road ASAP."

"No, what we need to do ASAP is rest." Naren replied. "You two have been in three major fights in two days, we've been in one, and Sera is going to be exhausted when she gets back. We'll be safe for one night. Let's rest and get on the road in the morning."

Nadine sighed. She knew Naren was right. "Fine," she muttered in reply. "Are you going to come, Victor?"

"Well… I mean, I can't stay here anymore, and it'll be better if we stick together now, no?"

"Agreed," Naren said. "Do we know where he's located?"

"The autonav in the elcycle is programmed to a coordinate in San Diego." Nadine replied.

Naren turned to face Victor. "You said you ran here from Chicago. Think you can run that far again? The cycle only seats two.

"Honestly, I have no fucking clue. I haven't had to run that far in a long-ass time. But do I have a choice?" Victor replied.

"Sure you do. Sera or I could carry you," Naren said with a smile.

"No, no. I can definitely run it," Victor said with a smirk back.

"Then it's settled," Naren said. "We leave for San Diego in the morning. I'm going to go fly over the hideout and wait for Sera. She'll be able to see me against the night sky. But before I go…"

Naren glared at Edgar.

"…let me say the following. Edgar, you're a fucking moron for getting my sister captured."

Edgar felt anxious, but only for a moment, since Naren's glare started to soften.

"But also, thank you for going to get her, and for helping us take out Tank. I don't know what would've happened if you hadn't been here."

Edgar breathed a sigh of relief. "Let's just call it even, ok?"

"Even it is." Naren replied. "And Victor, thank you for sheltering us. You had a good thing going here. It's a lot to give up."

"Yeah, well, I was starting to get lonely," he said, causing everyone to laugh.

"Ok, I'm off. Sera should be wrapping up soon," Naren said as he gathered himself and turned to take off.

"Oh yeah, I never got a chance to ask. Where is Sera now?" Edgar inquired.

Without turning around, Naren replied "Unleashing 20 years of pent-up fury on the last two androids."

Chapter 13

It's… it's dead. Sera thought as she flew back to New Orleans.

"It's dead!" she shouted as she spun through the air, a smile on her face and tears of joy streaming down her cheeks. At long last, the obstacle that had been standing in her way for twenty years was gone. Now only Can and Russ remained, and she knew how to deal with them. Her mind refocused on the task at hand and her smile fell away. Her jaw clenched and her eyes slightly squinted as her thoughts alternated between her battle strategy and the memory of her parents on that fateful day, twenty years ago.

"How do you do that, Russ?" she thought, mouthing the words as they came to her. "How do you just mow people down without caring? You saw me there. I know you saw me. I glow like a fucking sun! You knew they had a six-year-old child, and you killed them! I hate you, Russ. I hate you!"

Sera wiped her eyes and saw she was nearing New Orleans proper.

But I won't have to hate you much longer, she thought.

She started looking for the two gunmetal grey androids. Russ's form was almost humanlike. From a distance, it could pass for a broad-chested, six-foot-tall male. Its body was lightly armored, at least in comparison to Tank, and built to be much more agile. A small laser cannon sat just above its right hand and a machine gun sat atop its left. Electric blades were stored inside both of its bulging forearms and could extend out from the pinky side of its wrists for close-quarter combat. Jet boosters were built into its feet, and half a dozen stabilizing boosters lined its waist. Sera knew that Can and Russ were likely going to be near each other. Since its nonhumanoid body type would stick out like a sore thumb, and since it was her first target, Can was the one she was scanning the streets for.

She checked near headquarters first. Not there. She figured they might be making rounds, checking places with valuable equipment, making sure no civilians were trying to take advantage of Tank's absence. She checked the credit processing center next. No androids, just a handful of soldiers inquiring if their paychecks had gone through. She turned to head to her next target, and there they were. Both androids were walking down the street on their way to transport storage.

"Could they know I'm coming?" she thought. "No. They think I'm captured, and Tank was way out of range of their weird psychic comm system. There was no distress call. They know nothing."

She turned and saw the sun behind her. Even if they bothered to look up, they could never make out her small frame against the glare.

Ok, enough stalling, she thought. *You got this.*Sera took a deep breath.

"Go," she whispered to herself.

Sera plummeted to earth at full speed. The wind seemed to be screaming in her ears and her eyes burned from going so fast.

Faster, as fast as you can, god damn it! she thought.

Can and Russ were getting bigger and bigger. 300 yards away.

200. 50. 10.

A crescendo of noise roared across the city as Sera smashed into Can's chest. Bone impacting metal. Metal being wrenched and twisted. Pieces of debris flying off in every direction, each one booming and echoing as it slammed into a building or the street.

Fuuuuuck that hurt! she thought. She checked her fingers to see if they were broken. They weren't, but they hurt like hell and the skin on her knuckles had torn away. She turned to see Can lying on the ground in two big pieces and thousands of smaller ones. The lower half wasn't moving, the upper half was slowing down fast. A high-pitched metallic screech belched from its upper torso just before it went lifeless.

"A signal for backup, maybe? Whatever. Next step!" Sera thought. She launched towards Russ, who by now was taking off into the air while taking aim with its laser cannon. Russ fired and Sera rolled right in anticipation of the shot. It zipped past her and blasted a small crater in the street below. Before Russ could get off another shot, she was on top of it. She grabbed both of its forearms and, twenty feet in the air, kept them angled above her head. Russ had no shot with its guns and its blades were just a touch too high. Russ struggled with all its mechanical strength to lower its arms and get a good angle. And slowly but surely, Russ was winning. Another millimeter lower. Another two millimeters. Another two millimeters. Sera pushed back as hard as she could, but it wasn't enough.

Shit, bail! she thought as she ducked her head and threw Russ's arms to the right just as the blades came out. Unphased, the android rotated back and caught Sera with a vicious elbow to the side of the head. The hit dazed her for only a second, but it was enough to send her tumbling to the ground. As she popped back up, Russ took aim with the machine gun and opened fire. She flew forward and under the android, and took her eyes off of it just in time to see four soldiers lining up in the street to open fire as well. They had about ten feet in between them, separating in order to cover as much of the street as possible.

Perfect, she thought.

She pressed forward and was on top of them before they could take a shot. She took a hold of the first soldier by the neck and tossed him over her back, where he was eviscerated by the ceaseless shots from Russ's machine gun. As the bullets hit the first soldier, Sera made a hairpin turn and grabbed the second and third, one of their necks in each of her hands. Then she spun and let go, sending one soldier flying down the street and the other face first into the ground. In the next instant, she had her hands wrapped around the shoulders of the final soldier. She ripped him off the ground and with another hairpin left was angled back at Russ, with the soldier between her and the gunfire. Russ did not let up. It continued firing on its subordinate as Sera pushed closer. Finally, one of the bullets made it through the soldier's mangled torso and hit Sera in the left shoulder.

Shit! Ignore the pain. It's nothing. Ignore it! she thought.

She forced her way through the agony and continued upwards. When mere inches separated the lifeless soldier and Russ, she threw the body aside and grabbed Russ's arms again. She had a better angle this time. She caught the android at the wrist, right behind where the blades left its forearm. With her legs angled outward, the two of them started to rotate. Where they once were perpendicular to the ground, they were now turning closer to parallel, with Sera on top. They kept rotating farther and farther over, while Russ tried in vain to bring its blades down on Sera's shoulders. The pain from Sera's wound was excruciating, but she fought it with everything she had. After several seconds of struggle, they rotated so far that Russ's stabilizing boosters couldn't keep it in place, and the two of them propelled to the ground. Russ slammed into the pavement and Sera started dragging it along the cracked roadway as she flew. The sparks from metal hitting road subsided as Russ was pushed down so hard that it sank through the street. When Sera could push no more, she let go of the android's left hand and flipped forward, pulling Russ over her head. The blade on its right hand came within inches of her face as she brought Russ around, but it did not connect. Sera landed as she completed her flip and slammed the android down on its stomach. She stood on its back and pushed down with her leg while pulling back on the arm as hard as she could. Russ's left hand flailed wildly, trying to land a blow, but to no avail. The right arm bent farther and farther back until it snapped off at the shoulder. The blade on the now separated arm remained protruded, and while it had de-electrified the instant the appendage came off, it was still razor sharp. Sera plunged the arm blade first into Russ's left shoulder. It pierced clean through and pinned the android to the ground. She launched back up into the air and despite Russ's boosters going at full blast, the android could not move forward. When she thought she had enough height, Sera turned around and descended back to earth as fast as she could, aiming for Russ's waist. Meanwhile, Russ changed tactics and pushed up against the blade with its one good arm, trying to pull it out of the ground. It made a little progress, but not enough before Sera crashed back down right on its waistline. For the second time, a loud metallic wrenching sound filled the air as Russ's torso was separated from its legs. Sera darted forward and grabbed Russ' left wrist and pulled on the still attached arm. With the blade she'd stuck in the shoulder still anchoring the android to the ground, the last appendage popped off with the smallest of effort. At last, Russ was now defenseless and defeated.

Sera stood with one foot on Russ's torso and both hands on her hips, gasping for breath. When she felt she had recovered enough, she turned its torso over to look at the android's face. It was still functional. Its sensory inputs seemed to be scanning in desperation for a way out or for backup.

"I like that," Sera said, exasperated. "I like that you're still looking around. Makes me think you can feel fear." A wicked smile crossed her face.

"You can understand me, right? Yea, you definitely understand me. You probably don't remember me. I mean, you remember me from yesterday, sure, but you don't truly remember me. Don't remember that day 20 years ago, when you murdered my parents. Well I do, asshole!"

The scream was too much. She had to stop talking and take a few deep breaths.

"I remember that day. Far too well. And as a result, I've spent a lifetime planning this day. I needed help to do it. A lot of help. Not to destroy you, mind you. You were easy. But I couldn't do anything to end you with your bigger buddy still in the picture. It was taken care of a few hours ago."

When she uttered those words, Russ's sensors stopped darting around and trained on her.

"Oh, so that's who you were looking for, eh?" Sera continued. "Yeah, Tank was the first to go. That investigator you've been working with? He's a LO-EC, just like me. Just like my parents. He outsmarted all of you, and with the help of his badass sister, they ended Tank. And with big buddy out of the way, nothing could stop my vengeance on you. I hate you, Russ. I fucking hate you! You don't deserve to walk this earth! God, I want to tear you to shreds and leave nothing for anyone to find!"

Sera paused again to catch her breath. The pause helped her refocus. The wicked smile returned to her face.

"But I can't tear you asunder, Russ. I need you. At least part of you. You see, what Naren told you was true. I was building a garden this whole time. It was for a few hundred people who for whatever reason consider me a god returned to earth. And a god needs to feed her people. So, I had been powering the garden myself with this."

She pulled away the cloth on her right shoulder to reveal the metallic hole at her arm's apex.

"Only problem is, I can't power my garden anymore. I just took part in destroying the world-famous androids. I have to go on the run. That's where you come in, Russ. Naren tells me that whatever powers you three, it's self-contained. You generate your own power somehow, and you do it from right here."

Sera tapped on Russ's chest.

"A few of my followers are brilliant electrical engineers. So, it looks like you'll be powering the garden in my place. Just part of you, though. The power part. I don't need this silly sensory, memory, information-processing part here."

Sera tapped on Russ's head.

"Now, this isn't what I want, mind you. If I had it my way, I'd want the sensory part to remain intact as long as possible. I'd want you to see me as I tear you apart into little bitty pieces. If you feel agony, if you feel fear, I would want to give you all of it for as long as I could. But I can't have that. Part of you is too important. So, I made a little compromise to my philosophy, to my vengeance. Just a little feeling that I'll hold onto that'll give me some satisfaction. Naren told me that when I smash your stupid face, that's it. No memory, no information, no conscience. But just once, I'd like to think he's wrong. I'd like to think that there's some little self-aware piece of you tucked away in your chest. Nothing major, just something that knows that you, a once mighty android, are being used to power a garden for the very same people who you viciously oppressed. Some part of you that knows that and will continue to know that for all eternity. That thought, the thought that you'll continue to know what you've become yet be able to do nothing about it. That gives me enough peace of mind to move on. You're a scar on humanity, Russ. Or you were. Now…"

Sera chuckled.

"…now you're just a generator. Goodbye, Russ."

The smile fell from her face and was replaced by a look of sheer rage.

"and good riddance!"

Sera cocked her right arm all the way back and threw a single thunderous punch down on Russ's head, sending hundreds of pieces flying off into the street. What little of Russ's face and neck remained attached, she ripped off and tossed as far as she could. She looked down at the grey torso at her knees for what seemed like an eternity.

"Get out of your head, Sera! We've got work to do. Deliver this thing while you still have some semblance of energy," she said as she shook herself back into reality.

She heaved the torso onto her good shoulder and took off for the outskirts of the city. When she was surrounded by nothing but old abandoned buildings, she descended and strolled inside the very same one where Naren and she had reunited all those months ago. She walked down the stairs to 200 people running up and down row after row of vegetables and starches, all at various stages of growth so that nothing went to waste by over ripening or spoiling.

When she walked in, everyone stopped and ran over. She looked pretty beat up. Clothes torn, hands bruised in places and ripped open in others, the side of her face swollen from Russ's elbow, and blood still trickling from the bullet wound on her shoulder.

"You're hurt, Serafina!" Alison cried as she ran through the crowd.

"I'll be fine Alison, it's nothing serious," she replied.

"That, that metal thing you're carrying. That's… you did it?!"

"It's done," Sera said with a smile.

A huge cheer swelled up from all corners of the massive room. Tears began to stream down Sera's face. Everyone ran up and hugged Sera and each other, while Russ's torso was still slung on Sera's shoulder.

"Umm, I don't mean to take away from this moment, but this thing is getting kind of heavy," she said.

"Oh, my word I'm so sorry!" Alison replied.

Everyone backed up and allowed her to walk over to the battery she had stolen many months prior. She put the torso down next to it.

"Can I ask for one last meal before I go? I don't think I've ever been this hungry," Sera inquired.

"It's already prepped, take a seat."

Next to the battery was a long row of hand-sewn and stuffed cushions to sit on. Sera sat on the nearest one and was handed a huge plate of food. It might've been because she was so hungry, but it was the most delicious thing she'd ever tasted. While eating, she couldn't take her eyes off Russ's torso.

"I only did damage to his extremities," she blurted out during her last bite. "There's no reason the power source shouldn't work."

"We'll figure it out, child," Alison replied.

"The garden is going to be self-contained now," Sera continued, standing up from the table. "From the outside it'll look like just another decrepit building. As long as you're careful about entering and leaving, whoever comes in to replace the androids will have no reason to suspect this place."

"Again, we'll figure it out, child," Alison reiterated. "You have done so much, we can handle it from here. It's time you go out there and help the rest of the world."

Sera's eyes started to well up again.

"Do you, do you have my other uniforms?" she asked.

A man came over with several other Kung Fu outfits of all different colors, folded and tied up together. He handed them to Alison, who in turn handed them to Sera.

Tears started to stream down Sera's face once more. "I won't ever forget you. Not ever! Ok?" Sera sputtered out.

Everyone encircled her for one last long hug, and she made her way outside. She took one quick look back at the building, and with a smile, took off to the North-North West.

I, I did it, she thought to herself. *It's over. It's over. Mom, Dad, I did it. It's over. I did it. It's over!* "It's over!" she screamed aloud.

She continued to cry for what seemed like ages. When the emotional rush did subside, the stresses of the day caught up with her. She was exhausted. Sera flew for another twenty minutes until she found herself nearing a wooded area. Against the greens and browns of the forest, she could see Naren's feet glowing like a beacon. She rushed down to Naren while Naren rushed upward to greet her. They embraced and spun around through the air. Sera planted a big kiss on Naren's lips and Naren couldn't be happier, he wanted the same thing. When their lips unlocked from each other, Naren held Sera out at arm's length and looked her up and down.

"Let me guess, should've seen what happened to the other guy?" he said.

Sera cackled with laughter, the bad joke being a welcome respite after the pain and emotion of the day.

"Everything went to plan. Well, almost," she said, as she glanced at her shoulder.

"Let's head down. We'll get you patched up," Naren replied as the two of them started descending.

"How are your fingers? And did Nadine and the other guy get injured?" Sera asked.

"Other guys, actually," Naren replied. "It's a long story. Everyone got injured during the fight, but we couldn't have done it without all of their help. Nadine's humerus is broken. Our mystery man, his name is Victor, has a severely dislocated shoulder, and the other guy, Edgar, has a fractured ulna. I'm still in pain but I'll be ok. Lots of happy things going on to keep me distracted," Naren said with a smile.

Sera smiled back. "It's funny. Everything that happened today, and the thing I'm most nervous about is meeting your sister."

"Well, you won't have to be nervous much longer," Naren replied as they landed.

They walked the twenty paces to Victor's camp. Everyone was standing and waiting, having seen Naren and Sera descend. They arrived, and Sera found herself standing across the small clearing from Nadine, her arm in a makeshift wooden splint and hung in a makeshift cloth sling.

She's beautiful, Sera thought. *Even now, after everything that's happened today, she's so gorgeous. She fought so hard, got so injured, and did it without even needing a reason.* "Umm, you must be Sera. It's nice to meet you." Nadine said with a little smile.

"Shit," she thought to herself. And overcome with immeasurable gratitude, she sobbed and ran over to hug Nadine. Nadine turned just in time to protect her injured arm from Sera's tight embrace. Sera buried her head in Nadine's shoulder and wept. Everyone was frozen in place, unsure of what should happen next. The freeze thawed when Nadine wrapped her good arm around Sera and hugged her as tight. Tears began streaming down Nadine's face as she leaned her head against Sera's. Once Nadine started crying, no one else's eyes were left dry either. Everyone was overwhelmed at the sight of an immense, emotional pain lifting right in front of their eyes.

After a while, Nadine let go of her embrace and pulled Sera in front of her, their faces inches from each other.

"Naren explained everything," she said. "I don't have words for how glad I am that I could help bring you and your parents some peace."

Sera wiped her eyes and smiled from ear to ear.

"Let's get you patched up and get some food in you." Nadine continued. "We'll fill you in on everything and then we have to get to bed. Tomorrow before dawn, we set out on our first adventure together."

Chapter 14

"Naren. Naren! We got to get up." Victor said in an urgent whisper.

Naren undraped his hand from around Sera and popped up in the center of the lean-to. "What happened?"

"The birds started chirping, that means we have an hour till sunrise. We should get moving."

"Urgh!" Naren groaned as he rubbed his eyes. "Ok I'm up, I'm up. How are you so awake right now?"

"Umm, well the birds are always my wake-up call. But I couldn't sleep much with her so close," Victor said while looking at Sera, her glowing face peeking out from under a blanket.

"It takes some getting used to," Naren replied. "But wait, wouldn't you be used to an orange glow? You don't light fires at night?"

"Only when it's freezing cold. And I don't sleep then, either. I get worried someone will see."

"Guess that's something you won't miss about this place, huh?"

"You're not wrong," Victor said with a smile.

Naren shook Sera awake and then looked over at Nadine and Edgar at the far end of the lean-to. Nadine had fallen asleep on Edgar's lap, and Edgar in turn had fallen over onto Nadine during the night.

"Oy! You two!" Naren shouted.

Edgar and Nadine shook awake, realized the position they were in, and jumped out of the lean-to.

"Time to get moving," Naren continued with a smirk. Edgar turned bright red, and Nadine started laughing.

"Oh, damn it!" Sera exclaimed as she rubbed her arms as if they were irritated. "I got too involved in our conversations last night!"

"Ugh, we both forgot," Naren said.

Edgar was about to ask what they forgot, but remembered just before the words left his mouth.

Sera walked with urgency past the lean-to and deeper into the forest. As she walked away from Naren, Edgar and Nadine approached him.

"How'd you guys sleep?" Naren asked.

"Decent, I guess," Edgar replied. "But it was hard to fall asleep with her around."

"I was about to say the same thing!" Nadine followed.

Victor burst out laughing. "Hey, we all agree on something already!" he managed to blurt out as his laughing fit died down.

"So… how do her clothes stay on despite her, you know, basically exploding?" Edgar asked.

Naren chuckled. "That's not a bad description. She said usually she disrobes before letting off energy. That outfit she's wearing is special. Most of the concussive force just passes right through the fabric, and what doesn't is somewhat negated by the fabric's strength. It doesn't hold out forever though. She'll get maybe two more uses out of that one before it's too tattered. So she uses them sparingly, only when she may have to use her blast in combat."

No sooner had Naren finished his sentence than the roar of an explosion echoed through the campsite, followed by a stiff breeze that caused the surrounding trees to sway. Edgar was awestruck.

"So she has to do that every day?" he asked.

"At least twice a day, sometimes a third but rarely."

"Christ. I can't imagine having to deal with such a burden," Edgar said.

"Burden?" Nadine asked. "It's a gift and a curse, just like anything else, Edgar. It is a heavy inconvenience, but she is also basically a god among ants. We have to hide our powers, but her? She can shine as bright as she wants, and with Tank gone, there isn't a soul on this planet who could stop her."

Victor heard this and realized he was much the same. He had the gift of his speed, the curse of his shaking.

"You're right. Of course you're right," Edgar replied. "Why do I feel like I'm going to learn a lot hanging around you guys?"

"Anything's possible," Nadine replied with a smirk.

When Sera returned to camp, everyone quickly ate and started loading everything they could onto the elcycle. With all of the injuries, only Naren could manage to carry a pack. Edgar might've been able to as well, but with Nadine's arm in a sling, she needed to hang on tight while he drove, so a pack on Edgar's back just couldn't happen. Edgar hit the autonav button on the elcycle's console and the coordinates in San Diego popped up. With some help from Nadine, a route was chosen that took them off road whenever possible and avoided the major cities. With that done, they were off, Naren and Sera flying low overhead while Victor ran alongside. They spent the first half of the ride in silence. The only people who could hear each other over the wind were Edgar and Nadine, and she passed out the second she sat down on the cycle.

About halfway to San Diego, they stopped to eat again and so Victor could catch his breath.

"You ok?" Naren asked.

"Just… a little… winded," Victor replied in between breaths. "I'll be fine. I feel… good… muscles aren't… twitching… as much."

"I did notice that, but it didn't feel right to mention it," Naren said. "You have those involuntary muscle spasms a lot. Is that normal?"

"I guess so? I've had them as long as I can remember. I think they're why I'm fast, or maybe they're caused by the same thing. Whatever, I don't know," Victor said.

"It doesn't hurt or anything right?" Naren asked.

"Nah, just annoying sometimes. And speaking of annoying, there was something I thought about during the ride that's bugging me. What the fuck are we going to do when we get to San Diego?"

"I don't follow," Naren replied.

"How are we going to get into San Diego without being spotted?" Victor asked?

"Thank you!" Edgar exclaimed.

"I was wondering that myself!" Sera said. "I've never even heard of San Diego, are the peacekeepers there weak or something? Cause we can't fight for shit right now."

"There are no peacekeepers in San Diego," Naren said.

"Oh…" Sera replied.

"The reason why you haven't heard about it is because the whole city is abandoned. Has been for some time. Nadine and I know about it because the peacekeepers in LA were in charge of sending patrols there to make sure no one was raiding the old government facilities. I don't think there's much there besides abandoned buildings, and apparently this Symon guy."

"Well that makes life easy!" Sera said.

"Well, sort of," Nadine replied. "It makes it easy to get in there, but if we intend to stay, there's no telling how hard it will be to avoid patrols. Plus, finding food and resources could be tough. Hopefully Symon has all this figured out."

"Sounds like there's a lot to hope about Symon," Victor said. "We're putting a lot of faith in him to have answers, but we have no way of knowing if he's bullshitting us."

"He helped us fight Spidre and gave us the cycle to get cross country," Edgar said.

"Yeah. You said he also used to know Spidre, and that Spidre wants LO-ECs for some reason," Victor said. "What if this is all some big plan to lure us all out? What if they're working together?

"You're being paranoid," Edgar replied.

"Fucking right I am," Victor snapped back.

"And you bring up a good point," Naren interjected. "Symon helped us, a lot. And from how you described their fight, it seemed like Spidre wanted him dead. It's safe to assume he is not working with Spidre. However, we have no idea what his own intentions are. He is a stranger with an unknown agenda, and until we know what that is, we should remain cautious."

"So how do we do that?" Sera asked. "How do we find out if we can trust him?"

"Well, we're going to be asking him all sorts of questions, right?" Nadine said. "About us, about the battle or war or whatever the fuck happened that wiped LO-ECs out. So we want to try and get specifics, because if he is trying to mislead us, that would be the best way to trip him up. We should also try and get him to talk about his own past, because he may still have some sort of proof to back that up. It isn't perfect, but depending on what he reveals, it might be enough."

Everyone nodded after a few seconds of thought.

"Okay, so it's settled," Naren said. "We hear what Symon has to say, about our history, his history, and why he helped us."

Everyone nodded again.

"Let's get back on the road, then," Naren said.

They rode the rest of the way in silence. Not long before sunset they arrived at the coordinates on the autonav, with no signs of patrols. The building at the coordinates was a house, or at least it used to be, among a row of houses in similar disrepair. The place looked ancient. The roof had caved in and now only the first floor stood erect. Whatever color the house used to be had faded years ago. Now it was just bare faux-wood siding framing busted windows and a tattered front door. The front of the house was nearly flush with the street, leaving a substantial backyard given the size of the house.

"So uh, this is the place…" Nadine said, unimpressed.

"Christ, this looks like it's been abandoned for decades!" Sera declared.

Naren walked up to one of the window frames and peered in.

"It's not any more promising inside," he said.

"Let's check around back, maybe?" Nadine suggested with obvious pessimism.

They walked around the left side of the house, past a side door that was just as tattered as the front, and into the backyard. It was as unimpressive as the rest of the house. The ground was all dirt and gravel, and surrounded on three sides by a plastic picket fence that was falling apart. The back fence was in shambles, and the backyard on the other side was overgrown with brown grass. The fences on the sides of the yard were standing a bit straighter, but grass could be seen creeping over the tops of them as well.

"This fucking sucks," Victor said.

"Yea…" Naren replied. "But at least it's a decent place to camp out for the night. Let's get the elcycle off the street and we can—"

At that moment, a 5 foot by 4 foot patch of ground near the house flew open as if on a hinge. After a moment, a head poked out from inside the hole.

"Well uh… I sure hope I have enough food for five of you," Symon said through a beaming smile.

Everyone breathed a sigh of relief.

"Go get the elcycle and bring it in through here. I didn't hear any patrols for a while, but they were very active yesterday. Probably due to our little stunt in LA."

Edgar went around to grab the cycle in the front while Symon came out to meet everyone.

"So, I didn't catch your name when we met two days ago," Symon said extending his hand to Nadine.

"Nadine," she replied.

"Symon. It's nice to meet you." Symon said. "Did you uh, did you know you were going to be coming with this many people?"

"Definitely not. I only went for him," Nadine said, looking at Naren. "He's Naren, my brother."

"It's nice to meet you sir, thank you for all the help you provided to my sister," Naren said.

"Ugh. You called me sir. Worst word ever. Just call me Symon. Sir makes me feel my age."

"Can do."

Symon then turned to Victor. "So you're not the second brother, huh?"

"Not quite. I'm Victor, and I didn't know any of these guys till yesterday."

"That sounds like it will be quite the story," Symon said and let out a little chuckle. He then turned to Sera. Since she was standing behind everyone else, and it was still light out, he hadn't noticed her glowing till now.

"Hi. I'm Sera, thanks for taking us in!" Sera said with a smile.

"Uh, no problem," Symon replied, his eyes transfixed.

Sera's smile started to wane. "Umm, no offense, but you're kind of creeping me out right now," she said.

"I'm sorry! It's just you're…" Symon caught himself before saying the dumb thought in his head. "You're gorgeous, child."

Sera turned away, her smile returning and growing larger than before.

Edgar brought the elcycle downstairs, and everyone followed him in. Through the threshold was a tiny unfinished concrete room, barely big enough to fit the two elcycles. Naren crossed through that room to another door at the far wall and opened it into another area that was much larger. To the immediate right was a simple bathroom with just a toilet and shower. On the left was a larger room with a lot of old medical equipment shoved up against the wall. In the center of that room was what looked like a two-burner hot plate and a small freezer that were hooked up by wire to a 10' x 10' flat grey box mounted to the wall. Ahead of Naren and extending to the right past the bathroom was a larger open area. The right-hand side had a large wraparound desk. Past the desk was what was left of a staircase that led to the side entrance they had seen earlier. The rest of that area in the front of the house had chairs ringing the three walls with a mattress plopped down right in the center of them. Naren took this all in for about twenty seconds while everyone else entered the room.

"This was a dentist's office?" he inquired of Symon.

"Very good!" Symon exclaimed. "Although I guess I shouldn't be that surprised you recognized it. Dental equipment has changed very little in these past centuries."

"Centuries? So nobody before you lived here for a while?" Nadine asked.

"Easily over one hundred years before I arrived, maybe longer than that."

"Then how did you find it?"

"Months of searching. To be honest, it's surprising I found a place like this. Basements are a rarity here. When I found it, the backyard was all paved over and the metal storm door was exposed. So I took whatever dirt and gravel I could find, covered the pavement, then used the unopened glues this dentist left behind to bond some dirt and gravel to the storm door and hide it. Now if the peacekeepers come, they won't find the back entrance, and if they force their way through the side, they'll see the broken staircase and move on. The mattress I found before finding this basement, but the hot plate and freezer I didn't find for another few months. And then it took even longer to map out all the edible things growing in the area. But I found a lot, plenty to sustain all of us for a good long while."

"Pretty smart," Nadine said. "And you're sure the peacekeepers won't be able to find us?

"Well, we'll have to be careful. Spidre is going to be sending peacekeeper search parties to any place he thinks we might be hiding. San Diego has to be one of those places. Fortunately, the vehicles they use are loud as shit. We'll hear them before they hear us. So, we keep our movement outside limited to the back yard, only venture further out for necessities, and if we hear them nearby, we all head inside and stay quiet. I think we can handle that, right?"

Nadine nodded as she glanced over at his food preparation area. "Your electronics get power?"

"Uhm, the dental equipment doesn't," Symon replied. "Although if I needed to hook up the X-ray I bet I could…"

"Not the dental equipment!" Nadine exclaimed. "The hot plate and freezer. How are they getting power?"

Symon chuckled. "I knew what you meant, I'm just having some fun. They get power from this big boy," Symon walked over and patted the large flat box on the wall. "Any of you ever see one of these before?"

Everyone shook their heads.

"Not surprising. The one's you might've seen are a lot smaller, a 2'x3' box at biggest. It's a LO-EC battery."

Everyone was wearing a blank stare.

"Seriously? None of you ever saw your parents walk up to a grey box on their wall and put their palm up against it?"

"Oh. Yeah, maybe," Naren and Nadine said simultaneously.

"Well that's the same as this, but this is one of the first models. I guess the people who lived here were one of the first people to adapt the technology. LO-EC tech wasn't so popular when it first came out, but those who did adapt it first were people who wanted as little to do with government services as possible. They went LO-EC to stop using government power. The one's who had a lot of money took it a step further and had an eternity septic system and ground well installed, so they didn't need the city's sewage or water either. The people who lived here must have been some of those anti-government folks. I imagine their grandkids or great grandkids moved away when the Trans-Continental Transport hub in LA was finished, and that's when the place was abandoned. Everyone in those generations moved near the TCT hubs, so I imagine the house was just never sold and eventually fell apart."

Everyone was stunned silent as they tried to digest the onslaught of new information Symon had just thrown at them.

"You uh, you know a lot about LO-ECs, eh?" Victor asked.

"No, I wouldn't say I know a lot," Symon replied.

Everyone's heart sank.

"A lot is not strong enough of a term. I would say I know everything about LO-ECs," Symon continued with a smirk.

"Please, tell us everything," Naren pleaded. "We've been searching for answers for as long as we can remember."

The other four nodded in agreement. Symon looked around at the five young adults staring at him.

"How much do you guys know, or recollect?" Symon asked.

Everyone stayed silent.

"Holy shit," Symon said. "Well let's unpack the elcycle and get some food up. We'll have a meal and I'll tell you all I know."

Chapter 15

As the last of the food was dished out, everyone gathered in a circle and caught Symon up on their most recent fight and other pevents that Symon didn't know about. Symon, in turn, filled everyone in on the generations of LO-EC history that the younger LO-ECs had been sheltered from. He only paused his story once, when he revealed that the explosion in Boston had been caused by one immensely powerful LO-EC user. At that revelation, everyone stopped paying attention to Symon and turned to look at Sera.

"It wasn't me!" Sera exclaimed. "Christ, I've never even been to Boston!"

"Well, regardless of who it was or the reasons behind it, the UN now saw the LO-EC population as a threat to be eliminated and sought answers," Symon continued. "They granted the head of UN armed forces full discretion in taking action to stop the LO-EC threat. The head of the armed forces at the time being none other than Bartholomew J. Spidre."

"Christ," exclaimed Naren.

"At the time, I was a head of LO-EC research and development. Our lab was providing diagnostic services to some born LO-EC users, but our real efforts were cutting-edge work on new ways to use LO-EC tech. Given my high-profile status and the nature of my position, Spidre contacted me and said if I helped him, I would not be considered a threat. He told me that violence would only be used if necessary, and fully funded new research in several areas. He funded our LO-EC artificial intelligence project, our Body Heat Armament project, and our energy-suppression project, which only months later resulted in the invention of…"

Symon hesitated. His audience looked at him wide eyed. Symon took a deep breath and continued.

"…resulted in the invention of the BEOS, or Body Energy Offense System that the peacekeepers use, the LO-EC energy suppressor, and the androids."

The five faces around Symon turned angry. Sera stood up as Symons' eyes watered.

"I didn't know what was going to happen," he said.

"You're the reason those monsters existed! The reason we've all had to run all our lives! The reason our entire families are destroyed!" Sera screamed.

"You think I don't know that!? If I had known what Spidre was planning, I would've smashed it all myself!" Symon yelled back.

Sera turned for the exit, Naren stood up to follow.

"Please, don't leave! Please let me explain!" Symon cried.

"If I stay one more second, I'll rip you to shreds!" Sera boomed in reply.

"Good! Do it!" Symon yelled back. "You might finally bring me some fucking peace! It won't change the fact that I didn't know what Spidre was planning until that fucking bomb fell on Salt Lake City! And I haven't been able to sleep since!"

Sera turned around and clenched her fists. Naren backed away, there was no way he could stop her, even if he wanted to. Sera bared her teeth and prepared to leap at Symon. As she did so, from the corner of her eye, she could see Edgar. He wasn't looking at her or at Symon. She turned her attention to him fully and saw he was staring at the floor. Symon noticed the break in Sera's concentration and looked at Edgar as well. From his angle, Symon could see that tears were pouring from Edgar's eyes. Symon was the first to realize what was going on.

"Who'd you lose?" Symon asked Edgar.

"My parents," Edgar replied. Tears welled in everyone's eyes.

"I'm so sorry," Symon replied. Suddenly, a thought occurred to him.

"I can prove it!" he yelled. "I can prove Spidre acted on his own. Please, just a few more seconds! Give me thirty seconds. Sera, please! After that you can leave, kill me, whatever. Just thirty seconds."

Sera stood motionless, fists clenched at her side, staring Symon down. Symon dove under his mattress and rummaged around. He came out holding a very dusty and dirty mobile. He frantically cleaned the back of it, where there was a connector for a microtransformer.

"Edgar, I am sorry to ask this of you, but please power this up, then search the photos, you'll know which one to stop at." Symon pleaded.

Edgar obliged. He cradled the phone in his right hand and when he felt the connector and his microtransformer link, he activated his power. The phone's screen instantly came to life. He grabbed the earpiece and put it in his ear.

"Photos," he instructed the phone. A holographic image illuminated in front of him, displaying several digital images stacked on top of each other. He glanced at each one, then glanced down, which flipped to the next photo. He stopped when he reached a picture of Symon and a woman standing on a set of old train tracks with green water on their right and red water on their left.

"Edgar, please tell everyone what it is you're looking at," Symon requested.

"It's the Great Salt Lake. Salt Lake City was right next to it."

Symon nodded. "And before I was taken into Spidre's employ, I lived there. The woman in the photo was…"

Symon couldn't get the rest of the words out. Eyes softened all around the room. Sera sat back down and Naren followed.

"Finish your story, Symon," Sera said.

20 Years Earlier

A series of mechanical clicks sounded off one after another. Symon breathed a sigh of relief. He took a white handkerchief out of his lab coat and wiped the grease off his hands. After leaning down to check all the connections up close, Symon backed up to see the full picture. There stood Byron, the newest and by-far largest recruit to the special forces program. He was wearing a piece of bright-red armor that covered his chest, back and right shoulder. On his right forearm was another, more girthy piece of armor that had successfully connected to the upper arm for the first time.

"How does it feel?" Symon asked.

"Still heavy," Bryon replied as he lifted his arm. Despite talking normally, his voice boomed off the white walls of the lab, causing some lab assistants to shudder as they tinkered away at various mechanical projects.

"Not as bad as the last one, though," Byron continued. "I can work with this."

Symon breathed another sigh of relief. "That's excellent. Want to try and take the weapons system for a run-through? If it works, we are all done."

"Thank fucking Christ," Byron replied. He straightened his forearm as if taking aim.

"Weapons cycle begins on my mark. Proceed to the next weapon also on my mark," Symon said.

Byron nodded.

"Initiate weapons cycle now," Symon instructed.

With a flinch of his arm, Byron's armor whirred to life, a gentle hum becoming higher-pitched as the inner workings spun faster and faster.

"Initiate punch assist."

Byron cocked his arm back, then thrust forward. As his arm reached full extension, hydraulics at the front of his forearm activated, and a ring around his fist rapidly extended then retracted back into the armor.

Symon made a mental check mark of the device's success.

"Initiate electric sword."

Byron flicked his wrist and an unelectrified blade slid out of a compartment at the top of the apparatus. Another mental checkmark. The blade was not supposed to carry a current yet in this test model of the armor.

"Initiate shotgun."

Another flick and the blade receded back into Byron's forearm. A slight turn of the wrist then rotated the armor and caused a shotgun barrel to pop up. A few clicks of an empty chamber were a clear sign that this attachment was working as well.

Symon's heart started racing. Only one more component to get right.

"Activate machine gun," he instructed.

Byron flicked his wrist and then turned it, same as before. The shotgun attachment receded into the armor but was followed by a loud mechanical groan. Byron turned his wrist again, but the groaning continued with no movement.

The armor had failed. Symon clenched his teeth and tried his best to not show his frustration. Byron had no such qualms.

"God damnit, I want to be out of this lab!" he bellowed as he punched downwards into a nearby metal desk. The punch assist in his forearm activated, splitting the desk clean in half. As the hydraulic press retracted, the mechanical groaning stopped and the whirring sound slowed to a complete stop.

"Calm down!" Symon yelled.

"Fuck you!" Byron yelled back. "I didn't sign on to spend my days waiting around in a lab while you slap pieces of useless machinery on me!"

"You aren't going to be doing much else out there, all signs point to Spidre going the peaceful route." Symon replied. "But if you want to get out of the lab for now, then you're free to go for the day."

"Oh hell no," Byron replied. "I'm staying right here and you're fixing this thing right fucking now!"

"Just assessing the damage you did to it when you wrecked this table will take the rest of the day," Symon said. "Either go to your apartment or get on the next transit back to wherever the hell you came from. I need a strong subject with a high average body temperature, not a fucking child!"

Byron and Symon stared at each other. All work had stopped in the lab, and every eye was on them. After several tense moments, Byron ripped the armor off his body and trudged out of the lab. Symon unclenched his hands, which he hadn't even realized had balled into fists.

"Jesus Christ," one of the technicians said. "Symon, no offense, but I don't think you could've taken on that monster."

Symon thought for a moment. "Tough call. He's younger and huge, but I'm a LO-EC. If the punch assist was still working, though, I would've had no chance," Symon said. "I knew he would back down though. He was acting like a child, and children give in to threats pretty easily."

The tech nodded.

"I am a little rattled, though. I think I should call it a day." Symon continued.

"Of course. Don't worry, we can handle the cleanup here," the tech responded.

Symon wasn't rattled, but he was frustrated. The projects Spidre had him working on had all been like this. A frenetic pace where everything that could fail did, until there was nothing else that could happen but for the project to work. And now he was close with this one, his last one. Just a couple more weeks till he was out of this military-only compound and back home.

Symon hopped on his elcycle and the autonav guided him from the lab at military headquarters to the research division's apartment building across the city. His cycle coasted to a stop inside the building's garage. He strolled through the building to the elevators, and as he passed through the lobby, the conversations around him gave Symon an unsettled feeling, like somehow everyone was talking about the same thing. He shrugged it off and continued into the elevator and up to his apartment. Exhausted, he grabbed some leftovers from the night before and threw himself into bed. He pulled out his mobile and put the earpiece in.

"Livestream, channel seven," he instructed.

He was expecting to see a history show. Instead, the image was live news footage.

"—a clear message to the LO-EC communities around the world. This UN is no longer going to deal with this threat civilly or peacefully. This is a declaration of war."

The images on the screen were out of focus, but were of some giant plume of smoke, with several fires scattered around the bottom of the image.

"I'm being told we just finished drawing up an infographic to show the scope of the devastation. Is it ready to be put up on the screen? Yes? Yes."

An old satellite image popped up of a city with a large, two-colored lake next to it. The city had a red circle drawn around it with a diameter marked as 48 miles.

Symon's hands started shaking, his grip on his mobile getting so tight it hurt.

"Everything and everyone inside that circle on your screen is likely destroyed. Salt Lake City was entirely a LO-EC population, so the casualties to regular people are—"

The red of the circle on the screen spread and encompassed Symon's entire vision. His mind was blank. No thought, just action. Just walking out of his apartment, taking the elevator back down to the garage, getting back on his elcycle and pulling up to the back entrance of headquarters. He kicked in the door and approached the stairwell in the middle of the lobby. Two guards standing there jumped in surprise, and before they could recover, he grabbed one by the shirt collar and threw her across the lobby. He grabbed the other under his chin and held him against the wall.

"Spidre. Where?" Symon asked.

"S-Seventh floor. S-Strategy meeting," The terrified guard replied.

Symon turned and threw that guard across the lobby as well. As he stormed up the stairs, he could hear the first guard he threw muttering. An alarm followed, and Symon could hear doors to the stairwell opening above him. He started running and came across another guard as she was entering the stairwell. Symon lowered his shoulder and blindsided the guard before she ever saw what was coming. He ran up a few more flights and another guard stood above him, aiming down.

"Don't make this any wor—"

She expected Symon to stop. He didn't. He continued running forward at full speed and levelled her as well. Not long after, he made it to the seventh floor and exited the stairwell. There was a wide, long hallway ahead of him with offices and conference rooms glassed off on either side. At the far end was an open common area with floor-to-ceiling glass windows that looked out the front of the building. Standing in front of those windows was Spidre, flanked by five huge guards. Symon charged at Spidre, who remained motionless while his guards charged forward instead. Symon was much faster than them, and they converged about 20 feet from Spidre. Despite the guards' size, it was still a desperate struggle to get Symon under control.

"He is secure," one announced once they felt confident Symon wasn't getting away. He struggled again, to no avail.

"Why!?" Symon yelled.

"I had no other choice," Spidre replied with no emotion in his tone.

"You could have signed a peace treaty! Could have used the

energy suppressors!" Symon exclaimed.

Spidre shook his head. "No, your 'energy suppressors' were not an option. The only thing sure to work is this."

Thoughts started racing through Symon's mind. About Salt Lake City. About her. The rage inside him grew again, and he struggled against his captors once more. This time he had the strength. He wrenched his right arm forward sending the guard holding it flat to the floor. He stomped on the guard's head and pushed into the soldier at his back, causing the man to stumble and fall over. Symon brought his left arm to the center of his body while bringing his right knee over, plunging it into the stomach of the soldier holding that arm. With only two soldiers left, one holding either shoulder, he jumped backward. The two guards were not strong enough to maintain their balance. All involved fell over and as they hit the ground, Symon freed his arms and punched both guards in the face. The soldier that had been at his back tried to get up, but Symon was too fast. He swung his right arm around as he stood up, hitting the peacekeeper square in the jaw.

Symon charged at Spidre and as the two of them locked arms, Symon realized he was the far weaker man. Spidre spun him around and slammed him up against the glass at the front of the building. Spidre threw his right arm out to the side and created an energy blade from his hand. He held it there just long enough for Symon to see it, to understand the secret Spidre had been hiding, before Spidre slashed upwards across Symon's chest. Spidre let go of Symon as the wound started bleeding profusely. Before Symon could fall to the ground, Spidre kicked him in the chest and sent him through the glass window and down seven stories to the ground below.

Symon felt bones snap all over his body. He looked around and as his vision started going blurry, he noticed he'd landed right next to a military-issue standard electric motorcycle. He swung his body around and grabbed the handlebar with his right hand, slowly pulling himself on to the cycle.

"I knew it!" Spidre yelled from above. "I knew all LO-ECs were dangerous! If you had the gall to attack me, any of you could!"

Symon looked up and saw Spidre standing at the shattered window's edge, taking aim down. The energy blade leaped from his hand and just missed Symon's torso. It instead pierced through the electric motorcycle. Symon heard a faint hiss and knew the battery had been pierced. He threw himself away from the motorcycle as hard as he could, just as the battery exploded in a massive fireball. The ground shook and windows shattered at the ground level while Symon was thrown through the downstairs lobby and out through the back entrance. People all around screamed and ran for shelter. Symon was in agony now. Unbearable searing pain radiated through his torso. He looked down and saw that his shirt had been burned away by the fireball, as had most of the skin on his arms and abdomen. The burn was so bad it had cauterized his slash wound shut. Symon felt himself passing out from the pain. He tried to get to his feet, but several bones in his legs gave out. He dragged himself across the ground towards his elcycle. Every foot he traveled felt like another step towards unconsciousness, but he made it to the elcycle and pulled himself on. He energized the cycle and gave the autonav one simple instruction, South, before passing out.

When he woke up, he did not know how long he had been out or where he was. He was lying face up in the middle of a highway, surrounded by abandoned buildings he did not recognize. The elcycle was a few feet away on its side. Symon attempted to roll over but couldn't summon the strength. He closed his eyes and focused. He tried rolling over again but only managed to lift his left arm before it fell again on his left hip. The burns he had were still excruciating. He had trouble sensing or focusing on much else. And yet, there was something else he felt, something hard in his pocket that his hand hit when it fell. He focused and guided his hand into the pocket to pull out whatever it was. He propped it up on his leg and saw it was his mobile. Even blinded with rage, some part of his brain must have remembered to put it in his pocket.

He powered it on to see if it was connected to the net. It was not; they couldn't track him. His eyes focused past the icons in the holoimage and onto the background. It was the photo of him and the woman he loved, after they had just taken a walk across the ancient train tracks that separated the two sides of the lake. The woman that he would not see ever again, because of Spidre.

In that moment, Symon told himself he would not die. He would recover from this, and one day figure out a way to bring Spidre down. The first step towards that was to get over to his elcycle. He focused again, and this time he was able to roll over onto his forearms. He pulled himself towards he elcycle and gripped one handlebar. He powered it on and checked the autonav screen to see where he was. The screen displayed a city called San Diego. An abandoned city, close enough to LA to make supply runs if needed, far enough from Spidre to hide out. It would do.

———————

Symon concluded the story of the day he lost. During the telling, he had taken off his shirt to show off the burn scars all across his chest and arms. With the story now completed, he threw his shirt back on.

"Salt Lake City was exclusively a LO-EC population," he continued. "I assume Spidre had some qualms about dropping any sort of bomb on other cities with more mixed populations and opted for military assaults instead. In two years' time, the entire world's population of LO-EC users had been wiped off the face of the earth. The world thought of him as a hero who'd destroyed a threat, and he had the entire world's armed forces at his beck and call. So when the UN demanded that he relinquish his power, he had them wiped out, too. With no one left to stand in his way, Spidre took his current position as High Ruler of Earth."

"Another three years' work after that, and all of the world's remaining nuclear resources led to the world's first fusion reactor coming online, but it didn't work right, and with the only other sources of power being the five supermassive solar arrays, many now old and not working at full capacity, large and long blackouts plagued the globe. As a result, the economies and infrastructures of the world's major cities took a tumble. Meanwhile, Spidre's paranoia got the best of him, and he took the public net offline to keep any remaining LO-ECs from uniting and organizing. In that time, Spidre also built and activated the force field around his compound. That thing requires an obscene amount of power, which further added to the energy issues the globe has to this day."

Symon concluded his story there, and everyone sat in silence for what seemed like an eternity. Finally, Sera stood up and embraced Symon. When the hug ended, she turned and headed for the back door.

"You're leaving?" Symon asked.

Sera shook her head. "Just gotta go blow off some steam," she replied.

"There is one thing I don't understand," Nadine said. "Why did he kill off all the LO-ECs when he could have just rounded them all up and forced them to be used for energy."

"Jesus," Naren exclaimed.

"What? The guy is clearly a monster. Why would a man with no conscience give up an opportunity like that?"

"I'm sure that option was promoted by a few of his strategists, but he would have rejected it outright," Symon replied. "Spidre is a monster, but he has his own twisted sense of morals. To him, death was ok, enslavement was not. The death of LO-ECs was ok, and the death of normal humans was not. The only time his morals seem to break are when his own safety is concerned, and now that he is behind that force field, he is as safe as can be."

Chapter 16

Symon spent the rest of the meal and clean-up time getting filled in on the finer details of everyone's adventures over the past days. By the time they were done, Sera had returned.

"I'd ask if you ran into any issues avoiding patrols, but if you were able to avoid detection in New Orleans for decades, I imagine you would have no trouble staying under the radar here," Symon said to Sera.

"Yup, it's not a problem," Sera replied with a chuckle. "As long as I leave at sunrise and sunset and stay just above the buildings, I'll see any patrols long before they see me. Still, I made sure to fly much farther away than I usually would. I don't know the area and wanted to make sure no one could hear my blast."

"Nadine and I were just discussing a related topic," Symon said. "Please continue Nadine, it sounded like you were leading up to a question."

"Well, Sera is clearly our most powerful, being able to do something that amazing," Nadine said. "But from what you were saying earlier, it sounds like she could become even more powerful than she is now. All of us could."

"That's absolutely correct," Symon replied.

Everyone stopped what they were doing.

"More powerful how?" Victor asked.

"Well, more powerful is a subjective term," Symon said. "Just by getting better trained in fighting you will, technically, be more powerful. However, that training, or any other sustained physical exercise, will also make you 'burn hotter', like I mentioned earlier. You will literally have more power coursing through your body."

"And that's... good?" Naren asked.

"For some of you, yes. Just from what I know about Edgar, if he worked out more, pushed his body to its limits, his body could start creating enough energy that both his blades could work at once. For someone like Victor, though, that may not be a good idea. The way your body is constantly twitching suggests it is already having trouble with the energy you've built up, so you might have to be very careful how you train."

Victor gave Symon a frustrated look. Edgar was gazing down at his own hands.

"Does that mean I could shoot off an energy beam like Spidre can?" Edgar asked.

"Uh, no," Symon replied. "I mean, maybe if you took a nasty shot to your chest or shoulder, something powerful enough to sever the entire network in your arm, your energy would, in theory, shoot off having nowhere else to go. But taking a hit like that would almost certainly kill you. Frankly, I don't want to think about what Spidre had to do to himself in order to shoot off energy the way he can. It must have been a lengthy process, and painful. And I'd be amazed if he walked away from it without some lasting nerve damage."

"Whoa," was all Edgar replied.

"Nadine, I'm sure given enough training, the microtransformers in your hands would function, giving you the control you'd need to fly. Naren, you can fly because of the position of your microtransformers. The fact that they are between your toes gives you a level of control Nadine doesn't have with them on her heels. However, given the stories I heard about your fights yesterday, you need to learn proper fighting and landing techniques more than anything."Nadine beamed with excitement. Naren looked annoyed.

"Then there's Sera," Symon said as he turned to her. "I assume you have multiple functional LO-EC devices inside of you. It would explain your power, and all their networks intersecting and energy running into itself is the only explanation I can think of for your glowing skin. I imagine you must be able to control your power output somewhat. There's really no other explanation for how you can fly."

"Uh, I guess?" Sera replied. "I mean, it isn't a conscious decision on my part, though. I've just sort of always known how to fly."

"No, that makes sense," Symon said. "All of you must have some level of subconscious control over your power. If you didn't, you would've undoubtedly sliced your bed in half or boosted through a wall or ceiling while you were sleeping. But perhaps you could work on the part of your control that is conscious. You may be able to focus your mind and hold on to your energy for longer without it hurting. You'd be able to produce a larger explosion, but there is no telling what kind of damage that would do to your insides. I'd have to give you a medical exam to be sure. Actually, I probably should do that for everyone."

"You can do that here? With this crap?" Nadine said.

"Most likely yes," Symon replied. "Old dental equipment isn't perfect for the job, but if I can get it running, then it should suffice."

"We'll know our strengths and weaknesses," Sera said with a smirk at Naren. He grinned back.

"What the fuck are you two smiling about?" Victor said. "Why do you all even care about this?"

"What do you mean?" Nadine asked.

"All this shit about getting more powerful, what's the point? Why are we even worried about it?"

Everyone looked dumbfounded.

"Isn't it obvious?" Edgar asked. "We plan on fighting back."

Nadine was surprised, not only at Edgar picking up on where the conversation was heading, but also his apparent readiness to go along with it.

"Fighting back? Against Spidre?" Victor exclaimed.

"Why shouldn't we?" Naren replied. "We're powerful, we can get more powerful, and Spidre has no way of finding us or predicting our next move. I mean honestly, who can stop us?"

"No one," Victor said. "So, what? We stay here until we're healthy, then all go attack Spidre at once?

Naren shook his head. "We can't touch Spidre, at least not yet. He has a force field surrounding the San Francisco compound, and taking that down is too complicated for us to handle right now. Luring him out isn't going to work, either. He likely came out last time assuming he would only have to fight one LO-EC, and had that been the case he would have succeeded. Nadine, Symon, and Edgar together were almost an even match for him. Now that there are more of us, he won't risk coming out of his safety net again. Our best option for eventually getting to him is by attacking a different city and using it as the base of operations for a rebellion."

Victor was unimpressed.

"No one can stop us, Naren. No one can stop us," Victor said, putting a heavy enunciation on the second 'one'. "If we attack a city, we won't be up against one of anything. Don't most cities have entire armies guarding them?"

"We'll start small," Naren replied. Victor's expression did not change.

"We'll choose our first target carefully, and work as a team," Naren continued. "We have two people who can fly. With Russ gone, that means we will be unchallenged from the air. We have two operational elcycles, the fastest road vehicle ever created, with three capable riders. We have a master strategist with knowledge of the military in me, a genius and master of combat in Nadine, someone with in-depth knowledge of LO-EC and military technology in Symon, another skilled fighter in Edgar, and you, a man who is so fast that he can sneak around anywhere without fear of detection. We have a good team here, a great team."

"Fine, let's say we take a city," Victor said. "What's stopping Spidre from sending in even more troops from other places to stop us? Or sending troops in to take the city back when we leave? Or just bombing the city into the ground to send a message?"

"Well, he won't send troops stationed at other cities to support one we attack," Naren said. "He knows we have elcycles, therefore he knows we're fast. He would suspect that if we attack one city, and see that troops are coming from another, that we would just leave and attack the new, unprotected city. The more likely scenario is that he sends in the reserve forces, who are housed in New York and in Seoul. The reserves in New York double as the armed force protecting the Net tower in Manhattan, a valuable target he would not want to leave vulnerable. He is, above all else, a paranoid man. He wouldn't risk keeping those forces deployed at length to retake a city unless he had to. The forces in Seoul would be a little more expendable, and they're the ones with heavy artillery, which would be essential to taking back a city he lost. So if we choose a city in the Western hemisphere, the Seoul forces would take several hours to get to us in sufficient numbers to make a difference. Plenty of time to organize a defense. If he mobilizes them after we're gone and tries to retake the city, we'll just return and take it again. If that happens enough times, he'll realize whatever city he's attempting to reclaim isn't worth the troops he's losing."

"Fine. And the bombs?" Victor said.

Naren shook his head. "Using a nuke on normal civilians is different than when he used it in Salt Lake. At the time, that city was viewed by most of the world as a threat. But now, the world might see the use of a bomb on a normal population as a threat to all of them as a whole. It could cause a worldwide rebellion. That is a situation which Spidre wants to avoid at all costs, because it is a situation he cannot win. Civilian net might be crippled, but it is not gone. Word of something that major would get around."

Victor still had a skeptical look on his face. "I don't know," he said.

"Victor, I understand where you're coming from," Sera said. "Two days ago, you were living a quiet life by yourself, with no knowledge or thought about any of this. When Naren first told me about his idea to fight Spidre's army, about there being more fights after the androids were gone, I thought it was a crazy idea too. It took me a long time to warm to the idea. Right now, while we heal, we have nothing but time. If we decide to stay and get stronger, we'll have even more time. So don't decide today. Think about it. Maybe you'll warm to the idea, too."

Victor nodded.

"At the very least, you should let me conduct a physical on you," Symon said. "Even if it's just for you to know where you stand."

"I guess," Victor replied. "I don't know, I can't think. I'm too fucking tired."

"I'm with you there, buddy!" Edgar exclaimed.

"Agreed, we all need sleep," Symon said. "Victor, I guess you'll be my first patient tomorrow."

"Fuck no he won't," Nadine said. Everyone looked at her in surprise.

"What you need more than a physical is some real fight training. Hiding isn't going to be the same as it was, Victor. You need to know how to use that speed to your advantage. I saw the fight you and Naren had, and I've got to say, both of you were pretty pathetic."

"But I was winning…" Naren said.

"You were staying alive," Nadine snapped back. "Your basic fighting skills kept him off you, but you still can't mount an offense for shit. You and him are with me first thing tomorrow, no question."

Everyone looked at Symon to respond.

"Well I'm not going to argue with her," Symon said. "Sera, I guess you're with me first tomorrow, then Edgar."

Edgar and Sera nodded.

"I uh, I think we can all agree that the couple should get the bed, yes?" Symon said.

Edgar, Victor, and Nadine nodded in agreement.

"Oh, thanks so much!" Sera exclaimed.

"The rest of us should jump upstairs and camp out on the first floor. That's the only place where there's room for four of us to spread out. Just please when you jump, be gentle about your landing."

"Or we could just walk out the back and through the front door." Edgar pointed out.

"Er yes, I suppose we could do that, too." Symon said. "Shit, I guess I need to go find a ladder at some point so we don't have to walk outside every time."

As everyone stood up, Symon noticed the bare feet of Victor, Nadine, and Naren.

"I think I should try to find you all some shoes too. There is just one more thing that needs to be discussed before we go to bed, and I think I've been nice about this long enough."

Everyone looked at Symon with wide eyes.

"I understand you've all had a very stressful past few days, but it doesn't change the fact that you are all filthy. So before bed, can everyone please take turns and use the shower? The rest of my living space will thank you."

Chapter 17

"How on earth did you find so many blankets?" Edgar asked.

"You'd be surprised how much easier it was to find covers and tarps than to find a useable mattress," Symon replied. "When I first got here these were all I had to sleep on for the first month or so. It worked out in the end. The blankets were easier to carry around before I set up permanent residence."

Everyone had finished showering and as a result felt more relaxed, able to unwind for the first time since their adventure started. It was sure to be a peaceful night's sleep. Sera and Naren settled in on the mattress downstairs, while everyone else lugged tarps upstairs to lie on and blankets to keep them warm. Symon settled down closest to the broken staircase, followed by Nadine, Edgar, and Victor.

"Hey, Edgar?" Nadine asked. "Before we go to sleep, I have to ask. You seemed really on board with the idea of fighting against Spidre. I'd go so far as to say you were even enthusiastic about it. That's a big leap from having not known about any of this three days ago. Why?"

"Well, the other option is going back out on my own, struggling to survive again," Edgar replied. "And it seems like Spidre was the reason me and my family had any struggles to start with. I'll take my chances if it means we don't have to deal with that anymore."

"You've lived a tough life because of him," Nadine said.

"Eh," Edgar replied. "Had some tough moments I guess, but my Aunt and Uncle are awesome."

"They're still alive?"

"Sure are. They aren't LO-ECs, just normal people. They still live with their two kids in the apartment they raised me in on the outskirts of Las Vegas. The power is decent there and they have good jobs at the Trans-Continental Transport. They're the reason I knew about the tournament, and how I got to LA."

"They sound pretty well off. Why did you have to enter the tournament in the first place?"

"Oh I, uhh, wasn't living with them. Haven't been since I was like 13. They made good money but sometimes there were things we needed that they just couldn't buy. When that happened, I just went out and stole it. They didn't want me to, and I didn't listen. Then one time I got caught. And attracted a lot of attention from the peacekeepers. And had to use my powers to get away. With soldiers looking for me, it was too risky to stay with them anymore, so I lived out on the road."

"That's why you looked so tense when they took your photo at the tournament!" Nadine exclaimed. Edgar nodded in reply.

"After that I lived on my own for years and years and only came to them if things got bad, if I was desperate for food or money. It wasn't the most ideal situation for either of us. So the last time I visited, about three months ago, they told me about the tournament and that if I wanted to enter, they'd get me to LA."

"You're a good person looking out for them like that despite the risks," Nadine said. "Still, how did you not go ballistic when we saw Spidre?"

"What do you mean?" Edgar asked.

"He's responsible for your parents' deaths, responsible for the hard life you've had to live. You had to have figured that out at some point before today. How did you not completely lose it and just try to shred him when you saw him outside of San Francisco?"

Edgar shrugged. "There were just other things I had to do. If I had just gone off and tried to end Spidre, he would've killed me. Then I wouldn't have accomplished what I came there to do in the first place: help you escape."

Nadine felt her cheeks flush.

"There's a time and place for everything, and two nights ago outside of San Francisco was not the right time or place to end Spidre. It will come though, I just got to be patient."

"I guess you're right. Hey! Did you just teach me something?"

"Anything's possible," Edgar replied with a coy smirk. Nadine chuckled.

"So, who do you want vengeance on?" Edgar asked.

"Like, who do I want to kill?" Nadine said.

"Exactly," Edgar replied. "Sera had Russ. I have Spidre. I mean I guess we all have Spidre, but Sera wanted personal revenge on Russ. Is there anyone like that for you?"

"Umm, well. I don't know a specific person. But I would like to see the Special Ops unit gone," Nadine said.

Edgar could hear Victor stirring behind him. He leaned in closer to Nadine so he could whisper.

"What is the Special Ops team?" Edgar asked.

"They're the force that invaded Chicago," Nadine said. "Well, part of it. I don't remember a lot of what happened in Chicago, but what I do remember, I'm starting to piece together based on what Symon told us. I'm guessing Chicago was another big LO-EC town. My dad was an investigator for the UN peacekeepers, but at that point he and my Mom must have been helping the resistance keep Spidre's army out, because all I heard for months was talk of holding off the UN forces. People would come to our house all the time, normal-looking people like, no uniforms, and my mom and dad would go into the back room with them to talk for hours. Of course, Naren and I weren't allowed in. One day, I think right around the same time as Salt Lake City, people came over and never made it into the back. They just started talking right in the main room. They mentioned Special Ops coming. I had never seen my parents so nervous before. They packed bags for us and ran us over to the TCT. My dad used his military ID to get us on a transport to my grandma in Seattle, then he gave his ID and his watch to Naren. They starting crying as they said goodbye to us. And that was the last time I ever saw them."

"Christ," Edgar said. "So, you figure your vengeance should be against the forces who invaded the city?"

"Yes," Nadine replied. "Getting revenge on one person would be impossible. I have no idea how my parents ultimately met their end. But liberating Chicago, being responsible for the decimation of the peacekeepers there and making it a free city again, that would feel good. And be pretty damn poetic."

"Without a doubt, but Chicago is a big town, how…"

Edgar's words were cut off by a strange, repetitive sound.

"You hear that?" Nadine whispered.

"Yea," Edgar replied. "What is it?"

"It sounds like, pieces of metal banging together? But over and over again?" Nadine said.

"Whatever it is, it's coming from downstairs." Edgar observed.

"It is? It is! Wait. No…"Nadine was cut off by the sound of muffled moans coming from the basement. The moans got louder, and Nadine and Edgar could clearly make out that it was Sera.

"Oh my god," Edgar said, holding his hands over his mouth to contain his laughter.

"Oh god damnit!" Nadine blurted out before covering her mouth and face. "God damnit," she whispered. "Oh, fuck that's so gross!" She started kicking at the air under her blankets out of discomfort.

The moans got louder and louder, and it got harder and harder for Nadine and Edgar to contain themselves. Out of nowhere, Symon jumped to his feet and stomped on the ground.

"Hey! I don't think we'll have to worry about the patrols outside anymore,'cause they can hear you all the way in Los Angeles right now!"

Sera and Naren's apology could barely be heard over Nadine, Edgar, and Victor bursting into a fit of laughter. They laughed so hard their lungs hurt, and every time they started to slow down, one look at each other would start a new fit all over again.

"All right, all right! Can we please focus on getting some sleep here?" Symon pleaded.

"I'm sorry, I'm sorry," Nadine replied, as she wiped tears from her eyes. It was getting late, and all that laughing had made them much more exhausted. Victor lay back down, and Nadine and Edgar laid their heads on their pillows facing each other.

"Goodnight, Edgar," Nadine said with a bashful smile.

"Goodnight, Nadine," Edgar replied, with his own smile back.

Edgar closed his eyes, and the last thing Nadine remembered doing was studying the lines of Edgar's face as she drifted off to sleep.

The next morning, everyone came downstairs for breakfast, and Naren turned bright red upon seeing everyone. It was more difficult to tell what color Sera had turned. Not because of her glowing skin, but because as soon as she came back from letting off a blast, she hid under the covers and refused to come out from sheer embarrassment. She finally got out of bed when everyone went outside to train, and Symon asked to start the medical examination.

"Ok," Nadine said as everyone got outside. "The first thing I need go to over with you all is stance," she said to Naren, Edgar, and Victor. "Now, I won't be able to fully demonstrate, so do your best to imagine it, or for the basic ones you can follow Naren and later on…"

"Why the fuck are we learning stances?" Victor interrupted.

"That's always the first thing you learn during combat training," Nadine replied.

Victor looked skeptical. Nadine looked annoyed.

"In order to fight hand-to-hand with competence, you need to know where your power comes from. That's what learning stances teaches you," Nadine said.

"But what does it matter? I'm not going to be fighting any of you guys. I'll be fighting normal people. They don't stand a chance." Victor snapped back.

"You don't know what secrets the peacekeepers might be hiding," Nadine replied. "Spidre himself is a LO-EC and we didn't know till three days ago. And even supposing every peacekeeper in the world is just a normal human, there are things I can teach you that will be helpful. Like how to combat multiple assailants at once."

"Ok, that sounds helpful," Victor said. "Just teach me that."

Nadine shook her head. "Doesn't work that way. Those techniques would only be effective once you learn how to use your speed to your advantage in a one-on-one fight."

"But my speed is already an advantage," Victor replied with obvious annoyance in his tone.

Nadine took a frustrated breath. "How is your shoulder feeling Victor?"

"Uhh, much better now that I've slept. But what…"

"Awesome," she interrupted him. "So I'll give you the benefit of the doubt. Fight me."

Victor was confused. "What?"

"Fight me. Right now. If you land a hit, we can skip the stances."

"You're injured."

"I am."

"It wouldn't be fair for me to fight you. What would it prove if I win…"

"I didn't say win. You definitely won't win. Just land a single hit on me and we'll skip the stances."

"You're being ridiculous."

"And you're being cocky when you shouldn't be. I'm telling you that right now, with your speed and my injury, you still won't land a single hit on me. If you think you can, then come prove me wrong."

"Fine," Victor replied through clenched teeth.

Nadine turned her injured arm away from Victor and squared up to fight. Victor ran forward and cocked his arm back. As he approached, he brought his arm forward to punch, but Nadine blocked and threw his arm to the side. She then brought her hand back and landed a punch square to Victor's face. Victor jumped back in surprise.

"I thought the point was for me to try hit you," he said.

"It is," Nadine replied. "What? You thought that meant I wasn't going to hit back? This fight has to end sometime."

Victor had graduated from annoyed to angry. He ran back in and again, Nadine threw his arm out of the way and brought her clenched fist back to Victor's face. He came around with a left hook, but as soon as he started swinging, Nadine moved to her left. Victor hit air and Nadine kicked him in his side. He started swinging wildly and Nadine alternated between dodging and blocking. Every time she blocked a hit, a punch or kick would follow. Taking so many hits took its toll, and Victor was exhausted. He took a half step back and went for one last desperate kick. Nadine caught it and threw his leg up, sending him backwards into the ground. She then jerked forward and down and slammed her knee into his stomach, knocking the wind out of him. He stayed down, unable to catch his breath.

"Jesus Christ," Edgar said aloud.

Nadine stood over Victor, looking down and shaking her head as he rolled around holding his stomach. After about twenty seconds, he managed to take a deep breath again and looked up at Nadine standing over him.

"How?" he muttered in between gasps for air.

"You're fast Victor, but the moves you choose to use are predictable and slow," Nadine replied. "You cock your arms all the way back to punch. Makes for a more powerful swing but also gives your opponent longer to block or dodge. You also only aim for the face when punching, don't leave a hand up for defense, and don't use your legs enough. It's probable that there are some peacekeepers in the world who have better combat training than I do. And while you may be able to eventually overpower them, they'll give you enough trouble that other soldiers can get involved in the fight. And when that happens…"

Victor sat up and put his hands on his knees, still catching his breath.

"Ready to learn some stances?" she asked.

Victor nodded.

"Good. Sit there and watch while you recover. Edgar and Naren, line up!"

Chapter 18

As the day went on, fight training continued while Symon pulled people out one to do their medical evaluations. When he was finished, everyone gathered together and discussed the results out in the open. That was Nadine's idea; she wanted to make sure everyone knew what each other's strengths and weaknesses were so they could better cover each other in battle.

"I think that's just about everything," Symon said as he concluded. "Does anyone have any questions?"

Everyone stayed silent for a couple of seconds.

"I have one," Victor said. "Naren, what do you know about Chicago's soldiers?"

Everyone looked at Victor.

"Uhh, a good amount actually," Naren replied. "Looked up the defenses for a lot of cities while I was helping the androids with their investigations. Why do you ask?

"I overheard Nadine and Edgar's conversation last night before you, umm, interrupted them. Nadine said she wanted revenge on the people who invaded Chicago. From her story I figured you felt the same way. And I could go for a little revenge against those fuckers myself."

Everyone smiled. Victor was on board with their cause, and they knew it.

"I would love to retake Chicago, Victor, but that may be too tall a task for us right now," Naren replied. "Whatever forces were sent in to take a city during the war are the ones who stayed to govern it. The androids took New Orleans and stayed, the battalion that took LA stayed, and I a group called Special Ops were called in to take Chicago. Special Ops are still there, in addition to two full battalions of regular peacekeepers."

"Jeez that's a lot of manpower. They must have put up one hell of a fight during the war," Sera said.

"I'd be willing to bet you're correct," Symon concurred. "Special Ops were the last project I worked on before, well, you know. They were elite special forces allowed to use custom BEO systems due to their abnormalities."

"Abnormalities?" Sera asked.

"Wait, what's a BEO system?" Edgar asked the same time as Sera asked her question.

"It's the armor with built in weapons that the peacekeepers use," Naren replied to Edgar. "What did you say it stood for? Body Energy Offense?"

"Correct," Symon said. "Now to answer your question Sera, I should first explain how the BEO system works. The armor covering the person uses body heat already escaping the skin to charge weapons attached to the armor. Unlike the LO-EC device, it doesn't circumvent the body's natural ways to cool down, so its power is limited to how hot a person can get. Normal humans run at about 98 degrees, and can get up to, at maximum, about 102 degrees before either sweat starts bringing their heat back under control, or they start suffering from heat stroke and dehydration. BEO systems use this energy to power the attached armaments, so they're very taxing on the body, and can cause body temperatures to rise very rapidly. Therefore, usage must be monitored and controlled. No putting on excess armor or adding more weapons because you'll overheat too easily. But the peacekeepers in Special Ops are regular humans that through natural variations in genetics have a higher internal body temperature than the average human. Not much higher, their regular homeostatic temperature is at most, 101 degrees. But it's enough that they have to worry less about overheating because the armor is already getting a higher amount of base energy. So, where a regular soldier can wear only one weapon on their armor, Special Ops can wear two or more, and are given special permission to switch out and customize their loadouts. That makes them particularly deadly, especially if a population is preoccupied fighting off two regular battalions like Chicago was."

"And like we would be if we attacked," Naren followed up in a defeated tone.

"But wait, why are we assuming we would be attacking alone?" Nadine replied.

"What do you mean?" Naren asked.

"I'll explain in a second. Symon, was Chicago an all LO-EC community like Salt Lake?"

"No. It was one of the most mixed communities in the world," Symon said. "With most cities, the LO-EC populations tended to bunch together and take entire neighborhoods off the grid. Chicago wasn't like that. About a third of the population was LO-EC, but they were scattered all throughout the city. I'd assume that's why Spidre didn't just nuke them."

"It sounds like Chicago put up a hell of a fight back in the day, enough of one that Special Ops had to be called in. LO-ECs are powerful, but there's no way we held off that kind of force on our own. That entire god damn city had to have fought back and kept the battalions at bay. Why are we assuming that fighting spirit is gone? There must still be people alive who remember that. A lot of them. People who would've told their kids with pride that they held off Spidre's army. And Chicago has one of the most extensive underground net links in the world. They want to resist. They just need a real, credible force to lead them."

Everyone remained silent for a good long while, swallowing the last of their food and digesting the thoughts Nadine just voiced.

"Nadine is right." Sera finally said. "If we launch and attack in Chicago, the people will be behind us."

"Nadine is right about some things," Naren replied. "Chicago does have a lot of net links, and it does seem unlikely that their LO-EC population was left to fight on their own. Still, it is just a hunch, do we want to risk our lives for that?"

"Why does it need to stay a hunch?" Edgar replied. "Why doesn't one of us just go do some recon?"

"It's not that simple, Edgar," Sera replied. "The peacekeepers know what we look like. They'll have sent bulletins to major cities to look out for us."

"Not all of us," Nadine said. "The only people who know that Victor exists are either in this room or are being found dead next to a broken prison transport."

A wave of smiles washed over everyone in the room.

"Okay, this sounds like a decent plan, but a lot has to happen first," Symon said. "You all need to be healthy, and I would recommend some serious training before attempting this."

"I agree," Victor said while he and Nadine looked at each other in acknowledgement.

"When do you think I'll be up and running again, Symon?" Nadine asked. "I can't go all out in training Victor while I have a broken arm."

"Unfortunately, you're going to be the last one to heal. A broken humerus is a long recovery time. Even with the rapid recovery of a LO-EC user, you're looking at three or four weeks, most likely."

"Ugh, alright," Nadine said. "Victor, in a month when I'm fully healed, the real fun begins. You'll have Naren and Edgar to spar with in the meantime. Sera is a little out of all of our leagues, I think."

"Couldn't hurt to learn a few hand-to-hand tricks from the master. I'll be there every day," Sera said with a smile.

"Training with you guys is going to be the most intense workout ever," Edgar said.

"How long do you think it'll take to get me well trained enough that I can hold my own?" Victor inquired.

"Tough call, everyone's different," Nadine replied. "But you have speed on your side. That's a huge advantage. If we work at it hard every day, I'd give it three weeks from the time I'm able to swing with both arms until you're ready to go."

"So I think what I'm hearing is, two months till Chicago," Sera said with a chuckle.

"Two months till Chicago," everyone else responded.

With that, everyone got to cleaning up and preparing for bed, intent on working hard in training for the next two months.

Chapter 19

Victor was getting frustrated. It had been five days since he'd arrived in Chicago. Five days since he'd made yet another cross-country run and begun his effort to check out the city. After two months, everyone was healthy and trained well enough to put the plan into action. Nadine, Naren, Symon and Sera had told him everything to look for and look out for. So far, everything they said had been right. Everything they needed to know about the city, he found out on day one. Everything except the most important thing.

"Where are the god damn net access points?" he growled to himself as he repositioned the backpack he was carrying. He found himself walking along the coast of Lake Michigan, searching for any sort of clue to the whereabouts of an illegal connection to the military communication network. That, according to Nadine, would be the only safe place to talk with locals about the plan to take over the city. Going up to someone on the street was out of the question; there was no telling who they were or who might be listening. If someone was using the net access point, at least they were involved in some sort of subversion of Spidre's control.

The best thing to do in public was avoid contact, and Symon said that wouldn't be a problem. He said that one of the things he hated most about human nature was their aversion to people with disabilities. Symon was positive that people would see Victor's shaking and avoid interaction unless Victor engaged them. He had been correct. Even the peacekeepers barely acknowledged his presence. This allowed Victor to focus on the information Naren and Sera asked for. The broad stroke of the plan was to use the Chicago River and old highway 55 as barriers to defend the city once it was taken. Naren wanted to know where the military was headquartered and the city layout. Sera was concerned about where the civilian population lived in relation to the food dispensaries. Victor was no strategist, but even he could see that the placement of all these important things was not ideal to their plan. He rehearsed all the information in his head again, wanting to make sure he didn't forget a single detail.

There was a multi-building megaskyscraper complex on the east side of the river that housed a large portion of the population. On the west side of the river was a luxury building for those who worked, and a few other scattered megaskyscrapers. There were more than 25 river crossings in the area Victor was surveying.

There were two military headquarters, one on each side of the river, that also served as barracks. They seemed to use the river as a border between their jurisdictions. If they crossed over and interacted with the other side, Victor had not seen it. The infamous Special Ops team seemed to reside at both locations and came and went as they pleased. They had no visible patrol or assignment.

The thing that concerned Victor most was the location of the food dispensaries. Chicago had four of them, but only one on the east side of the river. However, the locals had somehow gotten away with farming along the shore of the lake. Victor figured the eastern battalion had too much on their hands dealing with the megaskyscraper complex to worry about illegal farming. Regardless, it was more food. He would leave it up to the smarter folks to figure out if that was enough to keep the population fed after they took the city.

Victor finished rehearsing the information in his head and realized again that it was all worthless if he couldn't find that net access point. Naren was confident that between the six of them they could take the city. Defending it was a whole different story. They would need help from the local population for that, and if that help wasn't guaranteed, neither was this plan.

He strolled near the lake for another hour or so before noticing something. A young woman was holding hands with a child. Her son, Victor imagined. He had noticed the two of them walking around the area the past few days. She would come down to the shore, someone would give her a couple ears of corn, and she would walk back to the complex. This time, she instead ducked into what looked like an old, abandoned hotel.

That's when Victor remembered something Edgar had told him. Victor liked Edgar, who seemed like the only other person who wasn't a god damn genius talking in big fancy words. Not coincidentally, Edgar never asked Victor to gather any information for him, nor did he provide Victor with any major pieces of advice. Edgar did mention one thing, though. He said net access points were places most people went to only when they, for one reason or another, wanted to find out what was happening in the world outside of their city. Everything else was a pattern, a routine. And the old hotel was not part of this woman's routine.

Victor looked around. There were a few peacekeepers about

two blocks to the west, and others even farther away to the north. None of them were looking in his direction or seemed to have noticed or cared where this woman was going. Victor hurried over and entered the building.

The interior looked like it had not been lived or worked in for hundreds of years. Huge pillars in the middle of what used to be the lobby kept the structure upright, but the interior walls were collapsing, and the floor had numerous holes. The front desk, or any furniture that might have once been there, had long been either taken or turned to dust. There was no sign of the woman anywhere. As Victor looked around, he heard the sound of metal scraping, as if it were being pushed.

He darted through the building at full speed until he found the source of the noise. Near the back of the building, he stopped just in time to see a set of elevator doors closing.

"That thing still works?" he whispered to himself. This wasn't like the elevators he had in the megaskyscraper growing up. This thing was ancient, so old that it should not be working. And yet there it was. He could hear the elevator as it made its way up the shaft. Not only was it working, it was working so well that it scarcely made a sound.

Victor stood there waiting for the elevator to come back down. After about two minutes, he got tired of waiting and put his ear to the door. No sounds: wherever the elevator had stopped it had stayed there.

"What the hell?" he thought. "Why doesn't it come back down? Can't it tell I'm here?"

He stood there staring at the elevator doors for a few more moments before he realized these were not like the elevators in the megaskyscrapers. Those would sense someone was waiting and just go to the floor they needed to. These elevators must be too old for that. He backed up and looked around for some sort of control. The only thing that even looked movable was a small brass button sticking out of a metal plate of the same color. He pushed the button and sure enough, the elevator sprang to life.

The doors opened about a minute later and he stepped inside. He turned and saw a panel with over 20 buttons that looked the same as the one outside the elevator.

"God damnit!" he yelled aloud. He grimaced and pressed every single button on the panel. He wasn't sure which one finally made the doors close, but they did, and the elevator started moving. It wasn't until then that he realized how small the elevator was. He looked around at the walls, and his heart started racing. He could feel himself breathing heavier and heavier as the walls felt like they were getting closer and closer. Feeling himself getting dizzy, he stumbled against the back wall, shut his eyes tight, and shoved his head into his hands. He didn't look up until he heard the elevator doors slide open. When they did, he looked only forward and walked into the room ahead. A crowd of people looked at him as he exited the elevator gasping for breath.

"S-Sorry," he said to them. "I don't like small spaces."

They nodded and went back to their conversation. The room Victor had entered was large. It looked like someone had destroyed walls to combine multiple smaller rooms with the hallway. The windows were all boarded, and the only light was coming from modern lighting fixtures retrofitted to the building's electric circuits, which were somehow still working.

Victor walked among the several dozen people and their several dozen conversations, trying to find one that stood out, one worth engaging further. As he neared the far wall, he saw two men talking, and suddenly he couldn't take his eyes off one of them. Victor couldn't quite figure out why, but something about this person made him want to go up to him. He walked over and realized he had no idea what to say. He continued strolling towards them and leaned up against the boarded-up window. He looked down and focused on their conversation, piecing together the words.

"Nah, that's bullshit man," one said. "Why the hell would a military investigator be involved?"

"I told you, he was only pretending to be one!" the other man exclaimed. "He was really one of them, a LO-EC."

"Fucking Christ. That must have Spidre quaking, that one of them was right there among his ranks and he had no fucking clue."

The other man nodded.

"Still, it sounds unbelievable. The androids wiped out a whole city's worth of LO-ECs. How could four of them bring the androids down?"

"It was five of us," Victor said with a smirk.

The two men turned to him and each raised an eyebrow. As they stared at Victor, their eyebrows fell and their eyes widened. Their breath started getting shallow and rapid. Maybe it was his twitching, maybe it was the way he had entered the conversation. Either way, the two men knew who they were in the presence of. Victor brought his finger up to his mouth, a sign for them to keep quiet. He then turned his finger and motioned for them to come closer.

"My name is Victor. I'll tell you everything, but I also need to ask you for help."

"I—I'm Tim," said the one who'd caught Victor's eye at the onset. The other man introduced himself as well, but Victor didn't hear it. He was too focused on Tim.

Victor proceeded to tell the two men every detail that led to him standing in the room with them. His campsite, the fight with Tank, and finding out that Edgar, Nadine, Naren, Sera and himself were all far more powerful than regular LO-ECs. Powerful enough to maybe even take the world on.

"So, this all leads to one question," Victor said as he concluded the story. "If we were to attack Chicago's forces, would we have help defending it against the reserves?

Victor had been speaking to Tim the whole time, including his most recent question. The other man nodded at Tim and stepped away. He knew where Victor's interests were, and it wasn't him.

Tim nodded back and turned to Victor with a smile. "Oh yeah. You've got help. Follow me."

Tim led Victor to the other side of the room, to the wall behind the elevator shaft. There was one area where a group of people were standing more tightly packed. Tim and Victor waded through the crowd and at the center of it sat a single person at a desk, looking at a box with green letters running across a black screen.

"What is that?" Victor said.

"That's our underground net connection," Tim replied. "It's an old computer, from like the end of the 20th century. Old computer connects to an old version of the net and use an old version of sending messages via the net. It's so old that the military's computers can't even recognize it as a message being sent. Conversely, the military's tech is so new that this computer can't decipher what they're sending. All our computer can do is tell when the military is sending a worldwide broadcast, and then if we need to send a message out, we do it. It gets broadcast with the military's signal and deciphered only by people with the same computer setup around the world."

"That's so fucking cool," Victor replied.

Tim nodded. "I don't know if someone already knew this connection still worked, or if they found it after Spidre cut off civilian net use, but either way when word got out it existed, the whole community came together to make it work. We have some brilliant electricians here in Chicago. Like, helped design the worldwide electric grid brilliant. They got the elevator working and rewired the building so it could use the modern electric systems. Then we destroyed the stairwells. Any peacekeepers that come snooping around will see the broken stairs, assume the elevators are broken, and just leave."

"But why have all of this? Why do you and the rest of the world even bother communicating?"

"Well, I don't know why the rest of the world does it, but we do it because we have been waiting to hear about the right time to strike."

Victor looked confused.

"Look around, Victor. Look at all of these people. Do you notice anything similar about them?"

Victor gazed around the room.

"Everyone is young," he said as he came to the realization.

"Exactly!" Tim responded. "Nearly everyone you see in this room was brought up under Spidre's rule. And most lost a loved one to Spidre's fucking war. Your friend was right, Victor. Our parents fought side-by-side with the LO-ECs when the military came. And every single one paid for it with their lives."

"So everyone hates Spidre for that?" Victor asked. "Some of the others were worried Chicago might blame LO-ECs instead. Like a 'we fought for you and got nothing but pain and suffering for it' sort of thing."

"There are some who feel that way. But LO-ECs weren't the ones who left the city without power for three years. LO-ECs weren't the ones who built a force field that requires so much energy it leaves the rest of the world with rolling blackouts. And LO-ECs weren't the ones who left us without a net. You didn't have to experience that, Victor. The net was how everyone spent most of their days. How we kept ourselves entertained and sane. You don't know what it does to people to lose that. They go crazy. They get bored. And the things crazy bored people are capable of…"

Tim looked down and clenched his fists. He took a deep breath through his nose to gather himself.

"Spidre had other options," Tim continued. "He could have instead used the net to his advantage, brainwashed the population into thinking LO-ECs were the enemy and the cause for all our problems. The older folks say that plenty of dictators have done the same in the past. Instead, he let his paranoia get the better of him, and it was his single greatest mistake. He left us to reach our own conclusions, and with everything he's done, there was only one conclusion."

Tim concluded his speech and closed his eyes in an effort to fight back tears. One managed to escape and roll down his cheek. Victor was unsure how to react. He felt his stomach grumble, and it gave him an idea.

"I uh, I have some food left in my backpack. I have to eat once more before I head back, but I don't think I can finish it all. Do you want to split it with me?"

Tim looked up and nodded. They walked over to a quieter corner of the room and sat down with the backpack in between them. They each unwrapped some of Symon's soy bars and started eating.

"So, you guys are really going to come here to liberate this place?" Tim asked, his tone hopeful.

"It seems that way. For all their hype, the Special Ops don't seem so tough, and I'm sure Naren and Nadine can figure out a plan to deal with the rest of the peacekeepers. We can defeat them, and if we have you guys to help us defend the city, we have a shot at keeping the city free.

"So, you guys do plan on freeing it then, not ruling it?" Tim asked.

"What do you mean?" Victor responded.

"Let's say we defend the city. What happens the day after? Do you rule in place of the peacekeepers?"

"I hadn't thought about it," Victor said. "Would you want us to rule Chicago?"

"Absolutely fucking not," Tim said. For a reason Victor didn't understand, the sternness of Tim's voice made him smile.

"Then it won't happen. I'll tell everyone that just so it's all clear. The plan is to free the entire world, so I don't think they plan to stay."

Tim nodded, that made sense. "Kill the peacekeepers that are here. Give us their weapons. You do that, and this city will never belong to Spidre again."

Tim was intense and excited. Even though they had just met, Victor was enjoying every second they spent talking. It made his heart feel heavy knowing the conversation now had to end.

"I—I'm sorry Tim, but I have to go. Finding out if we had help was the last piece of info I needed. I need to get back to San Diego so we can plan."

"Oh… ok," Tim replied. He too was sad Victor had to go. That, for some reason, made Victor happy.

"Is that ok?" Victor asked.

"Yeah, yeah of course. Just… I hope that after the battle, we get to hang out some more."

"Yeah, me too." Victor replied. He had no idea why he felt that way, but he meant it.

Victor stood up and slung the now-empty pack on his back.

"Spread the word, let people you trust know we're coming. When it happens, it'll happen fast. Be ready."

Tim nodded. "We'll be ready. Goodbye, Victor."

"Goodbye, Tim," Victor replied with a smile. He walked to the elevator, took a deep breath, and shut his eyes tight as it took him back to ground level. The second he hit the street, he was off running back to San Diego, a smile on his face, his mind thinking ahead to the next time he would be in Chicago.

Chapter 20

They drove all night in silence. When the sky started to brighten, they had a quick breakfast with Chicago's megaskyscrapers just within view. Even as they all sat eating, nobody talked. They were too focused on the many tasks that lay ahead of them. As they finished up, everyone took one last long look at each other, reflecting on the last two months they'd shared together. With that, they were back on the road into Chicago proper. They slowed their speed as they entered the city. All around them, civilians stared in amazement while soldiers stood confused as to what to do. As the elcycles turned, Victor pointed at a shorter building several blocks down. It was Edgar and Nadine's target. Nadine slowed the elcycle to a crawl and Sera lifted her into the air while Naren did the same with Edgar. They flew by the roof of the building and dropped Edgar and Nadine on top. Then, and only then, did Edgar break the silence that had lasted all evening.

"You ready to do this?" he asked Nadine.

"Not yet," she replied.

Edgar turned to ask what was wrong, and as he did Nadine planted a big warm kiss on his lips. After a couple of seconds she pulled back and smiled.

"Ok, now I'm ready," she said as she smiled and turned to face the roof access door while Edgar shook off being completely stunned.

One swift kick, and the door leading to the roof crumpled into the stairwell. Nadine darted down the stairs with Edgar close behind, his right hand blazing bright blue. Nadine reached the door to the top floor and kicked that one in as well, crushing the poor soldier next to it. They entered the room and faced several rows of soldiers rushing to put their gear on. Everyone stopped for a split second, a brief stare between assailants and soldiers, before Edgar and Nadine rushed into the room. Some soldiers started attaching guns to their armor and Edgar and Nadine barreled towards them. On the way, Edgar sliced through any soldier within reach. Nadine for the most part jumped and dodged around the unarmed soldiers, knowing she'd be back for them later. She was a flurry of movement as she bounced off the floor and ceiling. For a split second, a seam opened up in the crowd and she had direct line of sight at two of the armed soldiers. She took off with all of her might and jumped through the seam, slamming into the two soldiers and throwing them into the far wall. As their lifeless bodies crumpled to the floor, she turned, looking for other soldiers who were close to being armed. Across the room, Edgar's hands were a blur, slashing through anything that moved towards him, his blade bouncing back and forth between each hand as needed. Eventually, enough time had passed and enough soldiers had fallen that Edgar found himself staring at a soldier taking aim.

The gun is on his right hand, I roll right, Edgar thought to himself, remembering the lesson Nadine had taught him.

The soldier opened fire as Edgar ran right in a tightening loop. Some shots went flying into the ceiling or walls, some went flying into fellow soldiers. Edgar kept running until the shooter had to adjust his feet to continue firing.

"There it is," Edgar thought.

As the gunner adjusted, Edgar switched his blade to his left hand and charged in. The soldier attempted to dodge but reacted far too late, and Edgar's blade pierced his mid-section. Edgar then switched his blade back to the right side and continued running as the soldier fell to the ground. It had been only twenty seconds, but two thirds of the soldiers were down.

Nadine finished bouncing off the face of a soldier and landed on the ground. As her eyes trained on her next target, the sound of a loud bell filled the air.

There's the siren. Sera's time to shine, Nadine thought.

A hundred feet above the second building, Sera and Naren heard the siren. They looked at each other.

"I love you."

"I love you too."

Sera dove down as fast as gravity and her power would take her. As she fell, she caught a quick glimpse of a blur that could only be Victor running towards Edgar and Nadine's building, and another glimpse of Symon getting off the elcycle down the street. At twenty feet from the ground, she pulled up and slammed into the glass front of the building. She unleashed her explosion, and its familiar, cacophonous roar echoed off the surrounding buildings, the energy shredding cement and steel. The inertia from her flight carried Sera out the other side of the building while it started crumbling around her. As if there had been a planned demolition, the building's collapse was perfect. The bottom blew out and the levels above it imploded one by one. In ten seconds, a building that had stood for half a millennium was a pile of rubble and a mass grave for a battalion.

As the building came down, Naren landed on the other side of the bridge right next to Victor, who was outside the entrance to the building Nadine and Edgar were in. The air raid siren could just be made out over the sounds of crumbling concrete. As the noise died down, the dust cloud rose, and faint cries of soldiers could be heard coming from all directions.

"They're closing in on us," Victor said.

"You look South, I'll look North," Naren replied.

The two stood back-to-back just as the first wave of troops came around either side of the building. The soldiers seemed older in age, the youngest around 40. Their armor was fire red instead of the normal blue, and they all had electric swords on one hand and either a machine gun or a laser cannon on the other.

"Special Ops," Naren and Victor said.

As the soldiers facing Victor lined up and took aim, he threw his right arm up and across his body. The concussive air wave flung away from him and slammed into the soldiers before they could get a shot off. More soldiers came pouring around the corner. Victor continued to stand his ground, throwing his hands up in rapid succession and sending the soldiers flying the second they were visible. Pieces of the building began crumbling off the side as his shockwaves got closer and closer to the facade. A few blocks away, another wave of soldiers dressed in red came out of the dust cloud and over a bridge. Victor threw a shockwave, but it dissipated before reaching them. He rushed forward and threw a wave to his right while doing so, knocking back any soldiers that still hadn't yet rounded the corner. The soldiers down the street fired at him, but with Victor's speed none of them could manage a clean shot. In a matter of seconds, he was on top of them.

As he approached the front line of soldiers, the training he'd done with Nadine was a constant in his mind.

Throw all your body weight into the punch, he thought as he landed a blow and smashed the soldier's armor, sending her flying into the soldiers behind her. Another soldier came in to try and grab him. Victor ducked under and landed a jarring uppercut. Yet another soldier lunged at him, attempting to slash him with an electric blade. Victor ducked under again and, as the soldier continued forward, grabbed him and flung him over his shoulder, knocking over several peacekeepers who were attempting to flank.

Meanwhile, Naren had taken off in the opposite direction. Special Ops chased after him, shooting and missing as he serpentined through the air. He took a quick glance back at them.

"They ran at different speeds and spread out, just like Nadine said they would," he thought. He knew that since they were spread out, he could take them on one-by-one, with the soldiers in front blocking the shots of those behind them. He made a hard left turn and boosted into the frontmost soldier, pummeling him into the ground. The next soldier had stopped firing, afraid to hit her comrade, and was just taking aim again when Naren plowed into her. He continued back down the street and the strategy worked over and over again. When he arrived back at the building that Nadine and Edgar were in, he saw that a group of Special Ops had congregated at the entrance. He shot straight up in the air as they fired, then looped around the back of the building.

"They're going to expect me to come around the other side," he thought as he doubled back and returned the same way he had come. He darted down the facade of the building, then leveled out a foot from the ground. Sure enough, as he came around to the front, most of the Special Ops were facing the other way. He smashed into the pack of soldiers, then turned to face them again while landing with grace on the hard asphalt. In the next instant, he was blasting off again at full power, slamming into the last of the pack that remained standing.

Back inside the building, Edgar and Nadine had made their way to the third-highest floor. Nadine had found one last soldier holing up in the bathroom. With one violent kick, the soldier's face was in the main room again, via the hole his head had just made in the wall between the two rooms. The number of soldiers on each floor had decreased every time they had descended. The two of them were starting to feel winded but continued running to the next staircase. They hurtled downstairs, busted through the next door, and were met with an empty floor. The room was only rows of empty beds running between the support pillars and a deserted lounge area on the far side.

"Huh, that's interesting," Nadine said.

"What the hell? Did we clear the whole building?" Edgar asked.

"I doubt it," Nadine replied. "They must have all retreated and grouped together on a lower floor. I thought it seemed weird that there were less and less peacekeepers each time we went down a level. They're going to be waiting for us to bust through the door so they can launch an all-out counterattack."

"Well, what floor are they going to be on?"

"Tough to say. I doubt they'd be on the ground floor. They would just get sucked into the commotion going on outside and they'll want to leave that fight to Special Ops. Depending on how many troops are left, they may worry about too many people being on one floor. They would just wind up shooting each other, so they could have split up. Best guess, there are troops on the second or third floor, and another group a few floors above that. That way they'll avoid shooting each other through the floor as well."

"Winds up working in our favor," Edgar replied, "I needed to catch my breath anyway."

"Getting tired?" she asked.

"Not at all. You just got my heart racing before the fight even started."

The two of them smirked at Edgar's corny line and kept moving. They checked the bathrooms and showers as a precaution, but no one was to be found. They kept moving to the next staircase and next floor. It first appeared to be the same empty room, when Nadine noticed movement at the far wall. An elevator door closing.

"Oh, you fucking morons," she cried.

"Are they using the elevator to get to the lower floor?!" Edgar asked.

"They sure are," Nadine replied. "It's an older elevator. Let's wait to see where they stop. Then you cut through the door and the cables."

They waited as the lights of each floor illuminated and went dark again. When the light came to a stop, Edgar plunged his left blade through the door and severed the cables. The elevator could be heard screeching and scraping as it plummeted.

"Thirteenth floor it is," Nadine said.

They continued cautiously through each remaining floor without incident. When they reached the fourteenth floor, they took extra care to remain quiet so the soldiers below wouldn't hear and try shooting up at them. They opened the door to the stairwell. No gunfire, no one waiting for them at the bottom. They both took a deep breath and jumped down the stairs to the next floor. Nadine ran at the door full speed and kicked it with all her might. The door ripped off its hinges and flew into the main room, taking out multiple soldiers. Edgar saw the opening

the door had made in the crowd and rushed as far into the center
of the room as he could. The place was packed to the brim with
soldiers. Those who had guns strained to turn around and get in
a position to take a shot. Any soldier Edgar saw trying to get into
position was on the ground moments later. Those who had swords
were able to adjust more easily but flailed to keep up with his fast
movement. If their blades didn't hit air, they were hitting other
soldiers. Nadine used the distraction provided by Edgar to rush
into the room as well. A soldier swung around to take a shot at
her, and she threw his arm to the side, directing all of his shots
at the soldiers around him instead. In the next instant, her hand
was around his throat, and she slammed his head into the floor.
She released his neck and boosted into the crowd in front of her,
joining Edgar in the chaotic massacre. As the soldiers fell, dodging
became increasingly difficult. There were fewer people for Edgar
and Nadine to hide behind. They caught sight of each other from
opposite sides of the room and zig-zagged into the center. The
soldiers got confused and couldn't decide which target to shoot at.
Edgar did the circling trick he had used earlier and made his way
close enough to plunge his blade through a peacekeeper's gut. On
the other side of the room, Nadine boosted off the floor and leapt
through the air at the soldier shooting at her. He was too slow. His
shots always trailed behind her feet, right up until the point that
she tackled him and pummeled him into the floor. She stopped
only when sword-wielding soldiers, the only soldiers left standing,
charged at her together in one last desperate attempt to bring her
down. She boosted along the floor and rotated as they approached,
tripping all of them. They fell to the ground and were far too slow
to get up as Nadine's foot and Edgar's blade came down on their
heads one by one.

Nadine and Edgar stood hunched over, looking at each other, gasping for air. A splatter of blood covered their bodies and most of the room and corpses surrounding them.

"I don't… think they… split up… their forces… between two floors," Nadine said in between huge gulps of air.

Outside, Special Ops had wised up. One group had driven Naren away long enough to come together in a semi-organized circle. Those in the interior were firing up at Naren while the south-facing soldiers fired down the street at Victor, keeping just out of the effective range of his bursts of air. The troops weren't landing any hits, but Naren and Victor couldn't mount a counterattack either.

Shit, Victor thought. *I can't get close enough to them to do anything! And I'm getting winded. They're going to get lucky and shoot me long before those guns run out of ammo.* About a block south of the Special Ops circle, Victor noticed movement around the corner. A small group of regular soldiers was lining up to take aim at him.

Ugh, I can't slow down and take a clear shot at them right now! No, I have to. I don't know if I can handle dodging bullets from that many angles. Fucking god damn it. Victor slowed for a few steps and threw up his left hand, then his right. Two air bursts flew across the battlefield while several bullets whizzed past him. The whistle from their passing was so loud that Victor fell to the ground for cover, then scrambled to get back up as more bullets struck where he had just been lying. Down the street, his air bursts had made contact and knocked over several soldiers but didn't have the force to knock them out or kill them. They were getting back up and organizing a line for a second time.

Shit! Victor thought as he darted back and forth. *If they get that line up, I'm screwed. But I can't stop, that was too damn close last time. Don't tell me I'm going to be the first one to fucking retreat on our first—oh.* Victor's thought was cut off by an orange blur streaking through the sky and slamming into the line of regular peacekeepers. Sera popped up and started flinging the remaining troops into the sides of the surrounding buildings. She grabbed one of their lifeless bodies and, just like in New Orleans, threw the body in front of her as she flew towards the Special Ops team. Victor lined up behind her and made a mad dash down the street. A few soldiers diverted their fire from Naren towards the corpse flying at them, and Naren took the opportunity to dive. The three of them converged on the circle and hit it all at once. A good amount of soldiers fell, but the remainder moved to encircle their assailants. They started slashing with their electric blades while Victor, Naren, and Sera alternated between dodging and pummeling. When he had cleared out enough of the troops surrounding him, Victor noticed that a few Special Ops members had backed away from the action and were waiting for a hole to open so they could open fire. It was a trap.

"Fuck!" Victor yelled as he barreled through the soldiers he was fighting, away from the second set of Special Ops. As he pushed them aside, one of their blades caught his arm and the searing pain of electricity coursed through his body. He summoned every ounce of strength he had and continued to push his body in the direction he wanted. Sera and Naren heard him yell and took off before any shots were fired. Victor ducked around the corner of the building and threw himself to the ground and against the wall for cover. It was then that he heard a new round of gunfire.

"More soldiers? How are Naren and Sera not in cover yet?"

In the same exact second, Sera and Naren landed next to Victor.

"Can you get up?! Are you ok?" Sera asked.

"Nothing that won't heal," Victor replied, showing them a small, singed laceration on his right arm. "They almost got us. One of their blades caught me while I was clearing out.”

“It was a close call,” Sera said. “But it’s ok now. We’ve got help.”

Sera glanced into the street, guiding Victor’s eyes in the same direction. There he saw the Special Ops team being fired on by people running over the bridge, wearing a mix of armor and street clothes. The charge was being led by Symon.

“You and Symon finished off the troops on that side of the river and gave the armor and guns to the locals to help,” Naren said.

“Sure did!” Sera replied.

Victor smiled. “Let’s finish this.”

Inside, Edgar and Nadine had made their way through most of the remainder of the building and were just outside the stairs leading to the second floor. They were moving cautiously, knowing that if anyone was left in the building they were waiting down the next flight of stairs. However, they were now even more on edge, because for the first time in their entire journey through the building, the door to the stairwell was propped open. Nadine approached it warily. When she got close, she went flat against the wall adjacent to the doorway. She ducked down as low as she could and then peered around the corner and pulled back. No sooner was her head back in the room than the stairwell rang out with the sound of rapid gunfire, and the door became pock marked with bullet holes.

“A woman in red armor,” Nadine said. “We’ve got Special Ops.”

“They propped open the door thinking we were just going to run through?”

“It makes sense. We’ve been barreling into every populated room we’ve entered so far. They must have thought we were going to do the same now. Frankly I’m amazed we haven’t run into people in the stairwell yet. It’s a great defensive position.”

Edgar had a doubtful look on his face. "You thought of a way through this didn't you?"

"Of course I did. Keep her distracted here. I'll be back."

"Uhh, no problem," Edgar replied.

Nadine began walking back across the third floor while Edgar remained by the open door. He waited a few seconds, then stuck his hand out into the stairwell, drawing it back a split second before more bullets flew past. He then lit the blade on his left hand and plunged it through the wall, an effort to try and make the soldier think he was trying to get her through the cement. He waited another few seconds and stabbed through the wall in a different spot. Another few seconds, another spot. He kept this up until he heard muffled banging coming from the floor above. He ran back into position by the door and waited. The banging got louder and louder until the ceiling in the stairwell caved in. He darted into the stairwell just in time to see Nadine falling through the ceiling on top of the red-armored soldier. Nadine pinned her to the ground and Edgar ran up and plunged his blade into the side of her head. They looked down the stairwell at the door to the second floor. It was closed.

"Back to the normal plan, then," Nadine said. "No sense in being quiet after what we just did."

They ran towards the door and Nadine kicked it open once again. She and Edgar ran in and were faced with six Special Ops soldiers, three on either side. Nadine boosted right, towards the centermost soldier, drawing the aim of the two other troops on the right side of the room. Nadine landed in between the two soldiers closest to the door they had entered, and as they raised their guns to fire, she boosted away. Their shots sailed past her and into each other's chests. She ran up to the same soldier in the center, now a corpse on the floor, and picked him up to shield her from the remaining soldier's fire.

Guess this little trick Sera taught me will help after all, Nadine thought. The dead soldier was facing her. She wrapped the corpse's shooting arm around his neck and pointed it at the remaining soldier. She then reached out and clenched the dead body's fist. This activated the gun, which was drawing power from the still-warm body, and unleashed a barrage of bullets on the last soldier firing at her. At the door, Edgar had his back to a wall, keeping the closest soldier between him and the line of fire of the remaining two soldiers. The peacekeeper brought her gun up to fire on Edgar, and he sliced it clean off her armor. She then brought the blade on the other arm down from overhead, forcing Edgar to throw his blade up to block. The remaining two soldiers came around their comrade's left side and took aim at Edgar from less than a foot away. Edgar's hand had been forced. He threw open his right hand and a second blade came out.

"Christ, this still feels awkward," Edgar thought.

Edgar brought his right hand up and sliced off the arms of the two soldiers aiming at him. The swing of his blade continued around and plunged through the face of the soldier still blade-to-blade with him. As he withdrew his blade from her head, a barrage of bullets opened up from across the room and eviscerated the soldiers he had just severed the arms of. He looked across the room. It was Nadine, still operating the gun of the soldier she had used as a shield. The fight was over, the building was clear, and they had nothing more than a few scratches and bruises to show for it.

She dropped the body, and they walked across the room towards each other.

"You finally had to use them both, eh?" Nadine asked as she walked over.

"Yeah, but it still doesn't feel right. I'm glad I was standing still," Edgar said.

They grabbed each other's hands and peered into each other's eyes, beaming with delight that their fight was over. Then the realization hit them both that there was still a fight going on outside. They rushed across the room and down the stairs. They burst through the door out of the stairwell and across the empty lobby and into the street where they saw—

A celebration! Edgar thought. *We did it, we took the city.* In the streets, the locals were cheering and shouting. The Special Ops and battalion forces outside were now bodies strewn about the street. The only people not celebrating were the six LO-ECs.

"Wait! We shouldn't be celebrating yet!" Nadine screamed.

The crowd fell silent.

"She's right!" Naren continued. "This was only step one. Spidre knows about the assault, and he'll be sending backup. Now, we think it'll be the forces from Seoul that come, but there is a chance it'll be forces from New York, so we have five hours to get the best defense possible set up!"

"I need a dozen of you to run back to the megaskyscrapers. Use the PA systems to ask anyone who is willing and able to fight to come here," Symon yelled. "Everyone else who already has a laser or gun, follow the young lady in front of you south." Symon motioned towards Nadine. "Highway 55 will be our primary defensive line."

Chapter 21

Some of the locals ran back over the bridge towards the skyscrapers as Symon instructed. Nadine and Edgar walked over to their fellow LO-ECs.

"Building is clear?" Sera asked.

"Not a soul left alive," Edgar replied.

"Good," Naren said. "Victor, run in there and start tossing bodies out into the street. Sera and I will catch them, and Symon will help us strip them down. Nadine, you and Edgar get into position. Anyone who picks up a laser cannon will be sent to you; those will be most effective against the big artillery. It'll be up to you two to get them in position. We'll also send someone with food before the fighting starts."

"I appreciate that," Nadine replied. She turned to Victor. "There are dead Special Ops members on the second floor, most of the regular battalion was downed on the 13th, and the rest are all the way at the top three floors."

"Got it," Victor said. "Either of you want to take the top floors while I handle two and thirteen?" he asked, looking at Sera and Naren.

"Good call. I'll do it," Sera said.

As Sera spoke, Nadine turned to face the locals. "Ladies and gentlemen! If you'll please follow us!"

Nadine and Edgar took off running south with the locals close in tow. Victor ran into the building and in a matter of seconds was tossing bodies out the windows. Sera took off to the top of the building and proceeded to do the same. Naren did as best he could to catch the bodies as they fell, careful not to damage the now vitally important weaponry the bodies carried. As Naren caught the bodies, he brought them to the other side of the river, where Symon organized the bodies into piles based on what armaments they were carrying: sword, laser cannon, or machine gun. In a few minutes, the fastest and closest of the locals showed up.

"I need half of you to help me strip these bodies," he directed them. "Be careful when removing the machine guns. The ammo printer is built into the upper arm, so the upper and lower piece have to be removed together. The other pieces are a little more robust, but still be careful, we need all the weaponry we can get. The rest of you, run across the bridge, start stripping the bodies there, and bring the weapons back here. Try to keep them organized based on weapon type."

"Yes sir!" the locals shouted in unison.

A thought occurred to Symon as he looked down at the weapons system he created. "Do you have any good electricians living in the megaskyscrapers?"

"Quite a few," one local replied.

"Any that can hook up that to this?" Symon asked, pointing at the machine gun he just removed while opening the palm of his other hand and exposing his microtransformer.

"Without a doubt."

"Can you go find them and bring them here? Also, please tell someone to bring a good amount of food this way, anything they can spare. And on your way back, you'll see a huge, funny-looking, tan-colored motorcycle a few blocks south. Can you bring it here?"

"You can count on me!" the same local said, as he ran back towards the megaskyscrapers.

When enough people had arrived that they were stripping the bodies at the same rate they were being dropped off, Symon started equipping the newcomers with laser cannons and sending them south. Some time later, the drops from the 13th floor stopped, and Victor came running back down.

"How's it going down here?" he asked.

"It's going," Symon replied. "I want to get those weapons on the other side of the river as soon as possible, though."

"I'll start grabbing some then," Victor said.

"You feeling ok?" Symon asked.

"I'm fine, don't worry," Victor said sharply.

"Ok, just be careful."

"Fucking Christ," Victor replied. "Now is not the time to focus on my problems. Let's get this done!"

With that, he proceeded to run back and forth across the bridge, carrying one or two bodies with every trip. He finished moving them just as Sera cleared out the last of the bodies from the top floors. Their timing couldn't have been more perfect, as someone showed up at the exact same time carrying armfuls of food. The four of them stepped away from the body-stripping operation to eat and strategize.

"What's the status with the weapons?" Naren asked.

"I've been telling them to strip down the cannons and machine guns first. Swords are lowest priority. Most of the cannons have been given out and sent to Edgar and Nadine."

"We should save some of them for people defending the bridges. I'd say at least two at each crossing," Sera said. "Most of the heavy artillery will head south, but there is a chance some will still be sent over the river. We'll need to be prepared, just in case."

"I'll switch focus to the machine guns then and start sending locals with laser cannons to the crossings," Symon replied.

"We need machine gunners in place by the bridges. We have literally no one there yet." Victor said.

"The southernmost bridges will take top priority then." Naren said. "We'll need people up in the buildings shooting down, as well as people holding the line at street level. Alternate between sending machine gunners to the bridges and to Edgar and Nadine. Sera and I will keep an eye on the setup and when one bridge is fully defended, we'll direct the next arriving locals to the next crossing north. We'll keep up that pattern until every bridge is defended."

"We only have about three and a half hours left, at most," Symon said. "I don't know if we're going to be ready in time if the New York forces come."

"Neither do I," Naren replied, as he finished eating and turned to the locals to explain the plan to them. The last of the laser cannons were handed out and they left to their respective positions at the bridges. Sera and Naren took off to organize the machine gunners and get food to Edgar and Nadine. Symon and Victor continued directing their group. A few minutes passed, and the young man Symon had sent back to the megaskyscrapers returned, wheeling the elcycle on his left while a middle-aged woman holding a tool box accompanied him on the right. She was fit for her age, and wearing a light grey t-shirt, khakis and black boots.

"That took forever!" Symon said.

"I'm so sorry," the man replied as he wheeled the elcycle over to Symon. "I tried describing that thing in your hand to multiple electricians and a lot of people didn't know what to do with it. A few others knew, but they were too terrified of you. But then I found May here."

"I guess I should've expected that. We did just take out an entire army, I imagine that would intimidate some people," Symon said. "Nice to meet you May, thank you for coming. I'm Symon." Symon said, while flashing a smile at their new ally. "Think you can hook up a machine gun to my microtransformer?"

"Nice to meet you, too," she said, smiling back. "I could with the right parts, but I haven't had those for decades," she said.

"You have them now," Symon said, patting his elcycle on the handlebar. "Any part you need feel free to take it off this guy. I can always reassemble it later. I just can't disassemble it and attach the parts to myself by myself."

May took a long look at the elcycle. "I can have you hooked up in an hour."

"You're awesome," Symon said.

"No, you're awesome. A living breathing LO-EC, holy shit," May replied, looking Symon up and down.

"Gosh," Symon said, smiling and turning bright red. "And I'm not even the impressive one of us."

Symon then turned to the young man who had found May.

"What's your name, son?"

"Tim, sir."

"Ah, the legendary Tim," Symon replied. "You couldn't have done any better considering the circumstances. Thank you for all your help, but I need to ask one last thing of you."

"What do you need?"

"I think you already know that guy over there, yes?" Symon

pointed at Victor. "Grab a machine gun from him and head south. You'll find two people flying around down there, and they'll tell you where to go."

"Flying?" May said, perplexed.

"I told you, I'm not the impressive one," Symon replied to her. He then turned and shouted "Victor! Do you think you can get this guy set up with some machine-gun armor while this young lady hooks me up to a gun?"

Victor looked over the shoulder of the person he was arming and saw Tim. "Absolutely," he replied with a smile.

Farther south, Edgar and Nadine were getting those armed with laser cannons into place. They looked back towards the city and saw Naren approaching, holding food for them. He landed, and they inhaled what he had brought.

"How's it going? Naren asked.

"The laser cannon guys are in place," Edgar replied.

"But we need more gunners," Nadine continued. "We need the suppressive fire to keep all those ground troops at a distance."

"I know, and they'll be coming. But we have to split between sending them here and sending them to the bridges. Only a couple of the southern crossings have been set up for defense, and most of the northern ones only have two laser cannons guarding them right now."

Nadine sighed. "What else can we do to prepare then?"

"I'll make sure Victor is in place to help you guys well before the New York forces can be here. Other than that, all any of us can do is get what gunners we have in position as fast as possible."

"How much time?" Edgar asked.

"Two hours, two and a half max," Naren replied.

"I really hope you're right about the New York forces not

coming." Nadine said.

"Me too," Naren said as he turned and took off back north.

Nadine turned to the locals stationed on the highway. "Does anyone have a watch?" she yelled.

"I do ma'am," one of them shouted back.

"From right now, I want you to start counting down two hours. Announce how much time is left every half hour. Once an hour and a half has gone by, start announcing how much time is left every 15 minutes. When you hit two hours, announce how much time has passed every 5 minutes. Do you understand?"

"Sure do!" the young woman replied.

Nadine and Edgar worked to get every local who arrived into position as fast as possible. The woman who was keeping track of time announced an hour and a half was left. Then an hour. Then a half hour. Nadine looked over and saw Victor at the southwest corner of the highway. Still huge gaps in coverage on that side and on the east, and not enough coverage in the middle.

Once the timekeeper switched to five-minute announcements, the time seemed to start flying by.

"Twenty-five minutes left!"

"Twenty!"

"Fifteen!"

The middle was stronger, but still not enough for Nadine or Edgar to be comfortable. The east and west still needed a lot more coverage.

"Ten!"

"Five!"

"Zero. We've hit two hours!"

Nadine and Edgar got tense. The middle was solid, but the east and west still had obvious holes. They braced themselves for the onslaught the New York regiments would bring.

"Two hours five!"

"Two hours ten!"

"Two hours fifteen!"

"Two hours twenty… Twenty five… Thirty!"

Still no sign of troops. Still not a complete defense.

"Forty five… Fifty… Fifty five… Three hours!"

Nadine felt herself relaxing more every five minutes that were counted.

"Three forty five… Three fifty… Three fifty five!"

At the four-hour mark, Nadine finally breathed a sigh of relief. She told the timekeeper to stop making announcements. Naren was right. New York wasn't coming. And now they had all afternoon to get their defenses ready for the Seoul forces.Once the line was set up, Nadine and Edgar came together to strategize.

"So, I think when we see the arsenal coming, our top priority needs to be taking out the EMP cannons. If those things get a good shot off, they could disable entire sections of our defense at once. We should tell our guys to focus fire on the troops around those cannons first, then we'll run in and destroy them."

"How far out can they start firing from?"

"Pretty far, I think. But, according to Naren, they have to be aimed manually. All those electric coils and magnetic fields scramble automated aiming programs. We also have the cover of all the abandoned buildings as they come up the streets from the south, so they'll try to bring them in close before firing."

"And they won't try to fire it at us when we run up on it?" Edgar asked.

"It won't matter if they do, it wouldn't do anything to us," Nadine replied.

"What? Why?" Edgar inquired.

"EMPs only fry tech that runs on electricity," Nadine said. "All of our energy is biological, it doesn't get affected. Even Symon wouldn't get affected. But the BEO systems that the locals now have would be. That system converts body heat straight to electricity."

"So, it'll affect our guys' systems, but not the troops coming from Seoul?" Edgar said.

"It would affect them if they were on the receiving end of it," Nadine said. "The EMP cannon is like a mortar shooting invisible electro-magnetic 'shells'. Only electrical things in the blast radius of those 'shells' would be shut down."

"Okay, I get it now. So EMPs are everyone's top priority," Edgar said.

"Definitely. If we take them out before they get off a shot, it'll allow our laser cannons to create enough sustained fire to take out the tanks and any mounted missile or gun systems," Nadine replied.

"That sounds like a great plan then! But, umm, if the EMPs are that important, then why are we destroying them?" Edgar asked.

"What do you mean?" Nadine asked in return.

"Well, we're going to need to defend the city long-term, right?" Edgar said. "Sounds like having the EMP cannons would help with that a lot. Isn't there a way we can disable them without destroying them?"

Nadine was stunned. "That's... really brilliant Edgar. Yeah. I bet if we only destroy the control systems that adjust the cannon's position, we can disable them now and then rebuild or rewire the system later. And we can tell the laser cannoneers to try and only shoot to disable the other artillery! I'm proud of you. You may wind up becoming an expert military strategist after all of this."

"Well thanks!" Edgar said through a pride filled smile. "I do have one last question though."

"What's that?" Nadine replied.

"What do the EMP cannons look like?" Edgar asked.

Nadine put her face in her hand. "Aaaaand we're back to normal Edgar," she said, half amused, half frustrated. "It's a cannon, a 30-foot-long cannon mounted on a massive engine and wheels."

Farther north, Sera and Naren were perched atop a skyscraper ledge, also discussing strategy.

"So what do you think? Is everyone where they need to be?" Naren asked.

"Pretty much. I'm just worried about Victor," Sera replied.

"Victor?"

"Yeah. I mean, I understand the south is going to get hit hardest, but it's also going to get hit last, right?"

"So, you think he should start north, then work his way down as the Seoul forces start attacking in new areas?"

"Well, I think all three of us should, at least until we're getting pressed on all three sides. Then we'll all go wherever we're needed."

Naren thought about it for a moment.

"You're right. That makes more sense. I'll go tell them in the south. Will you let Symon know?"

"Yes sir!" Sera replied, saluting and sticking out her tongue.

Naren smiled. "Love you."

"Love you."

With that, they split ways. Sera flew over the northern defenses and was surprised to see Symon up in a skyscraper, peering through a busted-out floor-to-ceiling window over the center portion of the defensive line.

Sera flew over to the window. "Symon, what are you doing up he—holy shit!"

Sera got her first good look at Symon decked out with red

machine-gun armor on his left arm. Half a dozen wires were running from his wrinkled and callused palm up into his forearm and shoulder.

"I know, isn't it awesome?" Symon replied. "May rigged it up for me."

"May?"

Symon nodded his head to his left, where May was standing wearing her own set of machine-gun armor as well as a look of disbelief on her face.

Sera flew in through the window and landed.

"Nice to meet you, ma'am. It's awesome that you can work with LO-EC tech, and do it so quickly! Where'd you get all the parts?"

"You, you can fly," May replied.

"I can," Sera said smiling. She had been getting looks of disbelief all day, but had still forgotten that being able to fly was something others would be bewildered by.

"You can fly!" May exclaimed even louder.

"I can!" Sera replied again while chuckling.

"You'll never get used to being impressive, eh Sera?" Symon said.

"I'm sorry, I'm sorry," May said. "Symon told me I would probably see you flying around before the day was over, but seeing it up close? Holy hell!"

"Wait till you see the other trick I have up my sleeve," Sera said with a coy smirk.

"Oh, I've been told about that too, and I can't wait! But to answer your question, I still had my old toolbox from my electrician days, and the parts I got from his elcycle."

Sera turned to Symon. "You sacrificed your cycle for this? Symon, you didn't have to do that."

"I didn't sacrifice it. It can still function with just the one microtransformer on the right handlebar, and I can always put this one back on after the fight is over. Even supposing the elcycle is a total loss, it's worth it. This thing is built to fire using normal human body heat. Imagine the rounds per second it'll be pumping out attached to LO-EC energy. The Seoul forces are not crossing my bridges. They'll be too busy dancing around my bullets instead! Ha-ha!"

May and Sera smiled. "Well, I came to tell you we're going to rotate Victor up here for the start of the fight, since the north is going to be hit first. But you don't need him, so…"

"Oh. Well, I mean, if he's already on his way, might as well just let him come, right?" Symon said as he turned red. "I'll save him a couple peacekeepers to throw around, don't worry."

Sera chuckled again. "Oh yeah," she said as he turned back to May. "Wait till you see Victor in action, too. I have a feeling you'll be less impressed by my flying after that."

"We'll see," May replied with a smile.

Sera smiled back. "Good luck guys. I'll see you later."

With that she exited the window and flew back to her original perch. Naren met her there a short time later, just as the blur of Victor running could first be seen heading north.

Chapter 22

"Everything went ok?" Sera asked Naren.

"Yes," Naren replied. He was cradling several ears of corn, and as he approached, he repositioned a couple so Sera could grab them. "As long as we're on top of letting Victor know when he's needed south, Edgar and Nadine have no problem with it. Actually, they figured out a pretty solid strategy where he isn't needed much. They're going to focus on the EMP cannons first, and they're going to try to only disable them, not destroy them."

"So, we can use them to defend the city long term!" Sera replied.

"Exactly. And I'm sure Symon was relieved to hear he'll have some backup?" Naren asked.

"He was, but he thought of a pretty smart plan himself," Sera said. "He found this woman, an electrical engineer, and had her hook up a microtransformer from the elcycle to machine gun armor. He's going to be up in a skyscraper peppering the forces on the ground."

"That is smart," Naren said. "It's also fortunate he found someone who can work with LO-EC tech."

"Yeah, she seemed to know her stuff. And she was really

impressed at my ability to fly," Sera said, chuckling again.

"You met her?" Naren asked.

"She was up in the building with Symon. I told her if she was impressed by me, just wait till she sees Victor in action."

"Interesting," Naren replied.

The two of them stayed silent as Sera thought for several moments.

"So if we live through this, Symon is going to get laid, huh?" Sera finally said.

"What?!" Naren exclaimed.

"What? She's obviously got a thing for LO-EC users, and it must be fooooooorever since Symon got any action.""But how did you make that logical leap?""How did you not?! You never thought about this since we all came together?" Sera said.

"No, no, I did not.""Well I did!" He's the only one besides us that has ever had sex. Hell, he's the only one who had a chance to have any kind of sex life. We've all been in hiding and avoiding contact with normal humans who would give us away. He's the only one that didn't have to worry about that for at least part of his life. But it's been over 20 years. He must be dyyyying right now."

"Is this the best time for us to be discussing this?""Would you rather sit here eating in silence?" Sera replied. Naren sighed.

"Fair enough. I guess you're right," Naren said. "If anyone has had sex besides us, it's him. Nadine never bothered with guys while we were living together, and I imagine she would've told me by now if anything had happened while we were separated. Edgar is more likely, but still, I doubt it. He was too busy being on the run. And Victor, well, yeah."

"Ugh, I know," Sera replied. "I feel so bad for him. Being alone for twenty years is bad enough, but being alone at eight-years-old?!

That's a lot to work through as an adult, a lot to figure out."

"We'll help him through it," Naren said. "We'll help Victor figure himself out, and we'll help Nadine and Edgar figure things out too."

"Uhh, that's a little condescending of you to say.""What makes you say that?""I don't think we have to worry about Edgar and Nadine. Not as far as intimacy issues are concerned," Sera said.

Naren had a confused look on his face, surprising Sera.

"Wait, you're messing with me, right?" she asked.

"What are you talking about?""You never noticed Edgar and Nadine flirting?""No! What!?""Wait, seriously!?" Sera burst out laughing.

"How long has that been going on?" Naren turned bright red.

"Like, since the day I met them!""I don't know how I feel about that…""Why? Edgar's sweet," Sera said.

"He's a nice guy. But he's also… kind of dumb, no?" Naren said almost at a whisper.

Sera scowled. "You're really digging a hole for yourself right now."

"I'm sorry, but Nadine is one of the smartest people alive. Look how much she figured out for this plan. Edgar can't keep up with that. He almost never says anything when we strategize, and when he does, it's not anything particularly helpfu—"

At that point, Naren remembered who among them had thought up the idea of saving the artillery. He put his head in his palms to cover his now bright-red face.

"Are you ok?" Sera asked.

Naren shook his head.

"Just an idiot is all," he replied as he raised his head. "Edgar was the one who thought to disable the artillery rather than destroy it."

"Edgar thought of that!?"

"Sure did. All of us were so busy thinking about how to take and defend the city today while he was already thinking long-term."

Naren's head went back to his hand. "I'm sorry. I was wrong. Please don't tell Edgar or Nadine I said that."

"We'll all yell at you for it later. The sun is going down soon, we have to go make final checks on the defenses.""Okay, Okay," Naren paused for a second. "But seriously. You aren't going to tell them, right?"

Sera breathed a heavy sigh, then a thought occurred to her that made her smile.

"I won't tell them, as long as you promise me Symon isn't the only one getting laid tonight.""I promise!" Naren exclaimed.

The two of them started laughing as they slid off their perch and into the air.

"Love you," Sera said.

"Love you," Naren replied.

And with that they split off to either side of the city, making sure that everyone was in position at each crossing. As soon as the last bridge was checked, the sound of large motors could be faintly heard in the distance. A few minutes later, the troop transport vehicles arrived. Huge trucks, taking up nearly the entire width of the street and carrying hundreds of troops rolled towards the northern crossings and stopped just out of laser cannon range.

Damnit, Symon thought. *If they had just been a little closer, we could've blown up the truck and the troops with it. They figured out at least part of our strategy.*The troops piled out of the truck with remarkable efficiency. They didn't march forward though. They just stood there, down the street from the bridges, still just out of range.

What the fuck are they waiting for? Victor thought as he stood behind a line of troops at the Northwest corner. From his vantage point, he could see down the street from three bridges. One by one, he saw the trucks pull up, drop off troops, and pull away.

Oh crap, he thought.

They're waiting to attack all at once. Victor, Naren, Sera, and Symon all had the same thought at the same time.

What the fuck do I do? Do I stay here? Victor thought.

Sera and Naren flew over to each other.

"What do we do?" Sera said.

"We stick to the plan," Naren said. "This doesn't change anything. Victor is in a good spot and he can rotate over if he needs to."

"But if they're just going to stand there, we can fly over and tear them apart before they even attack," Sera observed.

"We could, but then we also risk getting bogged down in a fight while not being able to see the other bridges, not being able to communicate to Victor if he needs to rotate. The plan is good, let's stick to it," Naren said.

"Ok, you're right. Let's just keep a close eye on who needs help first.""No doubt."Victor watched as they split up and went back to their original positions.

*Guess everyone's staying put, I'll do the same.*Meanwhile, Symon continued to look out over the peacekeepers, who stared back.

"Our guys are doing well," May said to him. "Nobody's panicked and started trying to fire yet."

"Indeed," Symon replied. "The peacekeepers are still at a huge disadvantage being lower down. They'll be in range of our guns up high before we're in range of theirs. I think our guys realize that."

Farther south, Nadine and Edgar were just beginning to see the arsenal come into focus. It was extensive. At least half a dozen mounted weapons of some form, giant lasers or high-caliber guns, could be seen down every street. Surrounding the vehicles was a sea of soldiers. Just like their allies to the north, they were all waiting.

"Shit, they're all out of range!" Nadine shouted to Edgar, who was a couple streets down.

"What are they waiting for!?" Edgar shouted back.

That's when Nadine realized they should have been hearing gunfire from the north by now.

Fuck, she thought. "They're going to attack on all sides at once!" she shouted to Edgar and everyone else. "The second they get in range, I want machine gun fire tearing holes through those lines!"

Suddenly, the troops parted ways at every crossing. A faint rumbling could be heard all around the city. Then, at each crossing, an electric tank came into view. They were massive and black, with giant treads on either side, two machine guns sticking out the top, and the cannon in the center. The tanks rolled forward and passed the troops. The soldiers then proceeded to file in behind the tanks, running to keep up with them.

"They're using the tanks to block our shots!" Naren shouted.

He and Sera raced along the lines as fast as they could, telling the laser cannoneers to open fire and the machine gunners up high to try and focus fire past the tanks. Edgar and Nadine gave the order for their laser cannons to open fire as well. The city filled with the sounds of focused light beams cutting through the air and shells being fired back. The tanks seemed to be focusing their fire on the buildings, trying to take out the shooters there. No sooner had the fighting started than the EMP cannons came into view behind the southern line, four of them in total. One each on the far east and west corners, and two in the middle, equidistant from each other and the corner cannons.

Shit, with those tanks blocking our machine guns on the ground, they're not going to be able to open a hole for us, Nadine thought.

"Edgar!" she screamed at the top of her lungs. "We go now!"

Edgar barely heard her over the lasers and gunfire, but he knew she could only be saying one thing. He ran west until he found himself on a street parallel with the EMP cannon and leapt over the locals and onto the street below. While he clambered up the other side of the sunken old highway, farther east, Nadine boosted over the entire highway and hit the ground running. The two tanks down the street from Edgar and Nadine ceased firing up into the buildings and instead trained their turrets on the super-powered foes running towards them. As soon as they did, though, the laser cannoneers unleashed a barrage of fire on the tanks, taking out the machine guns. The big gun was able to get one shot off at Nadine, which sailed under her as she bounded down the street. She landed and boosted again, and her next landing put her face to face with the tank's main gun. As the turret adjusted to try and fire at her point blank, she jumped over it and came down on the barrel with all the power she could muster. An ear-splitting crash rang out down the street as the turret buckled and collapsed onto the tank's bow.

The troops behind the tank came rushing around to the front, and the tank operators threw open the hatches and leapt out. Nadine unleashed a barrage of punches and kicks on anyone who came within reach. As she did so, machine gun fire started ringing out behind her, coming from the locals, who had a line-of-fire from down the street. After a few seconds, enough troops were felled that Nadine had an opening and she boosted away. Laser fire whizzed by as she leapt through the air, taking out mounted weaponry as she passed them. She landed and took off again; the EMP cannon was only another leap or two away. Then she felt a strange sensation, first coming from her left hand, then the right. They felt the same way they did when she was connected to an elcycle.

Oh, what the fuck is going on now? she thought. As she landed, she took a quick glance and launched off again. Her palms had a blue glow, the same glow coming from the bottom of her feet, only much fainter.

It happened. It finally happened! she thought to herself. She tried to push out more energy but was unsuccessful.

Damnit. Just a little more power, and I'll be able to fly! She tried to reduce the power, turn it off the same way she turned off the jets in her feet. This time she was successful.

*Good, I have control. That'll be great once I gain enough power to really use them.*A gun turret exploded a few yards ahead of her, bringing her focus back to the situation. She landed. Her next leap would put her on the EMP cannon. She aimed for a raised metal platform on the right side of the massive barrel and took off. As she approached, she saw a peacekeeper on the controls bringing the engine to a stop. As she landed on the edge of the platform, the peacekeeper turned to use his electric sword but was far too slow. Before he could even start to swing, Nadine had leapt across the platform and kicked him over the guard rail. Nadine could hear the buzz of the electromagnets for the first time as she turned to look at the controls. It was rudimentary, a console mounted to the railing of the platform with a series of buttons on it, with wiring coming out of the back that led to the cannon. She hopped over to the other side of the railing and grabbed the wires. She boosted up and away from the platform as fast as she could, ripping the wires out and carrying them away with her.

One down, one to go. She leapt over the downed cannon and landed on the street. Farther west, she saw the other cannon was being adjusted to take a shot.

Fuck, I have to hurry, she thought as she bounded forward.

Edgar was facing similar problems nearby. The moment he clambered out of the trench that contained old highway 55, a tank trained its fire on him. And just like their counterparts who'd backed up Nadine, the locals armed with laser cannons behind Edgar focused fire on the tank, taking out the machine guns. Edgar darted to the right side of the street and then started running forward and left, trying to outrun the tracking of the main gun. The gun fired, missed behind him. Fired again, missed again. Before it could get a third shot off, Edgar had climbed on top of the tank, sliced the lock on the hatch open, and ripped it off its hinge. He jumped inside and started swinging with both blades, shredding the soldiers before they even had a chance to react. When the last soldier fell, he leapt back out of the hatch and into the mass of troops behind the tank. He extended both of his blades out in front of him and ran as fast as he could, plowing through the soldiers that stood in his way.

He was moving quickly, but he was still slower than Nadine. The first turret was being adjusted as he approached it. He ran under the platform and stabbed up through the grated floor, severing the peacekeeper's foot. The peacekeeper fell to the ground and Edgar stabbed up again, impaling him through the chest. With his left hand, he slashed along the platform's side and severed the wires from the console. With the cannon now disabled he looked right, down the street at the other turret. It was also being adjusted to fire.

Farther north, Naren, Sera, and Victor had their hands full. A few of the tanks had been disabled by an onslaught of laser cannon fire from the locals. The remaining tanks were slowed by the constant shots raining down on them. Since they were so slowed down, a few had opted to fire at the locals on the ground, obliterating them and allowing the troops to try and charge forward past the tanks. Sera and Naren were alternating between taking out the peacekeepers trying to cross and communicating to Victor where he was most needed. Victor was now at the centermost bridge, dodging tank fire and throwing out shockwaves, while Naren was a couple blocks south. Sera was flying in from the north, having finished off the last of the troops who had tried breaking through there. Symon and his group of locals had done well. All of the tanks were now disabled or destroyed and only one bridge was ever contested: the one Sera was heading back from now. She joined Naren in the fray, and they made quick work of the remaining peacekeepers. They stopped for a moment to catch their breath.

"The tank is down?" Sera asked

"Disabled right after he got off a shot at the ground troops. How's the north?"

"Peacekeepers are either dead or in full retreat. How are Edgar and Nadine doing?"

"Let's go find out."

They rocketed up above the skyscrapers and looked south.

"Two EMP cannons are moving, two aren't," Sera said.

"Yea, but where are… oh! I see them! Oh shi—"

I've got to make this, Nadine thought, taking one last great leap through the air.

That peacekeeper is getting ready to fire that cannon! If I don't make it with this leap… make it. Make it! Make it!

She soared through the air and the platform came closer and closer. She threw her hands to her side and powered up the tiny jets in her palm. It was the last little thing she could do to keep herself afloat just a little longer.

I'm going to make it. No I'm not. Yes I am! No I'm not! Yes I am! Nadine threw her arms up as the platform soared overhead and caught it with her left hand. She swung up in between the platform and its guardrail, scrambled to her feet, and flipped the cannon operator over the controls and down the side of the cannon. Nadine grabbed the control console and ripped it from the guard rail, the wires in the back snapping clean off. She dropped it at her side and looked down the street back at her defensive line. All she saw was a sea of dead peacekeepers, a disabled tank and mounted weaponry in various states of non-functionality.

The defensive line did well. I wonder how Edgar is doi—Nadine and Naren's thoughts were both cut off by the loudest, most deafening roar either of them had ever heard. It was so loud the entire city shook, and the roar was followed by a crackling electrical sound. All the gunfire on the western side, including those defending the large crossing at old highway 90, fell silent while the soldiers and the tank trying to cross were still rolling forward.

God fucking damnit! Edgar thought as he pulled his blade out of the cannon operator's side. He might have said the thought, might have even yelled it at the top of his lungs. He couldn't tell; all he could hear was the ringing in his ears after the EMP cannon fired. He had jumped up on the platform and plunged his blade through the operator's oblique seconds too late.

He turned to look back at his defenses. The peacekeepers' mounted armaments were down, but plenty of troops were still standing. On the defensive line, he could no longer see the muzzle flashes of the locals' guns.

*Fuck, they're defenseless now Fuck fuck fuck I fucked up! I got to hurry back now. They need me.*Edgar started running back towards the line. *Fuuuuuuck, I hope the others are on their way to help too."*

Farther north, the tank at the highway 90 bridge shifted its main gun and opened fire on the locals. Those in the building could do nothing but watch as the ground defenses were blown away by multiple shots from the tank, and a huge hole opened up for the peacekeepers to file through and fire on anyone left. They ran ahead of the tank, which was having trouble moving after taking so much laser fire.

"Go get Victor!" Sera said to Naren "I'll stop that tank."

Naren flew north while Sera flew south. She tried to dive towards the tank, but the troops turned to fire up at her, forcing her to stay at a distance.

*God damn it. I don't want that tank making it over that bridge. Our defenses need to look impenetrable!*As she went in for another dive, she heard howling winds rushing at her. She pulled up and saw the troops under her get thrown off their feet. She glanced north and saw the blur of a human that could only be Victor heading her way.

She smiled, and trained her eyes on the tank, which was now halfway across the bridge. She flew at it and just as she was about to make contact, she unleashed all of her energy. For a split second, the tank could be seen being blown back before it and the bridge beneath were consumed by the explosion. Pieces of concrete and carbon-fiber plating flew in all directions, while the larger remnants of the tank and bridge fell into the river below. Sera let the inertia from her flight carry her over the river and skidded to a stop on the other side of the street. The skid scraped and bruised her left arm, but otherwise left her unharmed. She shook off the dizziness and nausea from using her blast and scrambled for cover from the soldiers across the river. A few seconds later her power recovered, and she took off into the air, where Naren was waiting for her.

"That was their last hope of crossing a bridge," Naren said. "All the tanks are disabled and the only troops still left are those trying to break through in the southwest corner."

"I think it's time we sent a message to them, let them know this is our fucking city!" Sera replied.

They looked down on the troops who had made it over the bridge. Victor was leveling them with his shockwaves, which gave them an idea.

Just south of Naren and Sera, Edgar had caught up with the peacekeepers just before they crossed under the overpass that eventually descended to become highway 55. He was getting exhausted. The only things he could hear were ringing in his ears and his own heavy breathing. He was slashing at the troops around him as fast as he could, but they kept coming. He was all alone in the middle of a sea of peacekeepers, and all of them had their sights set on him. Edgar then heard something new, a faint scream. The scream got louder and louder until a peacekeeper landed right in front of him, putting some distance between him and the other soldiers. Another scream followed, and another peacekeeper fell from the sky, backing up the soldiers around him further. Another scream, another falling soldier. Edgar glanced up to see that Sera and Naren were taking turns scooping up troops who had crossed over the highway 90 bridge and dropping them to their deaths around Edgar. Naren dropped one last peacekeeper, then swooped down and grabbed Edgar. He lifted him onto highway 90 just in time to see Victor throw an air burst that levelled the last of the troops who had crossed. He then ran over to the overpass and threw a shockwave down at the troops, crushing some and forcing the rest back. Nadine charged in from the east and leapt onto the overpass about a block away. She turned to face the soldiers below her. Edgar's hearing had returned just enough that he could make out Nadine's bellowing.

"This city is ours!" Nadine cried. "You are all that's left of your pathetic fucking forces! Leave now or die where you stand!"

A silence fell over the troops as they stared up at Victor, Sera, Naren, and Edgar above them, and Nadine farther east. All the soldiers were wide-eyed, horrified at the fate that their fellow peacekeepers had just met, and terrified at the words Nadine had so forcefully spoken.

"Full retreat! Full retreat! Back to the TCT!" some manner of commanding officer ordered from within the sea of soldiers. They all turned and fled back to the trucks that had brought them in at the start of the battle. The five LO-ECs started to hear cheers from the defensive line. The cheers grew louder as the locals situated throughout the city heard and joined in celebrating. Nadine walked over to the rest of them, and they just stared at each other. After several moments, Nadine started chuckling. The chuckle turned into a giggle. The giggle turned into roaring laughter.

"We fucking did it!" Nadine screamed as she doubled over laughing. Almost infectiously, everyone joined in with her and fell to the floor laughing with sheer jubilation. Over the sounds of their cackling, they could hear a motor roaring up the onramp to the overpass. It was Symon on his elcycle, with the machine gun still attached to his arm and May at his back, her arms wrapped around his waist.

"Are you guys ok?" Symon asked as he pulled up. Victor pulled him down and wrapped an arm around him in celebration. May shook her head and chuckled as she unstrapped some food from the bike. She tossed it at everyone, one by one, and one by one they stopped laughing and started voraciously consuming what she had given them.

"So, what are the chances of them trying another assault

tonight?" May asked.

"Zero," Naren replied. "The CO called for a full retreat to the Trans-Continental Transport. They aren't just pulling back, they're getting back on the military trains that brought them here and going all the way back to Seoul. They didn't just lose, today: it was a complete and utter failure. All of their force and firepower and they only managed to make it across one bridge, a bridge that now lies at the bottom of the Chicago River. They also know that we now have substantial firepower to hold out for quite a while. They're going to go back to Seoul, and Spidre and his people are going to take their time thinking up another strategy. We have several days at the very least, and we have a lot of work to do tomorrow. We can and should sleep peacefully tonight."

May breathed a sigh of relief "We need to spread the good news," she said.

"We need to do more than that," Naren said. "They're going to cut the power to the city soon. We should run over to the net access point at the hotel and tell them to send messages out about our victory as soon as possible."

"They aren't going to cut the power. They can't," May replied.

"Why not?" Naren asked.

"The power grids are controlled at the fusion reactor plant. If they wanted to cut our power, they'd have to cut power to the entire grid that we're on. That would be all of North America."

Everyone was stunned.

"What?" May said. "I'm an electrical engineer, it was my job to know this stuff."

A sense of relief and happiness swelled over the entire group as they finished their food and looked forward to a good night's sleep.

"Still, we need to get a message out," Nadine said. "We need to tell everyone we can that downtown Chicago is free, and the rest of the world doesn't have to wait much longer to join us. Can you swing by a net access point before heading home?"

"Absolutely!" May exclaimed with pride. "Care to give me a lift?" she asked as she turned to Symon.

Symon smiled. "Of course," he said. He then turned to the other LO-ECs. "Should we all meet at the net access point in the old hotel tomorrow morning?"

"Sounds good to me," Sera replied. Everyone else nodded in agreement.

"Sleep well, guys. And congratulations," Symon said while beaming.

Symon and May got back on the elcycle and drove off into the night. Victor was the next to stand up.

"I'm going to see if I can find someplace quiet to spend the night. Although, I have a feeling with all this celebrating that's going to be impossible," he said with a smirk.

"Naren and I have a spot picked out," Sera replied. "Goodnight guys, we'll see you tomorrow."

"Goodnight," Victor said.

"Goodnight," Naren said.

"Goodnight," Edgar and Nadine said at the same time. They looked at each other and smiled.

Sera was right! Naren thought to himself but said nothing as he turned and flew off with Sera towards their earlier perch. Victor went running down the overpass in search of his quiet spot, leaving Nadine and Edgar alone on the highway. Nadine scooted over and snuggled up to Edgar.

As he wrapped his arm around her, she looked up at him and held out her palm.

"Look what happened today," she said as she powered her palm's microtransformer. The blue glow coming from the center of her hand was ever so slightly larger than it had been a few hours earlier.

"I told you you'd figure it out!" Edgar replied. "No wonder you're in such a good mood."

"I'm closer to flying than I ever have been, and my childhood city has been liberated from Spidre's army by our hands. Yeah, I'd say I have a lot to be happy about."

"So do I," Edgar said, looking at the beautiful woman at his side. They smiled at each other, then locked lips until they passed out in each other's arms.

Chapter 23

After eating the last bit of food left over from the night before, Edgar and Nadine made their way through the city to the old hotel. As they got closer, the commotion got louder. The celebrations from last night had given way to worry about the future of the city. They made it to the hotel, and the scene was utter chaos. Scores of people were there, yelling questions and concerns at a very overwhelmed Victor, who had been first to arrive.

"Oh, thank god!" Victor yelled upon seeing Nadine. "I don't know who to answer or how to answer them!"

"Can everyone quiet down please!?" Nadine bellowed. Everyone fell silent.

"I know you guys have a lot of questions, and by the end of the day we hope to have answers for most of them. But here's what you need to know for now. The forces we defeated yesterday were coming from Seoul. For those of you who don't know, Seoul is many hours away and on a completely different continent than us. They took an Inter-Continental Transport train across the Pacific ocean and then a Trans-Continental Transport train to get here. And when we beat them, they called for a full retreat. That means going all the way back to Seoul, and that means we have a few days to organize. So what needs to happen immediately is the following: Anyone with electrical or weaponry experience needs to go out and look at the artillery, see what can be fixed and used for defense. Others need to go with them to bring the artillery and guns within our new borders, which are the river to the north and west, the lakeshore to the east, and old highway 55 in the south. Who is up for that?"

A few dozen people stepped forward.

"Focus on the southern border first, over old highway 55. Pay special attention to the EMP cannons, but there's a lot of mounted artillery, and a whole lot of machine guns on dead peacekeepers."

Those who stepped forward nodded and ran out of the building. A few scattered people in the crowd ran out with them.

"We also need a casualty report. We lost a lot of people last night, and we need to know who they were. Anyone with extensive knowledge of the city's inhabitants please go to that."

The crowd thinned out even further.

"And I need a whole bunch of people to monitor the food distribution center and the farms and make sure they aren't looted. And I better not find out that you yourself looted while on duty."

More people left, leaving the old lobby about half as full as it had been. As the locals left, Sera and Naren arrived.

"Good morning!" Naren yelled to everyone. "Did anyone send out messages over the net last night?

"Sent them all night and sending them still," one local replied. "We figured there was no sense in keeping our data levels low anymore, so we've just been blasting them over and over to ensure they get picked up."

"Good call," he replied as he turned to Nadine. "What did you send them to do?"

"Assess and move the artillery, body count, and guard the food sources," Nadine replied.

Naren nodded and turned back to the crowd. "Anyone feel like checking out the government buildings to find anything that might be useful?"

A few people stepped forward and exited the building.

"We really need to figure out a long-term strategy and do it today," Nadine said. "You should've seen this place when we first got here."

"So, let's do it, what are we waiting for?" Naren replied.

"Symon. He's not here yet," Victor said.

Sera smirked as Naren put his head in his hand.

Naren sighed. "Does anyone here know where the electrical engineer named May lives?

A confused look crossed Victor, Edgar, and Nadine's faces while two people in the crowd raised their hands.

"Could one of you lead the way, please? Actually, why don't both of you come? It'll be good to have more locals around to help us figure this all out."

One man and one woman stepped forward and walked the five LO-ECs over to the megaskyscraper complex. The elevator looked like it had seen better days, but was functional, and brought them swiftly to May's floor. They walked down a hallway and stopped at a front door. Naren knocked, and a quick scuffling of feet could be heard. May arrived at the door about a minute later, looking somewhat disheveled.

"Oh Christ, did we oversleep that much?" she asked.

Over her shoulder, Symon could be seen in the room taking a seat on some pillows on the floor.

"Fucking called it!!" Sera yelled, as Symon put his hands behind his head, a look of smug accomplishment on his face. May's mouth curled into a smile.

"Well, I guess you all better come in," May said. "Strategizing in here is better than at that loud-ass hotel anyway."

Everyone filed in and took a seat on the pillows, the floor, or the mattress pad that was still rolled out. It was a one-room apartment with a shared bathroom at the end of the hall. The only window faced the inner courtyard, and the walls were bare except for a few hanging tools. The floor was littered with various pieces of electronics, and a small kitchenette was set up in the far corner, consisting of a single hot plate and a few pots, pans and utensils.

"So, the big question. What do we do now?" Symon asked.

"That depends what you mean," Naren replied.

"He means big picture," May said. "You've taken the city. You've defended it. Now what?"

"Oh. Well that's up to you." Naren said.

"What do you mean?" May replied.

"I mean exactly that. We can stay, help govern, help defend. We can stay and help defend only. We can leave after helping you set up. Or we can leave right now. When Victor came here a few days before our assault, one of the things he found out is that there was a good chance you don't want us to stay. I imagine after his visit, a lot of the locals discussed these options, no?"

"They did, and most people wanted you gone," May said. "Otherwise you're no better than the military. No offense."

"None taken," Naren replied.

"That being said, I wouldn't want you to leave without being sure we can handle this ourselves," May continued.

"Agreed, your ability to defend yourself is top priority." Nadine said. "There are more reasons for us to leave as well. Right now, we are the biggest threat to your city. If we stay here, that is all the more reason for Spidre to send everything he's got to this one location. We are powerful, and the fight this city put up last night was incredible. But we will not hold out against the might of the entire world's army, not forever. Not to mention there is still always the chance that as long as we're here, he'll send strategic missile strikes to take us out. The casualties from that… it's not worth the risk. We can help you organize today and tomorrow. But after that, we need to get out of here and make it known that we are gone."

"How are you going to 'make it known that you're gone?'" one of the locals asked.

"We attack another city," Nadine said.

A silence swept over the room.

"Have any of you guys heard of the term 'regional destabilization'?" Nadine continued, addressing everyone except Naren and Sera.

Symon nodded, everyone else shook their heads.

"It's a strategy that has been used countless times in the past, but it's a tricky one to get right," Nadine said. "Spidre's army is massive, but at the same time it is finite. He only has so many soldiers and so much artillery. Right now, he can send them all here. If we liberate another city, one as important as Chicago, that's two cities he has to focus on and split forces between. Meanwhile, every other major city in between sees its neighbors free and decides they want a piece of that. They start to revolt on their own. Now Spidre has to choose to either help keep the cities that are rebelling or focus on retaking the ones he lost. If it's done right, he finds himself in a rebellion so widespread that he can't contain it. But doing it right means not losing a single city. Chicago must stand on its own. So, what needs to be done to make that happen?"

Everyone remained quiet for a few moments, pondering Nadine's question.

"What about, like, police?" Sera put forward.

"What do you mean?" Nadine asked.

"Well earlier, you sent people to guard the food dispensaries to make sure they weren't looted. That can't be the only crime they would have to worry about, right? The army was here keeping people in line before, but with them gone, who is going to keep order? Now that there are so many guns in the city, I feel like that would be important, right?"

"Yes, yes it would be," Naren agreed. "May, is there any place most of the guns can be kept, somewhere they'll be out of reach for the general public, but accessible if you need to quickly organize and defend the city?"

"An armory," May replied. "Yeah, I think we'll be able to figure that out. I think some people should keep their guns though, people who would be first to the line defending the city. Only the people we trust most, though."

"That sounds fine," Naren said. "More relevant to you, though, is repairing the artillery. You know your way around electronics. I am inclined to think people are going to look to you to lead them when it comes to repairing all the heavy equipment. Think you can handle that?"

"No doubt in my mind," May replied.

"Excellent," Naren said. "I know the city is growing daily production crops by the lake. Between that and the food dispensary, is it enough to sustain the city in perpetuity?"

"I doubt it," one of the locals replied. "Most of the dispensaries were on the other side of the river."

"Can we just move the plants and grow them here?" Sera asked.

"I don't see why it wouldn't work," Symon said. "The crops in the ground in San Diego were daily production. When they were originally engineered, daily production crops were designed to grow anywhere bamboo could grow, so any halfway decent soil would do."

"Bamboo?" Edgar asked.

"That's what enabled daily production. Crops used to only produce edible food once or twice a year. Then there was a big effort during the 21st century to curb world hunger using genetically modified crops. Bamboo is the fastest growing plant in the world, it can grow like 3 feet in a day. So research inevitably led to its rapid growth genes being incorporated into other edible plants, and the tech was refined enough that certain crops could produce food daily."

"Huh," everyone else in the room said at the same time, fascinated by what they had just learned.

"So, we could send out a few parties to take food out of the dispensaries across the river while it is still peaceful," Symon continued. "What I would be concerned about is the crops taking too big a toll on the soil here. Hydroponic gardens don't take up much room, and you don't need to worry as much about nutrients running out. Planting in soil needs a lot more space, and dirt dries up and gets sapped of nutrients. If we're going to replant everything in the food dispensaries, we'll need more space."

"What about the area north of the city?" Nadine said. "The river empties out into lake Michigan again a few miles up, right? And that whole area can be cleared and farmed."

"It can, but defending and area that size would be tough," Naren replied. "It's a lot more access points, a lot more bridges.

Plus, if they come in from the far north, no one in the main city would know for quite a while."

"So let's blow up the bridges," Sera said. "If we do that, they would have to either rely on artillery for everything or assemble their own crossings to get into the northern area. Either way, someone on lookout in the megaskyscrapers would see them and could send word to ground forces."

"How would we blow all of them up, though?" Naren asked. "You won't be able to do all of them in two days. I guess we could use the artillery…"

"Or I could do it," Victor replied. "That could be my project."

"You think your shockwaves are strong enough to take down a bridge?" Nadine asked.

"Well, not just one wave. But if I keep hitting it over and over, it'll go down. Unless it's a big bridge like the one that Sera already blew up."

"I don't recall seeing anything that big in the north," Sera said. "But if a couple of them are too tough for you, just let me know, and I'll bring them down."

"Will do," Victor replied. "But why are we leaving any of the bridges up? Wouldn't it be easier to defend the city if they were all down, not just the northern ones?"

"It sure would have helped yesterday," Nadine said. "But the thing is, word is going to get out that Chicago is free. People are going to want to come here. Do we want to make it difficult for them? If we blew the bridges yesterday, or blow them now, they'll have to circle all the way south, and that will be the main area Spidre's forces will hammer."

"It's a decision the city should make, not us. Which brings up another issue," Naren said, turning to May and the locals. "You guys are going to have to set up some kind of government, a trusted group of people that can vote on these things and also voice the needs of the people. I had an idea that each floor of the megaskyscrapers can elect someone who represents them, and then those people could meet to discuss things. Whether or not that idea will work for you is your call."

One local nodded. "That's a pretty good idea. We'll bring it up when we get back to the hotel. And we'll let them know about everything else you guys said, too. Then they'll all spread the word amongst the skyscrapers."

"Excellent!" Sera exclaimed.

"I think that just about covers everything then," Naren said. "You two head back to the hotel. The rest of us should go see if the folks who went to repair and collect the artillery need help. Victor, if you're not needed there, then you can head up North."

As soon as they exited the building, the two locals headed east while the majority of the group walked south.

"Were you part of the group working on the EMP cannons?" May asked a large group of people as soon as they arrived.

"No ma'am. We were helping with the casualty report," someone in the front replied.

"Any estimates yet?" Symon asked.

"So far, we've only done the southwest corner, where the EMP cannon hit. 4996 people. The peacekeepers charging over the bridge just mowed them down."

Edgar's heart sank. *They'd be alive if it wasn't for me,* he thought.

"Did you identify anyone?" Symon asked.

"Yes. Everyone. We were heading back now to get more people to help us move them," the local replied.

"There was one guy who would've been wearing Special Ops

machine gun armor, his name was Tim." Victor said. "I never got his last name, but we did send him to the south…"

"I'm sorry," one person a couple rows back interrupted. "He was my next-door neighbor, and he was on one of the lines that got blown open by tank fire."

A look of sadness spread over Victor's face.

"You ok?" Sera asked them.

Victor stayed silent.

"Victor?" Sera asked.

"Sorry," he said. "I uh, I think I'll get started on the bridges."

"Uh, yeah, go for it," Sera said.

Victor nodded and darted north. The rest of them continued south and found a group of people standing in front of the easternmost EMP cannon.

"So what's the status of these big guys?" May asked.

"Well, some are better than others, but I think they can all be fixed." one woman replied. "The one farthest west was undamaged. They're working on moving it now. The two in the middle need new wiring run from the control module to the firing mechanism. This one is going to be a chore. The control panel was heavily damaged. It could take days to fix."

Nadine turned bright red and scratched the back of her head, embarrassed.

"Mind if I take a look at it?" May asked.

"Please do!" the local replied.

May jogged ahead while Naren walked up to the same local.

"What about the other artillery? The tanks and mounted guns?"

"A few of the mounted laser cannons are functional, and a couple of the gun turrets. The vehicles they are mounted on are not. The tanks can no longer move on their own, but all their main cannons work save one, which was dislodged from its moorings."

"Jeez!" Nadine exclaimed, turning bright red all over again. "I really overdid it, huh?"

"You did what you had to do to keep people alive. Not something everyone can say," Edgar replied in a depressed tone.

Simultaneously, everyone realized how guilty Edgar was feeling about letting the EMP cannon go off. Before anyone could respond, May yelled from the cannon's control platform "We're going to have to move this thing!"

"What do you mean, move it?" Nadine yelled back.

"I mean attach a rope to one side, have a whole bunch of people push on the other side, and roll this sucker," May replied as she descended from the platform. "The cannon is designed to fire or drive, not both at once. Right now, it's stuck in firing mode, and the control panel is fucked. We're going to have to assemble a new one. That'll take days, and I'd rather not be on this side of our borders working on it."

They all stared up at the massive gun, bewildered at the thought of moving it any sort of distance.

Symon sighed. "Can someone run to the megaskyscrapers or the hotel and see if anyone has a lot of rope?" he asked the group of locals.

"On it!" one of them replied as several of them ran north and east.

"In the meantime, we should organize into groups." Naren said. "The strongest locals should come with me to the back to help push this thing. Edgar, can you help push too?"

"Uhh, sure," Edgar replied, unsure why Naren asked him specifically for help.

Nadine was confused as well and was about to say something when out of the corner of her eye she caught Sera's gaze. Her eyes sort of said "It's ok, he's got this," so she stayed silent, and Edgar and Naren walked to the far side of the cannon while Symon, May, Nadine, and Sera awaited the arrival of the ropes.

Once they got out of earshot of the rest of the group, Naren spoke up.

"I'm surprised at you, Edgar. You're taking this hard," Naren said.

"How could I not?" Edgar replied. "People are dead because of me, Naren. Thousands of people are dead because of me."

"They aren't dead because of you. They're dead because of Spidre, and the Seoul forces, which you helped drive away," Naren said.

"You all played just as big a part in that, and you didn't get anyone killed," Edgar said.

"Of course we did!" Naren exclaimed. "It was my plan that put you in that spot, my plan that caused front lines to be blown apart by tank fire."

"Your plan didn't account for my being so slow," Edgar said. "If any of you had been there in place of me, that EMP burst wouldn't have gone off."

"That might be true," Naren replied. "But it would also mean we'd have a fourth EMP cannon that was immobile. Just look at what Nadine did. She rendered a tank useless and did so much damage to an EMP cannon that we have to fucking pull the thing. Do you think Sera would've been any less subtle than that? Or Victor?"

"No, probably not," Edgar agreed.

"A lot of people died because of that EMP cannon hit, but it's going to save far more. It could save this entire city," Naren said.

"Why, because it's intact? That wasn't strategy, Naren. I just stabbed the operator and jumped off without thinking."

"I wasn't talking about the cannon itself. I was talking about the blast it caused," Naren said.

"What on Earth are you talking about?" Edgar asked.

"Think about it from Spidre's perspective," Naren said "Let's say you made it to the cannon in time. You stabbed the operator just before he got the shot off, everyone retreated same as they did, and thousands more people are alive. Spidre's military strategists would look at that and say 'well, if we had just gotten a shot off with the EMP cannon, we'd have been set' and they would have sent forces back here within hours with more EMPs. We'd have no time to organize, no time to repair the artillery and set up more permanent defenses. No time to farm, to blow up bridges, to set up armories. But that didn't happen. They got a shot off with the EMP cannon, and they still couldn't do anything. The cannon brought down an entire section of our defenses, and still the best they could manage was to get a couple hundred soldiers over one bridge which no longer exists. Every part of their strategy was performed successfully, and they still failed. That means serious re-strategizing. It means scratching every plan they've had in place for decades and writing a new one. It means time for us."

"But again, it was pure luck!" Edgar exclaimed. "I didn't think about any of that stuff, I just reacted."

"Let me ask you this then. Who thought up the idea to just disable the artillery, not destroy them?" Naren asked.

"I did," Edgar replied.

"Let's say you didn't think of that plan, or at the very least didn't follow it," Naren said. "Would you have changed your strategy any? Would you have done anything different that would've caused you to be faster?"

Edgar thought about it for a moment, then nodded. "Yeah. I dove into the tank and killed everyone inside rather than just slicing through the main gun. That would've been faster. And I guess at the first EMP cannon, I was jumping up and stabbing at the operator and the wires when I could've just slashed through the moorings."

"So your strategy slowed you down, killed a whole bunch of our allies, but left us with three functional pieces of heavy artillery," Naren said. "Not to mention all of the artillery the locals and the rest of us would've destroyed had you not thought ahead. So I'm going to have to disagree with you. It wasn't just luck. It was a strategy that will wind up saving far more lives than were lost. It could very well be the most important aspect of this entire effort to take and defend Chicago."

"Now I feel like you're just saying that to make me feel better. It couldn't be that important," Edgar said. Naren sighed.

"Edgar, I know about you and Nadine," Naren said.

A shiver went down Edgar's spine. "Look Naren, we haven't done anything. We haven't even talked about what's going on. I mean we only just kissed for the first time yesterday."

"You kissed?!" Naren exclaimed. "No, not important, can't get off track here. Look, I didn't figure it out, Sera did. And when she told me, I'll admit I was concerned. You're a nice guy, and anything you find a passion for, you also seem to have boundless dedication towards. But Nadine is my twin sister. As far as I'm concerned, she and Sera are the most important people to have ever been born. And to be honest, I was worried that you, despite all your good traits, were not good enough for her."

"Okay…" Edgar replied, visibly offended.

"But I don't think that anymore, Edgar, and it was because of the plan to save the artillery that you thought up. It's that impressive, that important. So look past what happened yesterday and see what your plan has done for all of our futures. You're going to be the key to our success, Edgar, and you and Nadine, you deserve each other."

Edgar's eyes welled up. "Thanks, Naren,".

Naren smiled, extended his arms, and embraced Edgar in a big, long hug.

Meanwhile, at the front of the cannon, a related conversation was going on between Sera and Nadine.

"So, what was that about? Why did Naren pull Edgar away like that?" Nadine asked.

"Well, uhh, he may or may not know that you and Edgar are a couple."

"What?!" Nadine exclaimed. Symon started chuckling.

"What? Are you not?" Symon asked.

"I don't know. I mean, we never really discussed it. We only just kissed for the first time yesterday."

"You kissed?" Sera said, ecstatic.

"Yeah… twice."

"Details. Now," Sera said while bouncing up and down and smiling.

"I really don't—"

"Oh fuck no!" Sera interrupted. "I've wanted to talk about this for weeks. You are not holding out on me, god damn it."

Nadine sighed. "We were on the roof of the battalion headquarters, about to burst into the stairwell, and he asked me if I was ready. And I don't know what came over me. It was just something about the situation, or maybe how he asked the question, but I just, knew I had to kiss him."

Sera's eyes glazed over with tears. "How did he react?"

"I think he was stunned, more than anything," Nadine said. "I don't think he knew it was coming. He's smart, but he's also kind of dumb, you know?"

Sera chuckled. "That's an interesting way to put it. But I also doubt that he minded much, and I guess it must have been good if you both wanted to do it again."

"Jesus Christ, Sera," Nadine replied, turning bright red again.

"What?" Sera asked. "You said you kissed a second time, so you must've liked it. What's so embarrassing about liking a kiss?"

"It wasn't like that, the second one was just as spontaneous," Nadine replied. Sera looked confused.

"During the fight against the Seoul troops, this happened," Nadine said, as she turned her palm face up and a bright blue glow emanated from the center.

Sera and Symon's eyes widened.

"Huh, I feel like that's bigger than it was yesterday," Nadine said.

"Holy shit!" Sera exclaimed.

"Right?!""So can you fly now?" Sera asked.

"I'm not sure. I couldn't yesterday, but the jets look bigger now," Nadine replied.

"We'll practice later ok? I can give you tips on how to balance and stuff," Sera said.

"I appreciate it," Nadine replied.

"So wait I mean that's awesome, don't get me wrong, but what does it have to do with kissing Edgar?" Sera asked.

"Well after you all left, we were cuddled together and I was so excited that I showed him," Nadine said. "And then he got excited about it too, and the only thing that felt right to do in the moment was kiss."

"So that's twice now that you kissed because it was the only thing that felt right in the moment," Sera observed.

"Yeah, I guess so," Nadine replied.

"But you're not a couple?" Sera asked.

"I don't know!" Nadine exclaimed. "I mean we haven't discussed it or anything. Is that what makes someone a couple? When you talk about it and agree 'Yeah, ok, we're a couple now'?"

"No, I don't think you necessarily need to have a conversation about it," Sera replied. "Gosh, I didn't realize how complicated this was."

"Well when did you and Naren become a couple?""Hmmm. I guess for me, it was official the first time we had sex," Sera said.

Nadine sighed again. "I knew you were going to say that, and yet it still didn't make the thought any less nauseating."

"Sorry! But it's true," Sera said.

"But that can't be what makes every couple official," Nadine said. "Are May and Symon a couple now that they've had sex?"

"How did I know this conversation was going to lead to us?" May said.

"Sorry," Nadine said.

"It's ok," May responded. "Symon and I stayed up way later than we should've last night talking about it. And no, we are not a couple. We figured that he would not be staying, and even if I wasn't needed here, it would be far too dangerous for me to come with you. Trying to maintain a relationship given our situation would just be unfair to the both of us. Not so much the case with you and Edgar."

"That's true," Nadine replied.

"The way I see it, there are three ways you can feel about it," Symon continued. "You can feel indifferent, that being a couple won't affect you in any real emotional way. If you both feel that way, then a relationship just won't happen. Since we're having this conversation now, I doubt that's the case."

Nadine nodded.

"You can also feel like a relationship will make you frustrated or sad, in which case you shouldn't do it. That's how May and I feel about it. Or, you can feel like being in a relationship with someone will make you happy, like it is completing a piece of you, one you may not have even known was missing. If you both feel that way then, well, you know what to do."

"But what if something bad happens?" Nadine asked. "What if we make this investment in each other and then one of us doesn't make it through this?"

"That's a tough point to grapple with," May replied. "It all depends on who you are as a person. Let's say that kiss you had yesterday is as much as you two ever share. And let's say something does happen that separates you two forever. Are you going to be the type that says to themselves 'I made the right call not to get emotionally invested' or are you the type that will spend the next few years, or maybe even your whole life, wondering about what could have been? There is nothing wrong with either side of that coin, but everyone does pick a side."

"Which side do you tend to find yourself on?" Nadine asked.

"I can't go through life not knowing," May responded. "I have a lot of regrets Nadine, and they all come from wondering what could have been. I refuse to wonder anymore."

"Is that why you slept with Symon?"

"One of many reasons," May replied, causing a smirk to flash across her and Symon's faces.

"Hey, yeah, that is weird!" Sera exclaimed.

"Excuse me?" Symon and May responded.

The conversation was interrupted by a commotion all around them. The locals had returned, and they'd brought rope. The group lashed the ropes to the cannon, and everyone got in line and pulled while Naren and Edgar's group pushed from behind. The cannon rocked back and forth and started rolling forward. Once the cannon was in motion, keeping it moving was effortless. A few minutes later, the cannon was two blocks past the southern border. Edgar and Naren rejoined with the rest of the group and they walked together to the western border to check on its status. While they walked, May felt she had to continue the conversation they had started earlier.

"So what did you mean before we got interrupted? What's weird?" she asked Sera.

"I mean, from what I know of the war and everything that went on, I always felt like normal humans hated LO-ECs," Sera replied. "Or at the very least, resented us for being the catalyst that led to the current state of the world. I understand that Chicago was a little different demographically, so you guys might feel a bit more indifferent about us. Still, you take it even one step further. It almost seems like you're attracted to Symon because he's a LO-EC."

"I'm attracted to power, Sera," May replied. "And Symon is powerful, even if he doesn't think so."

Symon blushed.

"But more importantly, he's different. You all are," May continued. "I find that difference intriguing, many people find it terrifying. Story of humanity, I guess."

Everyone except Symon had a blank stare.

"Ugh," Symon groaned. "That went right over their heads May, they have no idea."

"No idea about what?" Naren said.

"Do you think we're the first 'different' people that humanity feared? Or even tried to exterminate?" Symon asked.

"We aren't?" Sera asked.

"Christ, no! Humans have been killing each other because of our differences for forever! And for way stupider differences then being super-powered walking power plants."

"Like what?" Edgar said.

"Jeez where do I even start?" Symon asked himself. "Ok, so you know, your skin color right? You know how most people are whatever color we all are. What would you even call it? It's skin colored. What else is the same color as our skin?"

"Uhm, that's a weird question," Sera said.

"Well it used to be an important one!" Symon snapped back. "Ok, so like, Sera, you're a darker complexion than the rest of us, right? When you're not glowing, I mean."

"Yeah, I guess so," she replied.

"And has everyone here ever met someone… lighter than us?" Symon asked. "I had a colleague in my lab whose skin was lighter. It almost had like a white/pinkish hue to it."

"Oh yeah! I knew someone like that!" Nadine said. "My grandmother's downstairs neighbor was a pale, pinkish color."

"I remember him!" Naren exclaimed.

"Yeah, so, that wasn't always uncommon," Symon replied. "Every continent had its own color, basically. People from Asia were a different color than people from Europe. People from Africa were a different color still, and they were all a different color than people native to America, and so on."

Sera had a skeptical look on her face.

"You're fucking with us, aren't you?" she asked.

"No, I'm serious! It's weird, right?" Symon replied.

"And people… cared… that their skin colors were different?" Nadine asked.

"Cared is an understatement," Symon said. "They fought wars

over it. They murdered and enslaved each other over it. And it wasn't just skin color. What country you were from, what god you prayed to, how much money you had, even if you were a man or a woman. Any little difference could and did make someone else fear you.

"Men feared women?" Sera asked.

"Sure did," Symon replied. "And women feared men too. Some nuances were even more convoluted. Like if you were a man who loved another man, a whole bunch of people wanted you dead."

"So, what changed?" Naren asked. "Why did people stop caring?"

"It was generations of work, hundreds of years," Symon replied "But as the years passed, people grew to understand each other better. Each generation, more so than the one preceding it, became aware of the innumerable similarities they had and dismissed their differences as unimportant. And in the case of skin color, as they came to realize their similarities, they started caring less about only forming relationships with 'their own kind'. Eventually all the skin colors had become so entangled with one another that there was no recognizable difference, save the occasional anomaly like Sera or your old lab neighbor."

"So you're saying the reason why people fear us is that they don't understand us," Nadine said. "I guess that makes sense."

"Like May said, it's human nature," Symon said. "But now we and normal humans have one glaring similarity, in that we both want to see Spidre gone. Nothing unites people quite like having a common enemy, and I suspect that you won't see too much overt animosity from normal humans as long as we're all fighting him."

Chapter 24

As the sun set that same day, a very hungry Victor came stumbling into May's apartment. None of them had eaten that day; they had been too busy getting the city set up for their departure.

"How'd everything go?" Sera asked.

"All the bridges are down," Victor replied dryly. Sera could see that something was still bothering him.

"More importantly, how'd the rest of the set up go?" Victor asked.

"Everything that can be set up is," Symon replied. "There was one undamaged EMP cannon that can now run up and down the western border wherever it may be needed. Two other cannons were damaged but are now functional and facing south, along with a smattering of heavy guns. It'll take a couple more days for the fourth cannon to be repaired, but when it's done it'll go on the southern border too. The heavy artillery it replaces will go to the northern crossings. That left only one crossing unguarded by some form of heavy artillery, so Sera blew that one up right before she ran off to train Nadine."

"Oh, how'd the training go?" Victor inquired halfheartedly. "Naren told me on the way back that we have another flyer among us."

"Still a little unsteady, but I was off the ground!" Nadine said. A smile flashed across Sera's, Edgar's, and her face.

"Fantastic," Naren said. "That going to be vital at some point during our fighting. Symon, what is that thing in your lap?"

Symon glanced down at a heavy-looking, foot-long box he was holding.

"Ah, this was a little gift from the people you sent to search the government buildings," Symon said. "They just grabbed it because it was heavy, had no idea what it actually was, but I sure do. It's a LO-EC battery. One of the last models to be made before the war started. I'm going to bring it with us."

"It can't still be charged, can it? What purpose is it going to serve?" Nadine said.

"It doesn't have a charge, but that's a good thing. They're quite a bit heavier when they're full. But any of you guys could charge the thing to capacity in a few minutes. I wasn't sure what the power situation was going to be wherever we go next, so I figured it would be good to have just in case."

"Yeah, umm, speaking of which, where are we going next, and when?" Edgar asked.

"Well, now is a good time to discuss that." Naren said. "May, is there anything else you think we need to help you set up? Any concerns that might have been brought up at the hotel?"

"Not a one," May replied. "If anything, everyone was awestruck by how much was organized in such a short time. With the current set up, all that heavy artillery and the EMP cannons, we can handle things from here."

"Excellent," Naren said. "Then unless someone else has an objection, I'd like to get a good night's rest tonight and move on our targets tomorrow."

Everyone was silent, and everyone except Nadine had a dumbstruck look on their face. Nadine appeared pensive.

"You just said 'targets', didn't you?" she asked Naren. As in more than one city?"

"I did," Naren said. "Is that a problem?"

Nadine thought for another few seconds. "But how would you keep the cars from being called out of the ICT tunnel?"

Everyone turned to stare at Nadine.

"What are you talking about?" Symon asked.

"What? Don't tell me I'm the only one who figured it out," Nadine replied.

Everyone continued staring.

Nadine sighed. "We're attacking Halifax and Gibraltar."

"Okay, how the fuck did you do that!" Sera exclaimed.

"I just used what I already knew," Nadine said. "We want to destabilize the region so that Spidre's forces have multiple areas of unrest to contend with. That means attacking a city relatively nearby, most likely on the same continent. It would further serve our goals to try and take a city that is also of geographical or infrastructural importance, a place that can serve as a jumping-off point for the next phase of the plan, whatever that may be. The fact that Naren wants to attack two locations means the cities are probably connected somehow. An ICT tunnel connects two cities, and having control over one of those would be invaluable for furthering our cause. And there is only one ICT tunnel that is less than a day away from us, the one connecting Halifax and Gibraltar."

Everyone remained silent for another few seconds, too stunned to speak.

"So, that was amazing, don't get me wrong. But umm, don't you mean a TCT tunnel?" Victor asked, breaking the silence.

"No, why would I mean that?" Nadine said.

"Well then, what on earth is an ICT tunnel?" Victor asked.

"Wait, seriously?" Nadine said.

"Yes," Victor replied.

"TCT stands for Trans-Continental Transport. ICT is Inter-Continental Transport." Nadine replied. "You really didn't know that?"

"Hey, I've been in the woods since I was eight, can I get a little slack on the worldly knowledge?" Victor snapped back.

"Sorry," Nadine replied.

"For all functional purposes, they're very similar," Naren interjected. "Have you ever taken a TCT before?"

"No," Victor replied, his heart racing at the thought of being in a tiny, closed car for hours.

"Ugh, that complicates things," Naren said "It's one very long pressurized train car, and it moves through vacuum-sealed tubes via electromagnetic engine. Makes them incredibly fast. But there are a few minor differences between the TCT, which runs over land, and the ICT, which runs through water. The ICT has an independent computer system that monitors and changes the rigidity and buoyancy of the tunnel to account for tides and any sudden movements in the water from storms. The same system coordinates the arrivals and departures of the cars. But the major difference is in the speed. The ICT is newer and faster. The route from Halifax to Gibraltar, the full length of the Atlantic Ocean, takes a little over an hour."

"Jesus," Edgar replied. Naren nodded.

"That's why controlling of one of those tunnels would be quite beneficial to our cause," Naren replied.

"Wait, one of?" Victor said. "There's more than one of those things?!"

"Of course there are!" Naren replied. "Remember, the forces that tried to take back Chicago from us came from Seoul, which is all the way across the Pacific Ocean. They took one of the other ICT lines to cross the Pacific, then switched to a TCT line to make it the rest of the way. There are multiple types of train cars, too. Cars for people, cars for cargo, and cars that can transport military equipment."

Victor stayed silent.

"We have to take the Halifax to Gibraltar line, though, and you're going to have to play a major part in that," Naren continued.

"Okay…" Victor said cautiously.

"To answer your question, Nadine, there are two emergency control stations for the tunnel, one on each side." Naren continued. "The stations are unoccupied because their controls can be remotely accessed, but in the event of an emergency, workers can also run over and start the shutdown procedures manually. If we coordinate attacks on both of the emergency stations at once, then the tunnel can never be shut down."

"Isn't that dangerous?" Edgar asked.

"Not at all," Naren said. "There has never been a single accident or malfunction on any of the ICT lines in their history. I imagine the stations were put there to placate riders when it was first constructed."

"So Sera will blow up one, and Victor will tear up the other," Nadine said. "But we can't risk all of us riding the ICT and being spotted, 'cause then they'll shut the line down. Which means you and Sera are going to Gibraltar alone. Do you think you two can take on their forces on your own?"

"I'm not sure," Naren replied. "But I'm fairly certain you three without Victor can fight off Halifax's forces. If Victor hopped in a car as it's leaving after he destroys the shutdown station, then Sera and I only need to avoid being shot for an hour before he comes and helps us clear out Gibraltar."

"Naren and I can synch up our watches, so we attack at the exact same time," Symon said.

"Awesome!" Sera said. "So does anyone know where the emergency shutoff stations are?"

"They're impossible to miss. I still remember them from when I was a kid," May said. "Small red buildings across the road from the main stations. Big signs on them and everything."

"Is there any worry about Spidre figuring out our plan and already having reserve forces from Seoul or New York already in place to fight us?" Symon asked.

"It is always a possibility, but not very likely," Naren said. "For one, if the New York forces didn't come to Chicago, I doubt they'd be pulled out to proactively protect some other city. If anything, we would still be dealing with forces coming all the way from Seoul. Secondly, it was incredible that Nadine figured out the plan, and Spidre has even less information than she did. He has no idea what our long- or short-term goals are. For Spidre, there are still too many unknowns to try and guess our next move and ambush us. But to be doubly sure, we could always do a little recon before attacking."

"So, no rushing in on the elcycles like we did here?" Victor asked. Naren nodded.

"We can leave the cycles outside of the city, then keep a low profile as we make our way to the station," Symon said. "I imagine Sera and Naren will have an easier time staying covert."

"So when do we meet up again? And how will Victor get back from Gibraltar?" Edgar asked.

"What do you mean?" Naren asked.

"When the ICT line goes down, you and Sera will be able to fly back, but can you get to Halifax while carrying Victor? Isn't that too far?"

"No Edgar, you have it backwards," Sera replied. "You, Nadine, and Symon are going to meet us in Gibraltar after defenses in Halifax have been set up. And we aren't taking the ICT line out completely, we're destroying every way to control it besides its own internal automation. It will continue running on schedule unless Spidre cuts the power. If he didn't do that when we took Chicago, I doubt he'll do it at all."

"Ok, now the thing that Nadine said about spreading the revolution makes more sense!" Edgar exclaimed.

Everyone smiled.

"So what time do we leave? And when do we attack?" Edgar asked.

"Sera and I will have to leave a few hours before dawn. We have way more ground to cover. You guys could leave around dawn, and we'll attack when both our watches strike seven."

Symon reached behind him and grabbed his modified machine-gun armor. "Sounds like we have a plan," he said as he grinned.

"Sera and I will need to get to sleep soon, then," Naren said.

Sera looked over at May and Symon. "Umm, maybe we should give them some alone time before we settle in? How about we all run for a quick shower down the hall first?"

"I appreciate it," Symon said, grinning even further as May shot him a dirty look.

"You guys go ahead," Nadine said. "Edgar and I will go get the cycle we rode in on. The locals brought it over to the hotel earlier."

With that, everyone left the apartment save Symon and May. Nadine and Edgar took the elevator downstairs.

"So, Naren got you out of that funk you were in earlier, huh?"

Nadine asked.

"Yeah!" Edgar replied. "Although truth be told, I think he pulled me aside to talk about you and me."

"Funny, that's what Sera wanted to talk to me about, too," Nadine replied. "Those crafty fucks. What did he say?"

"Just that he was ok with it," Edgar said. "Although I didn't have an answer for him as to what 'it' is."

"Yeah, that's where my conversation with Sera went also," Nadine said. "May and Symon got involved in the conversation, too."

"So that's why Sera asked May that weird question earlier!" Edgar exclaimed.

"Yup," Nadine replied. "They said a lot about being a couple, but it really came down to one question that May asked. If something were to happen to either one of us, and we never made that deeper commitment to each other, would we be happy we never took that extra step, or would we regret it for the rest of our lives?"

They both stayed silent for a long, long time, contemplating the question that May had posed and Nadine retold. By the time Edgar spoke up, they were two blocks from the hotel.

"Ugh. I can't figure it out!" Edgar said as his eyes welled up. "I don't know which of those people I am. I've never felt regretful about anything before, but I also have never felt the way I do now about you."

"I feel the same," Nadine replied, her eyes also glazing over. "All of this insanity going on around us, and the only thing frustrating me is what my future with your silly self is going to be."

She glanced up at Edgar and smiled, and he smiled back. The glance became a full stop, and they turned to face each other. That then turned into them holding each other in their arms.

"You'll figure us out," Edgar whispered. "Don't worry, you always figure everything out."

Chapter 25

"Can you read the departure board from here?" Symon asked Nadine.

"Sure can, there's a train leaving at 7:03 Think you can tear down that building and get to the station in less than three minutes?" she asked Victor.

"I'll have time to spare," Victor replied.

The four of them had cut up two of Symon's blankets and turned them into makeshift hooded ponchos, hoping that kept them unnoticed. So far, it was working. They had walked through the city without being noticed and without seeing any reserve troops from Seoul or New York. They were now outside the ICT station, a building that was several hundred feet long and split in half inside by a giant gap running north to south. The eastern half was the commuter area, with a waiting area, ticket machines, and rows of moving stairs and lifts that led to the ICT and TCT tracks below. The western side was almost empty. It was an enormous lift designed to transport military or industrial vehicles from the tracks below up to the surface. The west wall was designed to retract and led out to a large onramp that took vehicles around the station and onto old highway 111. When the wall was down, a single employee-access door was the only means in and out from the west. East of the onramp, and across the street south of the main station, was the emergency-shutoff building.

"Four more minutes till we make our move," Symon said, glancing at his watch. "Still too much time to just walk over and wait. Let's circle around the north side of the station again and walk through that park on the other side of the onramp. That'll bring us right to the emergency-shutdown station at the perfect time."

"I don't like this," Nadine said. "We're going to be fighting with this incredibly wide street for the troops to spread out on. Mounting an offense in that open space is not ideal."

"No, it's not, but it'll have to do," Symon said. "The road at the front of the station isn't any smaller, and we'd have to deal with civilians there. If I find an elevated vantage point to fire from, and you keep coming at them from the air, we should be fine."

Nadine was still uneasy, and Edgar could tell. He was also worried about Victor, who had seemed on edge since the fighting in Chicago.

"So uh, what are these troops called?" Edgar asked, trying to distract everyone from the stresses at hand.

"What do you mean?" Victor said.

"Well, we fought the Special Ops in Chicago, and the androids in New Orleans. So wouldn't the troops here have some kind of nickname too?" Edgar replied.

"Oh, they're called The Destructionators," Symon replied.

"Seriously!?" Edgar exclaimed.

"Of course not!" Symon replied. Nadine and Victor burst out laughing. Edgar was glad to have lightened the mood a little.

"Ok, time to focus up," Symon said, getting everyone's attention.

We make our move in ninety seconds."

They stood together, waiting for Symon's watch to count down, which aroused the suspicions of the three soldiers standing guard by the eastern entrance.

"Hey, you four! Keep it moving!" one of them shouted. The four didn't budge.

"I said get going. Now!" she shouted again. They kept ignoring her.

Two of the guards started approaching "If you all don't start walking away right now, you will be arrested for—"

"Now!" Symon yelled, and the four of them off their ponchos. Edgar and Symon leapt at the approaching soldiers while Nadine took off towards the guard at the door. Victor stood still and unloaded a barrage of shockwaves at the bright-red building ahead. In a matter of seconds, the building and soldiers lay broken on the ground. A few blocks away, a siren started blaring.

"The peacekeepers know we're here! Get going, Victor!" Nadine shouted.

Victor raced towards the station, smashed through the door, and dashed across the elevator floor. The soldiers on the commuter side took aim but were far too late. By the time they'd opened fire, Victor had leapt off the elevator and landed on the moving stairs across the gap.

"The 7:03 to Gibraltar! What track?" he shouted.

"T-track one!" a very nervous commuter managed to blurt out.

He darted down the stairs and through the crowds to track level. As he came off the stairs, a gap in the crowd opened up as they ran for cover, and two soldiers were standing there waiting for him. He ran right at them and landed a fist to each of their faces before a shot even went off.

"All aboard on track one, 7:03 to Gibraltar," an automated voice rang out on the loudspeaker.

Victor sprinted past the four tracks terminating to his left towards the further of two tracks ahead on his right. He passed through the doors of the long, windowless, metal train car and swung around to look behind him.

Come on, doors, come on! Close close close! He couldn't risk throwing a shockwave at the soldiers if they made it to the platform; if it damaged the train, the automated computer might abort the departure. That left fighting or hiding while trying to hold position in a small, contained space. The thought sent chills down Victor's spine. He hated small spaces.

The platform in front of him was clear now. He could see all the way down past the stairs to the empty cavern behind it that the massive elevator above would fill if lowered. He could still hear commotion coming from the bank of stairs he had just descended. It was the peacekeepers from the commuter area struggling through the crowd down to him.

Close! Close! Close! was all he could think. The commotion was being replaced by the sound of heavy boots pounding on metal stairs. He saw the soldier's feet make the turn to the last moving staircase and his heart started pounding. The first troop's body came into view. Then another. And another. And another. The first soldier made it to the platform. Another appeared on the stairs. The second soldier made it to the platform. Another soldier on the stairs. The first soldier brought his gun up to aim at the train doorway and Victor threw himself against the wall at the back of the train. In the next moment, the distinctive 'bing bong' of the closing doors blared through the train's speakers. The doors hissed and slid shut, and the train launched out of the station.

Victor sank to the ground, gasping for air and trying to bring his heart rate down. Faint classical music started playing over the sound system and video displays on the sides of the train lit up, showing a looped video of a serene ocean under cloudless blue sky.

"This ICT is scheduled to arrive in Gibraltar in one hour and twenty-six minutes," a female computerized voice said over the speakers. "Local time upon arrival will be 1:29am. Thank you for riding today."

Victor spent several seconds curled up with his back to the wall, staring at the floor. When he had calmed down somewhat, he lifted his head. The ICT was all one long car on the outside. On the inside it was separated every 50 feet or so by heavy ballasts with doors that slid into an airtight seal, a design element meant to contain any pressure leaks. Victor's eyes were now trained on the ballast, which every commuter who had boarded that section of the ICT before him was pinned up against. About forty people were there, trying to stay as far away from Victor as possible. He could see the look of terror on everyone's faces as they stared at him. He slowly stood up but continued to lean against the wall.

When he caught enough of his breath to talk, he said, "I'm sorry. I'm not going to hurt you."

The commuters all relaxed, if only slightly.

"Umm. When we get to Gibraltar, I would stay on this train if I were you," Victor continued.

The commuters all nodded in agreement.

Back in Halifax, things were going well. The soldiers were arriving in small groups from the east, down the much smaller southern street rather than from the northern onramp. Nadine and Edgar were dispatching the peacekeepers as fast as they arrived. Symon had gone into the ICT station itself, trying to find a way to the roof, but it hardly seemed necessary.

Nadine swooped in from above and drilled the last soldier of a group into the ground. "I didn't expect them to be so disorganized!" she shouted over to Edgar as he walked over.

"Guess you were worried for nothing," he said with a smirk. She smiled back.

The fighting had ceased for a moment, and so had the noise that accompanied it. The commotion from inside the station was also dying down and being replaced by another sound. A faint rumble, growing ever louder. After a few seconds, it was loud enough that Nadine and Edgar realized what it was. Footsteps, hundreds of them, coming from the north.

They raced back to the western end of the street and were met with a surge of soldiers running at them, the closest of whom were only fifteen feet away. The soldiers started firing, leaving Edgar scrambling to run back the way he came while Nadine took to the air. Most of the soldiers focused on following Edgar, leaving Nadine to watch from above.

"Keep running, Edgar!" she bellowed.

Edgar didn't run. He turned to fight. He slashed through the first few troops to arrive, but Nadine knew he would soon be overwhelmed. She dove down and flattened one soldier, then landed several shots on the other peacekeepers before she was surrounded and forced to take off again. When she felt she was at a safe height, she turned around and saw that Edgar was franticly slashing at any soldier who raised their hand toward him. Nadine started diving in again to help, but this time some of the soldiers saw her coming. They aimed up and fired, the shots coming close enough to force Nadine to stop her descent and watch helplessly. A soldier kicked Edgar in the back of his knee, and he fell to the ground. Edgar landed on his back and kept swinging. His blades were long enough that they were still able to reach the arms of the peacekeepers standing over him. He continued to slash at them to keep them from firing their guns or stabbing with their electric swords. The onslaught was so constant that he couldn't change focus and slash at the soldiers' feet, which were constantly stomping him and keeping him on the ground. One soldier managed to kick him in the head. Didn't hurt, didn't faze him at all. The second kick didn't either. Or the third. Or the fourth. Or the fifth. The sixth one hurt a little. The seventh hurt a lot. From that point on, with every stomp or kick that came down on his head, he could feel his consciousness slipping away.

No, he thought.

No!' Nadine thought.

It can't end now. Not without—they both thought, but were cut off by the sound of much louder and far more rapid gunfire.

From Edgar's perspective, the world was getting dark, but the stomps and kicks less frequent. He could not see what Nadine saw, that Symon had made it to the roof and was mowing down the troops surrounding Edgar.

"Get him out of there!" Symon shouted over the sound of his bullets. Nadine barely heard Symon, but she didn't need to. The second there was an opening, she dove down and grabbed Edgar by the shirt collar. She threw him over her shoulder but couldn't fly away with the extra weight. With a jump at all her might and her jets at max, she just cleared the heads of the soldiers around her. She landed and then jumped off of the face of one sending her rocketing up and the soldier tumbling to the ground. She then coasted away from the group of soldiers over to the park due west. Several soldiers tried to follow, but Symon shot them. He then turned his attention to the gunners. Edgar had taken out many of them, but Symon still aimed from one to another, taking them out as they raised their hands to fire at him. His hands and gun were too fast, no one on the ground could even manage a shot.

"We've got to get to the roof!" one of the troops shouted as the last gunner fell. The remaining soldiers, carrying only swords, desperately ran for the doorway on the west wall that Victor had splintered earlier. Symon aimed and fired as they got close. The pile of the bodies by the door grew ever wider as they tried in vain to make it through. When only a half dozen soldiers were left, they scattered in a last attempt to escape with their lives. Symon refused to let that happen. One by one, he took careful aim and one by one, they hit the ground. Not a single peacekeeper was left standing. Halifax was theirs.

When the last soldier's lifeless body hit the ground, Symon lowered his gun and breathed a sigh of relief.

"That was too close," he said aloud. He looked in the direction that Nadine had glided and saw her holding Edgar tight.

"Edgar's fine, he's fine," he said to himself. "That must have been scary for them. I'll leave them alone for now, they'll come back over when they're ready."

Symon grabbed the edge of the roof and swung over the side. He let go and landed on his feet after the long drop, a slight twinge in his knee when he landed.

"Ooof," he said. "That didn't feel great. From now on, it's steps and ladders to get down from up high."

He heard more footsteps approaching from the east. He turned and aimed his gun down the southern street and saw four civilians running up to him. He lowered his gun. They stopped running about teen feet away, putting their hands on their knees while trying to catch their breath.

"You're… you're the guys from Chicago… the ones they've been… sending messages about… on the net," one of them managed to say in between gasps for air.

"Yes. Well, some of them," Symon replied.

"We… we came to help fight!" the same young lady exclaimed.

"You're all a bit too late for that, I'm afraid. I will need help organizing defenses in case they try and take back—wait a minute."

Symon looked down at the four newcomers' hands.

"Why are all of you wearing fingerless gloves?" Symon asked. The four of them smiled.

About a hundred yards away, in the park, Nadine was sitting down and still holding Edgar tightly. She had him sitting up with his back against her chest and his very swollen face on her right shoulder.

"Wake up, Edgar. Wake up!" she said with force. "I can hear you breathing, so I know your still in there, just wake up already! I need to know you're ok. Please let me know you're ok."

Edgar let out a very muffled groan.

"God damnit, Edgar, let me know you're ok!" she bellowed.

Edgar winced. "Please stop yelling, my head hurts," he said weakly.

She smiled and wrapped her arms around him even tighter.

"You were right Edgar, I figured it out," she said. "I know what kind of person I am."

Edgar rolled his head back and looked up at Nadine. "I do too," he replied. "I… I love you, Nadine."

Nadine sniffled. "I love you, too."

Nadine cracked a smile, while a single joy-filled tear ran down Edgar's swollen cheek.

"But you're still an idiot!" Nadine exclaimed. "Why the fuck didn't you run when they were coming for you!?"

"It was my plan all along…" he said weakly before passing out again. Nadine thought for a moment and then understood. The man she loved was an idiot. The bravest idiot she had ever met.

Chapter 26

"This feels amazing," Sera said.

"It does, and the stars are a refreshing change from staring at water all day," Naren replied. When Naren and Sera had arrived at the Spanish coast, they'd surveyed the city from high in the air and not seen any large military vehicles, a soldier encampment or any other sign of extra troops from Seoul or New York. The two of them were now floating in the ocean hand in hand, just within sight of land, staring up at the stars as they waited for their time to strike.

"Ugh, I know. I never thought monotony could be so fucking exhausting!" Sera said. "Flying the length of an ocean in a day I can handle. Staring at nothing but ocean for a day… never again."

"I don't know about never again," Naren said. "But I hope it won't have to happen again for a good long while."

Sera's mouth curled into a serene smile. "How much longer till we have to go?" she asked.

Naren put his right hand up and squinted to see his watch. "Ten minutes and twenty seconds, although the only thing that has to happen then is destroying the emergency shutoff building. After that, it's a waiting game until Victor arrives."

"I hope he does," Sera replied.

"Does what? Arrive?" Naren asked. "You don't think the four of them can take Halifax?"

"Normally I wouldn't have a doubt, but for some reason Victor just seemed… off… yesterday," Sera said.

"Off?" Naren replied.

"Yeah. More withdrawn and abrasive than usual," Sera said.

Naren thought for a moment. "You might be right about that. But all he has to do there is destroy the shutoff station and run to the train. He can handle that, no matter what mood he's in."

Sera sighed. "You're probably right. Still, I'll talk to him about it tomorrow, now that we'll have some time to slow down."

Naren nodded and looked at his watch again. He stared as the seconds passed until the moment came.

"It's time," he said.

Sera nodded and took to the air as Naren did the same. They turned to look at each other and held each other's hands.

"Love you," Sera said.

"Love you," Naren replied.

They took off through the strait and veered left towards Gibraltar. The black, dark edifices of the megaskyscraper complex surrounded the ICT station, making it visible despite its sparse lighting. As Sera got closer, she could make out the red paint of the emergency-shutoff building just where May had said it would be. She aimed straight for it, and compared with the buildings and bridges in Chicago, the emergency-shutoff station came down with little effort. While Sera took the building down, Naren flew over the city.

I'm sure they all heard Sera's explosion and left headquarters, Naren thought. *Maybe they're all running down the same street, though?*Naren continued to fly and could only find small groups of peacekeepers spread throughout his flight path.

*Damn it, they're all split up! This is going to take hours even with Victor's help. Wait… Why does the northern part of the city look so desolate?*Naren flew north and saw the rows of abandoned buildings were interrupted by a large concrete clearing that cut the city in half.

This is… an airstrip? Naren thought to himself. *What the hell is this still doing here? Planes haven't been a thing since… Maybe they didn't need the land because of the megaskyscrapers in the south? Whatever the case, this is perfect.*Naren turned back south and saw Sera rising back into the air. He headed towards her, hearing occasional gunfire aimed at him as he whizzed past.

"You have a plan?" Sera asked when he arrived.

"I do," Naren replied. "Fly overhead and try to stay out of range of their gunfire. Lure them together into larger groups if you can. Then when Victor gets here, lead them all north to the airstrip."

"Airstrip!?" Sera exclaimed.

One hour and twenty-six minutes later, the ICT arrived at Gibraltar. The doors of the ICT slid open and Victor darted out at full speed. The station was different than the one in Halifax. All the platforms were above ground, and the station was empty, save one TCT car waiting in silence across the dividing platform. Victor could hear a massive commotion outside and raced through the station's main entrance to try and find Sera and Naren. He didn't have to search long. Sera's orange glow and Naren's light blue jets were obvious in the night sky as they darted around avoiding gunfire. Sera was closer, but Victor was confident she was having an easier time on her own than Naren was, so he followed the blue streak in the sky to the east. When he was close to catching up, he saw three soldiers firing upwards and barreled into them, slamming them into the ground. The sudden cessation of gunfire prompted Naren to look down.

"Christ am I glad to see you," Naren said as he descended and landed on the street.

"What's the plan?" Victor asked. "Just run around and pick them all off one by one?"

"I think there's an easier way," Naren replied. "There's an old airstrip north of here that cuts the island in half. It's a huge open area. If you hide out near there and we coax them all to follow us…"

"An airstrip?" Victor interrupted. "That's an airplane thing right?"

"Yes, they never built over the one here. I think it might have marked a border or…"

"What does it look like?" Victor said, cutting Naren off again.

"It's just a long concrete field to the north, you can't miss it."

Victor darted off as quickly as he had arrived. Naren was perplexed by Victor's abrupt attitude but shook the thought off. He had other things to worry about. He took off again and headed towards Sera. She saw him coming and headed his way.

"He's here," Naren shouted as they crossed paths, and Sera understood. She flew as low as she felt comfortable going, just above the building lines, and slowed down just enough so the troops could keep up with her.

"She must be getting tired, look how slow she's going!" one soldier yelled.

"Follow her!" another shouted.

Sera smiled. She was getting tired, but that wasn't the reason she was slowing down. When she felt she had a good number of peacekeepers following her, she headed for the airstrip. She flew over the pockmarked concrete plain, and the soldiers followed.

When she reached the far side of the airstrip, she shot straight up in the air and doubled back. The soldiers stopped to turn around and were leveled by a shockwave from the charging Victor. A few moments later, Naren emerged from the building line and the soldiers following him met a similar fate. They repeated the process two or three times apiece, and none of the soldiers expected the demolishing blow awaiting them. In a matter of an hour, only a few dozen scattered troops remained in the city, easy prey for Victor, Naren, and Sera.

With the fighting over, Naren found Sera and Victor to discuss getting the city reorganized.

"Were there people on the ICT you came in on?" he asked Victor.

"Sure were," Victor replied.

"Damn. Okay. Was there another transport in the station?" Naren asked.

"Uh, yeah, on the other side of the tracks," Victor said.

Naren breathed a sigh of relief. "That's a TCT line, the last one this city will see for a long time. Can you go back to the station and tell everyone who doesn't want to stay in Gibraltar to get on that train and ride it wherever it's going, whenever it leaves. Then I guess just run around announcing that's the last train out. Sera and I will do the same."

The three of them then parted ways again. When Victor arrived at the station, he saw that the empty platforms he'd left had since come to life. Many more lights were on, and screens showing departures had lit up. The first departure was the only one that wasn't going back to Halifax. It read, "Paris: 5:05 | Status: On Time." He told the people still hunkered down on the ICT car the situation, and they filed across the dividing platform to wait for the Paris train to open. Then Victor joined Sera and Naren screaming news of the city's takeover, and for anyone who wanted to leave to make their way to the station. About an hour passed when the now exhausted Sera, Naren, and Victor felt they had spread word enough and stopped. They bunked in an abandoned building near the airstrip, ate the last of the food Naren had taken with them, and lept for what little remained of the night.

The next morning, the sun shone brightly, an unwelcome sight in their groggy, under-rested states.

"Ugh," Sera groaned. "We need to find food. Not going to be easy with the entire city looking for us to answer questions."

"No telling how friendly they'll be either," Naren replied. He glanced over at Victor, who was still sitting on the ground, rubbing the sides of his head, and shaking a lot more than usual.

"Are, are you ok? We've got to get going," Naren said.

"Just give me a minute! Fucking Christ," Victor snapped at Naren.

"Okay, what the fuck has been up with you lately!?" Sera snapped back. "You've always kept to yourself and that's fine, but these past two days you've barely talked, and when you do, you're fucking mean!"

Victor locked eyes with Sera as she stood over him, their stares so intense they could've burned holes in each other. But after a few seconds, Victor's stare wilted as his eyes welled up with tears.

"I don't know!" He cried. "I don't know, and I can't figure it out and I want to sleep but I can't 'cause my head keeps thinking about stupid things!"

Naren was taken aback by the sudden burst of emotion. Sera wasn't.

"Naren, go," Sera said. "Victor and I have to talk, and you would do all the talking with the locals anyway."

"Yeah, no problem," Naren replied, still not over the surprise outburst. He walked out of the building and took off to the south. Sera sat down cross-legged in front of Victor, who had gone back to rubbing the sides of his head.

"So when was the last time you remember falling asleep?" Sera asked.

"Three nights ago, after we defended Chicago," Victor replied.

"You haven't slept in two nights!?" Sera asked.

Victor shook his head.

"Well, that explains a lot. I'd be an asshole too if I didn't get sleep for that long," Sera said. "And it's not physical? Just like your mind just won't shut up?"

Victor nodded.

"Well, what are the thoughts you're having?" Sera asked.

"I just said, it's stupid stuff! I don't know why the thoughts are even in there!" Victor exclaimed.

"Is it about our fights? Or something in Chicago?" Sera kept guessing.

"It's… I keep thinking about Tim," Victor replied with a sigh.

Sera thought for a moment. "I'm sorry, but I'm drawing a blank here," she eventually confessed.

"The guy I asked about after the battle. The one that died after the EMP blast," Victor said.

Everything clicked in Sera's head. "You liked him."

"I barely knew him," Victor replied.

"Doesn't matter," Sera replied. "Your thoughts at night keep coming back to him. About why, out of thousands of locals who died in the assault, he had to be one of them. And then you start wondering why, out of those thousands of people, he's the one that's sticking out in your mind. And then you think that if we hadn't attacked Chicago, he'd still be alive. Then you start wanting to get revenge, but knowing you can't because you have no idea who killed him or if the person who killed him is even still alive. And then you wonder why you want revenge in the first place. Then that cycle of thought keeps repeating. Over and over and over. Does that just about cover it?"

Victor was stunned. "How did you know all of that?" he asked?

"You think Naren was the first person I ever liked?" Sera replied.

"He wasn't?" Victor said.

"Of course not!" Sera responded. "The group that raised me after my parents died had kids of their own. Some of them were cute, all of them were nice. And everyone in that group gave up a lot to keep me safe. Some of them gave up too much," Sera said as her eyes started welling up too.

Victor cocked his head to the side. "I liked him…"

"There was a lot you missed out on during your years in hiding, Victor. Having a crush was one of those things. Losing that person was another," Sera said.

"Have all of you had to deal with this?" Victor said.

"I'd assume so," Sera replied. "Well, maybe except Nadine. She's a machine."

Victor smirked.

"So how did you deal with it? How did you forget about that kid you liked?" Victor asked.

"I never forgot about him. I just know he wants me to move on," Sera replied. Victor looked up.

"What does that mean?" he inquired.

"The group that raised me, they had this idea that when we die, it isn't the end of us," Sera explained. "Some part of us that can't be seen or sensed lives on, and becomes part of a larger, unseen power that looks over everyone who is still alive. They thought that

I was some messenger sent by this larger power, which was the reason they took me in and raised me.”

“I’ve never heard that before,” Victor said. “Is that true?”

Sera shrugged. “No idea. But supposing it is, that means a part of Tim is out there somewhere, looking over you, me, everyone. And if that’s true, do you think he would want you to have his image plague your thoughts for the rest of your life? Or would he want you to move on, live your life, and get the sleep you need to save the world?”

“He’d want me to sleep,” Victor replied.

“So then do right by him, and sleep,” Sera replied with a smile.

Victor started nodding weakly, then the nod got progressively stronger. Sera held open her arms and Victor hugged her tight.

“Try to get some sleep now,” Sera whispered. “Naren and I will handle things out there and bring you food.”

“Thank you,” Victor whispered back.

Chapter 27

"It's a good thing there are no planes anymore," Sera said as she looked out onto the runway from the building they were staying in.

"Huh, why?" Naren asked.

"Well, it just seems like all of these things we've been doing would be a lot harder if we had to fight planes," Sera replied. "The fact that we can fly and they can't seems to be a pretty big deal. Imagine if they had been able to send planes when we were in Chicago. Being up high in the buildings for defense would have been useless."

"Wait, they used to have planes for fighting?" Victor asked. His shakiness was still escalated, but in the nine days that had passed since they took Gibraltar, he seemed to be in much better spirits.

"Oh yeah!" Naren replied. "They had passenger planes for normal people, and then they had fighting planes that shot guns and dropped bombs and spied on people."

"So why don't we have them now?" Victor asked.

"I guess they were just replaced with better stuff. Like we have the TCT system now, which is just as fast as any plane, and before that, cars still had autonav systems. Planes might have been faster than cars, but I doubt very many people would have paid for a plane ride if they could just fall asleep in their car and wake up at their destination. And fighting planes would have been even more useless. The military has had spy satellites and remote-controlled missiles for hundreds of years. So planes would only be useful for fighting other planes, and what other planes would a unified world government ever have to fight? They must've just stopped maintaining them from lack of need."

"I guess that makes sense," Victor said. "Bet they would've kept a few of them working if they had known about us, though."

"Without a doubt," Naren replied. "Let's walk over to the net access point, I'm getting anxious to hear about what's going on in Halifax."

They all stood up and exited the building. It was the last one still standing that bordered the runway.

Sera glanced up at its facade. "I guess this one has to come down today, huh?"

"Yup," Naren replied. "The rubble from the buildings is a perfect barrier. Any invading force must cross the open runway while the city defends from cover. This is the last hole remaining besides the access route we want to leave open in the far east."

"I know it's silly, but I'm sad to see it go," Sera said.

"It's not silly," Victor said. "We've had peace and quiet the past few days. This building coming down means that's over soon."

"I will miss that, not going to lie," Naren said. "But our peace is being replaced by peace of mind that Gibraltar is finally defensible without us."

Victor and Sera nodded.

"I just hope Nadine, Edgar, and Symon had as much luck as we had," Naren said. "This has been easy on our end, but we don't know anything that's going on there."

"Well, we know they took the city. The net has been blasting word of it every day," Sera replied.

"I know, but we have no idea what challenges they're facing there. What if one of them got injured? What if they're having trouble setting up defenses? What if there is a military siege? What if the locals were allied with the military and give them a hard time?"

They arrived at the net access point, which was being housed in an old building on the side of a mountain. The moment they walked inside, they stopped in astonishment. In front of them stood Nadine, Edgar, and Symon, all facing the door. Sera caught a brief glimpse of Nadine and Edgar holding hands before they noticed her and threw their arms to their sides.

"You're here!" Sera screamed as she ran over and almost tackled Nadine with a hug, bringing a smile to everyone's face.

"We just got here about twenty minutes ago," Symon said. "We were about to ask these guys if they knew where we might find you."

"Took you guys long enough to get here," Naren said. "Not that I didn't mind the rest."

In the dim light, Naren had just noticed Edgar's face, which was still dotted with bruises.

"Looks like you guys ran into some trouble. Are you ok?" he asked.

"Yeah, I'm alright, just got in a little over my head is all," Edgar replied.

"I think you mean, 'took on an entire regiment on your own like a fucking champ'," Nadine said.

"It's true," Symon continued. "Edgar stood his ground while the regiment surrounded him, then took out as many gunners as he could. He knew they were going to beat him down and did it anyway. It allowed me to get into position and gun down the rest of them. If he had run, they would've chased and spread out. It would've made taking them all out way harder. Simultaneously the smartest and stupidest thing I have ever seen anyone do."

Victor, Naren, and Sera looked at Edgar and nodded, impressed with his bold actions.

"We didn't even have much trouble with the Seoul forces," Nadine continued. "They showed up two days in with some tanks and a few mounted guns. Child's play compared to Chicago."

"Seven days ago, eh? That's the same day that Montreal started rebelling," Naren said. "Looks like our plan is working. Other cities are starting to rebel on their own without our help, and spreading the reserve forces thin." Everyone nodded in reply.

"So what took you guys so long?" Sera asked.

"Setting up defenses," Nadine replied. "We had to block a lot of streets coming from the south and west, and there was a bridge to the north that the locals wanted gone. Not so easy to do with no explosives and no one to blow shit up."

"So how'd you do it?" Victor asked.

"A lot of planning and some well-placed cuts from Edgar and kicks from Nadine," Symon said. "Now there's only one road in and out. And with the defense there, I feel confident saying that we will never have to go back."

"That's a pretty bold statement," Naren said. "What makes you so sure?"

Symon grinned. "There were more LO-EC users there."

Stunned looks fell across the faces of the three who attacked Gibraltar.

"Four of them in total," Symon continued. "Some of the last people to have it surgically implanted, I imagine."

"That's awesome!" Sera shouted. "I want to meet them! Why didn't you bring them to Gibraltar!?"

"We asked if they wanted to come," Symon replied. "They refused. They said Halifax protected them for too long, and now it was their turn to return the favor."

"How were they never found?" Victor asked.

"They aren't sure of that themselves, none of them remember anything before living with their parents' neighbors," Symon said. "According to the locals, the military declared Halifax 100% clear of LO-EC activity, and yet, there those four were. They suspect that since they were born normal and had the surgery so soon before the war started, Spidre just didn't have a record of them yet."

"So their parents knew something bad was coming, left the kids with people they trusted, hoped the military didn't have record of them, and were correct. If that's true, then there could be more people around the world who survived the same way!" Sera said.

"It's very possible," Symon said. "In the years before the incident in Boston, thousands of young children were being implanted with LO-EC devices every day. If Spidre's list was out of date, then there might be a substantial population still out there."

"They're going to be coming out of the woodwork now, especially if even more cities rebel," Nadine said.

"Were there any new cities today?" Victor asked. "The last one we heard about was Toronto two days ago."

"Pittsburgh, rumors came in on the net just before we left," Edgar said. "The folks in Montreal and Providence are still holding on to areas of their city, too."

"So by my count that's six cities on the west side of the Atlantic where the local military is overwhelmed, and Seoul has to organize against. Yet there is only one city on this side of the ocean that can make that same claim. If you ask me, that just doesn't seem fair," Naren said with a smirk.

"Are you guys ready to move on here?" Edgar asked.

"We will be after today, just one more building to bring down by the airstrip. After that, the city will only have one road to defend at the far east corner," Sera replied.

"So where to next?" Symon asked.

Naren looked at Nadine. "Should I tell them or are you going to do your 'guess the next step of the plan out of nowhere' thing again?"

"Oh, I think you already know the answer to that," Nadine replied. "It's the same deal as when we left Chicago, try and destabilize the region so Spidre's forces are overwhelmed with multiple rebellions at once. So we're going to a city far enough away that other major cities are in between it and here, but still less than a day's travel away in the event we have to retreat. Additionally, Montréal's successful rebellion means you're probably thinking of a city with a relatively small standing army, leaving the larger armies in larger cities to the local population. That only leaves one option. We're going to Monaco."

Everyone looked at Naren. "She's right," he replied with a shrug. "And after defenses are all set up there, we'll head back to where all of this started, New Orleans. We'll drive out whatever force replaced the androids, and with Sera's connections there, it'll serve as the perfect area to monitor all the rebellions and wait for the opportunity to move on to the next phase of the plan."

A wave of excitement filled the room. "When do we leave?" Edgar asked.

"That depends. Did you bring the elcycles with you?" Naren asked.

"Sure did, along with most of the supplies we picked up in Halifax and Chicago," Symon said.

"Awesome. You can leave a lot of that here if you want, since we'll be coming back when we're done in Monaco," Naren replied.

"All we need are the elcycles and some food."

Symon nodded.

"So that means we can leave tomorrow morning to attack at night. Today we set up the last of Gibraltar's defenses, and tonight we rest," Naren continued.

"You guys need any help with the set up?" Edgar asked.

"Well, all that needs to happen is to fill one last hole in the wall we made. Gotta bring a building down to do it, and I'm kind of an expert at that now," Sera said. "But it couldn't hurt to get some fresh eyes to look at it, though, see if we missed anything."

"Good call, let's head over there now," Naren said. As everyone filed in behind him to leave, Symon motioned to Victor that he wanted to talk. Victor stepped over to him and they dropped a couple steps behind.

"You're shaking a lot more than you were nine days ago. I doubt I'm the first one to notice," Symon said.

"Sera and Naren both asked about it, but I feel fantastic, better than I ever have," Victor replied.

Symons's look of worry did not fall from his face.

"Look, I'll admit that after Chicago I wasn't feeling well. But I had a long talk with Sera, and she helped me figure out that it was all emotional stuff. I remember what you told me, alright? I've been looking out for any bad symptoms and nothing. If anything it's the exact opposite. I feel amazing, like I can do anything and everything."

"I'm glad to hear it." Symon said. "But if anything changes…"

"I'll tell you, I promise," Victor interrupted. "With how I feel right now though, I don't see that happening for a long fucking time."

Chapter 28

"So this last point is obvious, but I feel I have to ask," Nadine said. "You are sure the locals aren't going to run out of food?"

"They assured me they won't," Naren replied. "They have half a dozen food dispensaries around the city, and they were all well stocked before we invaded. The government workers at the dispensaries were all locals, and they're sticking it out to make sure everything stays up and running. They'll be ok."

"So, we're done here?" Edgar asked.

"We're done," Naren said. "By this time tomorrow, we attack Monaco."

Everyone smiled as they sat down and started eating. After the last abandoned building by the airstrip was brought down, the six LO-ECs moved into the net access point building. They were on the floor of the main room now, sitting on Symon's blankets.

"So what's the plan?" Symon asked.

"Monaco is a little bit different than the other cities we've taken," Naren said. "The country is connected to mainland on three sides. However, it is also surrounded by an undeveloped mountainous region. There are only two roads in and out, and a high peak to the north would serve as an excellent lookout point for both roads. So, once we take out the peacekeepers in the city, all we'll need to do is set up that lookout and help the locals strategize against possible invasion along those two roads."

"Well, that makes life easy," Victor said. "And what about taking the city?"

"The key will be finding the headquarters quickly," Sera said. "They only have the one regiment, and the locals here who have been to Monaco said all the soldiers are housed in one tower near an old fancy building they called 'The Casino'. If we get to that building fast, and I bring it down, then the only troops we'll have to deal with are the ones out on duty. We'll hold our ground near the headquarters and just wait for them to come to us."

"Holding our ground didn't work so well for us last time," Edgar said, the events that occurred in Halifax flashing through his mind.

"Things are different now," Naren replied. "In Halifax, you had the whole regiment coming at you. You also only had one person for air support, and only one person who could take down soldiers at range. Nadine couldn't provide enough of a distraction alone, and Symon needed to be in a strategic position to be effective. This time, it'll be three people in the air. The troops will be so distracted by us that they'll be easy pickings for the three of you. And with Symon and Victor on guns, you are not going to get overwhelmed."

Edgar took a deep breath to calm his nerves. He wasn't completely confident, but Naren's logic was sound.

"Okay, it's a good plan," Edgar replied.

"Let's finish up here and get everything ready for tomorrow," Nadine said. "We're going to need to move fast when we get to Monaco, so we should try to rest up as much as possible."

The six LO-ECs finished their food, moved the elcycles into place, and fell asleep. The next morning, they had a quick breakfast and got on the road. They drove all day, only stopping to eat. As the sun set, the city became visible through the mountain landscape. They entered the city proper and people began clearing the streets as they passed. North of the old casino, the military headquarters came into view, and Sera sped up. As she bore down on the building's black edifice, she threw her hands out in front of her and prepared for impact, the same way she had several times before. Her arms crashed through the building's glass panes and she unleashed her explosion. The power left her body and she coasted through the air to the other side of the building as it fell. Her vision was somewhat compromised as she broke through, but between the fingers of her outstretched arms, she could still make out an endless sea of dark orange uniforms.

"Oh fuck," was her only thought as she fell out of the air and the dust cloud consumed her. Farther west, the other five set up with their backs to a building. Nadine and Naren had taken to the air. Naren was floating above Symon, facing east, while Nadine and Victor faced west. Edgar stood in the center of them, blades out, waiting to see who would need back up first. Naren saw the first soldiers exit the dust cloud and his eyes went wide.

"Shit!" he yelled as he darted forward. Edgar followed him on foot while Symon opened fire. In an instant, there were too many troops on the street for Symon to gun down. Edgar ran toward a soldier who was raising his arm to aim. He sliced through the gun and down through the soldier's chest. By the time the soldier had fallen, three more were surrounding him. Edgar slashed one as he ran past, then plunged one of each of his blades into the other soldiers' guts. By then, there were six more soldiers around him, with even more being gunned down by Symon. Meanwhile, Victor and Nadine had focused their attention on soldiers coming from the north. Nadine weaved through the air and drew their gunfire while Victor mowed them down, but the soldiers just kept coming. More and more troops piled into the intersection and Victor began having trouble focusing on so many targets. Nadine kept dodging shots, but that task was becoming more difficult as well. Finally, the gunfire became so intense that she had no choice but to fly up out of their range to reset. As she did so, she looked out over the buildings and saw what they were fighting. In every direction for at least five blocks, all she could see was row after row of soldiers in orange armor, all converging on their location. Her eyes went wide.

Way too many, she thought.

They were surrounded and fighting an unwinnable battle. She turned to head back down to the street and saw Edgar surrounded, but most of the gunfire around him was focused up at Naren. The only soldiers paying attention to him were the ones in his immediate vicinity, whom he was dispatching with relative ease. Meanwhile, Symon had backed up against a building. He was closest to the elcycles and furthest from the incoming flood of soldiers. Victor, on the other hand, was surrounded. And in the brief time Nadine had flown out of the peacekeeper's range, all their attention had trained on him. She darted down and threw the soldiers around Victor away, then together the two of them desperately fought their way through the crowd towards the cycles.

Naren had seen Nadine fly up high and knew that the two of them moving towards the cycles meant they all had to get out as fast as possible. Nadine wasn't quite strong enough to lift Victor yet, so they had to fight through the crowd. Naren did not have that same problem. He descended in between bullet fire and flew just over the heads of the soldiers, hoping it made their shots more difficult. He skimmed along and thrust his hands out as he passed over Edgar. He grabbed Edgar under the shoulders and lifted him off the ground. Taking on Edgar's weight only slowed Naren down for a second, but it was enough for one of the gunners to catch up with him and put a bullet in his knee. Naren cried out in pain as he fell out of the sky. Edgar grabbed him and flung him down at his feet, then squared up as the mass of peacekeepers bore down on him.

"Get them away from me!" Victor shouted as he saw Naren go down. Nadine knew what he meant. She lunged at the soldiers in front of Victor and knocked them away, giving him just enough room to throw a shockwave at the crowd ahead. He continued to throw them in rapid succession, sweeping from the right to left, while Nadine shifted to his back and kept the soldiers there at bay. They made slow progress towards Edgar while he struggled to keep the peacekeepers off of him. Blows and bullets kept getting closer until shots started grazing his arms as he swung. By the time Nadine and Victor had made it to him, he had half a dozen wounds covering his extremities. Victor swung around to face the direction of the cycles, and Nadine and Edgar turned so that Naren was in between all three of them. Naren struggled to his feet as Victor started to throw air bursts in the direction of the cycles. Naren faced forward and caught a glimpse of Victor as he looked around.

"Why does Victor look so pale?" Naren thought, and as if on cue, Victor stopped throwing shockwaves and fell to the ground. His body started convulsing as Nadine swung around and stood over him.

"What the fuck happened?!" she screamed.

"I don't know!" Naren yelled back.

Naren tried taking off, but it was no use.

Shit! I can't get off the ground! he thought as he attempted to throw punches while all his weight was on one leg. *I can't even fly Victor out! Think! If Nadine or Edgar threw me then maybe I could… wait, that's it!* "We have to hold out till Sera gets here!" Naren yelled as Nadine threw blows around her. She immediately knew what his plan was.

"Edgar, when you see Sera, throw me as hard as you can, then prepare to hold out here for a few seconds!" Naren boomed.

"By myself?!" Edgar yelled back.

"I'll try to make it as short a wait as I can! It's our only way out!" Nadine screamed.

Edgar was not sure what the plan was, but he prepared regardless. A few more desperate moments passed, and Edgar saw Sera approaching from the east. He turned and threw Naren as hard as he could while Nadine did the same to Victor. Naren activated his jets as he was launched and breathed a sigh of relief as he remained afloat. Sera saw what was happening and dove to catch Victor. He fell in her arms as Nadine took off into the air, leaving Edgar alone. Edgar took a deep breath and swung wildly all around him. Bullets continued to sail past him and graze his arms as he fought with all the energy he had left. Then he heard the revving of engines, one heading west, the other straight towards him. He barely saw the cycle before it broke through the crowd. Nadine grabbed him as she passed and held on with all her might as she plowed through the soldiers in her way. Edgar's right leg and hand hit the ground for just a moment as he was grabbed, but it was enough to cover them in huge scrapes. The instant Nadine had enough clearance to lift him onto the back of the cycle, she did just that. Edgar looked ahead and saw they were catching up with Symon on the other elcycle, Naren flying overhead, and Sera flying even higher while holding Victor in her arms. His body was still convulsing, but no one could see any injury.

The air was thick with feelings of confusion and anger. For the first time since their whole adventure started, the six LO-ECs found themselves defeated and retreating.

Chapter 29

"Nadine, get my big bag from the net access building and bring it right back here!" Symon screamed as he brought his elcycle to a stop about 100 feet south of the wall they had built in Gibraltar. "I also need a knife and anyone in there with any medical knowledge!"

Nadine shook the tears out of her eyes and flew ahead. Edgar slid up to drive the elcycle and brought it to a stop at the same time that Sera and Naren landed. Naren hit ground and collapsed under his visibly wounded knee. Sera laid Victor on the ground, his body still convulsing.

"Edgar, hold his arms at his side, keep him from injuring himself!" Symon continued yelling.

Edgar did as he was told. "Can someone tell me what the fuck is going on?"

"There's too much power built up in his body, it's frying his nervous system," Symon said through gritted teeth. "He has multiple energy converters in his body and only one inaccessible microtransformer to contain it all. His body had been compensating, getting rid of the excess by shaking but now... where the fuck is Nadine?"

Moments later, Nadine landed, carrying Symon's bag and a small folding knife.

"What are you going to do?!" Edgar asked.

Symon snatched the knife from Nadine.

"Access it," he said as he plunged the knife into Victor's left pectoral muscle. "Nadine, open the bag and take the LO-EC battery out of it," Symon said as he cut through Victor's flesh.

Nadine was dazed from exhaustion but managed to rustle through the bag and find the battery. She brought it to Symon's left-hand side and sat down just as she felt herself passing out. Symon used the knife to fold back Victor's skin and muscle, revealing the dull grey color of an oversized microtransformer underneath. With his free hand, he grabbed the battery, turned it over so the connector was facing down, and jammed it into the hole in Victor's chest. The battery let out a subtle, high-pitched whine, and the lowest of seven indicator lights on the side started blinking. As the whine subsided, so did Victor's convulsing. Symon's knife work was deft. The hole he had cut through Victor's muscles was substantial, but relatively little blood was escaping. Edgar let go of Victor's now-motionless arms and rushed to Nadine's side. He laid her back against his knees and looked her over. Apart from being exhausted, she was unharmed, a trait that at the moment, only she and Sera shared. Everyone else was covered in cuts, scrapes and bullet wounds.

"Are you ok?" he asked her.

"I'll be fine," she said weakly. "Victor?"

Edgar looked over at Symon.

"I think he's going to live, but it'll be a while before we can tell if there was any nerve damage," Symon said. "God damn it! I told him to tell me if he was feeling ill. He shouldn't have been fighting at all if he was that close to burning out. And to have to fight so hard on top of it…"

Edgar could feel the anger swelling in his chest as he looked over at Naren. Nadine and Sera looked at him as well. Symon's gaze remained fixated on Victor.

"I should've known," Symon said, his voice dripping with guilt. "I saw the signs but trusted him to tell me the truth. I should've kept him from fighting."

"Stop Victor? From fighting? Not likely," Naren said.

"I should've…" Symon continued, "I should've seen it coming."

"Hey! Earth to Symon!" Naren raised his voice. "There was nothing you could've done!"

Naren's raised voice jarred Symon back into the present. He looked at Naren. "What happened?" Symon asked. "You usually see these things coming."

"I swear Victor said he felt amazing, and it didn't look like he was lying."

"He's not talking about Victor you fucking moron!" Edgar boomed, taking Naren aback. "You said we were going to deal with one regiment in Monaco, but there were hundreds of thousands of soldiers there waiting for us!"

Naren's face sunk. "I…" his voice stumbled as he choked back tears, "I knew that was going to happen eventually. I just didn't expect it so soon."

Nadine's eyes widened. "Wait, what are you talking about?"

"Those weren't just Monaco soldiers," Naren replied. "The regiment in Monaco wears standard blue peacekeeper uniforms. But almost everyone there was in orange, a color only worn by regiments from New York."

"God damn it!" Nadine cried out as she sat up, got light-headed, and lay back down.

"I don't understand," Edgar said.

"We walked right into a trap," Sera said. "Spidre and his men knew what our next target was and had plenty of time to move the New York battalions to wait for us."

"How could they have known what city we'd choose to attack next?" Edgar asked.

"The same way I did," Nadine said. "They looked at everything that's happened and figured there was only one option. We got too predictable."

"And Spidre got too desperate," Naren said. "Or I guess it's more accurate to say he got desperate earlier than I thought he would."

Edgar started to piece things together in his mind. "Did… Did you want the New York soldiers to come out?"

"That was supposed to signal the start of the next phase of the plan, Edgar," Sera said. "That's why Monaco was our next target. Rebellions breaking out on this side of the Atlantic would've caused Spidre to reorganize the Seoul troops. He would have moved them here to stop discourse from spreading across Europe and into Asia and Africa. The next city we would have attacked would have been New Orleans, so that every city between it and Chicago would've started rebelling too. With cities between Chicago and Halifax already causing Spidre serious trouble, it would've meant every city surrounding New York would've been in a state of war. His hand would've been forced. Spidre would have to bring troops out of New York to intervene."

"But you weren't expecting him to come to Europe to stop us," Edgar stated.

"I don't know," Naren replied.

"What do you mean you don't know!?" Edgar exclaimed.

"I mean that there were a lot of fucking possibilities, and I couldn't account for all of them!" Naren roared before getting light-headed and lying back. Sera scooted over, picked his head up, and placed it on her lap.

"Look," he continued in a much quieter tone, "the thought had crossed my mind that more soldiers than usual would be waiting for us. The thought had even crossed my mind that enough time had passed where troops from New York could've been moved and been well-fortified. But they know what we all look like now, so sending an advanced scout to check was out of the question. Then, we had so much success taking out a single regiment on our own, I figured even if there were double or triple the number of peacekeepers, we wouldn't have a problem. But that wasn't triple. That was far, far more. Then, Victor went down while we were trying to fight our way back out and…"

Naren couldn't finish his thought, he was getting too choked up. Sera brushed the tears from his cheeks. Edgar lowered his head, ashamed for letting his temper get to him. Suddenly, a thought occurred to him, and his head snapped back up.

"Why was it so important to pull troops out of New York?"

Naren sniffled. "What?"

"We've been liberating cities to keep the Seoul forces off our backs, to spread them too thin. Now you're saying the next phase of the plan was to create enough rebellions to get the New York forces involved. Why?"

"So that we could take down the communications tower in Manhattan while the soldiers were deployed elsewhere," Nadine said. "The reason he can communicate instantly around the world is that tower. That thing pumps out the wireless signal the whole world uses. If that were to go down…"

"Spidre would have to scramble to set up some other outdated communication network," Naren continued Nadine's thought. "It could take months, maybe even a year or two. In the meantime, the only way he would have to communicate would be to send someone in a high-speed vehicle. Military communication would be crippled for a critically long time."

"So we destroy the net tower to cut his communication systems. Fucking hell. Is it even possible?" Edgar asked.

"Possible? Yes. But really fucking hard," Naren replied. "Was anyone else paying attention to the uniforms of the New York soldiers?"

"The uniforms?" Nadine asked.

"Specifically, the patches on their uniforms, on the left arm. It indicates what battalion they're with. Queens has two flowers making an X, Bronx has an eagle perched on a shield, Brooklyn has a robed woman, Manhattan has blue, white, and orange bars, and Staten Island has a cityscape in front of mountains. I saw two, the flowers, and the eagle on a shield."

"I'm pretty sure I saw a different one. It was like a green mountain I think?" Symon said.

"I saw that one!" Sera said. "It was a city in front of a huge green mountain."

"That's Staten Island," Naren replied. "Did anyone see a different one?"

Everyone remained silent.

"So it's safe to assume the other two boroughs weren't deployed to Monaco," Naren said. "Meaning if we're going to do this, we'll have to deal with Manhattan and Brooklyn. Brooklyn being the largest battalion of the five."

"That's Captain Byron's battalion," Nadine said. Naren nodded before sinking his head into his hands. As he did so, the local medical staff arrived.

"We don't have to think about this now," Symon said. "We have to heal, and we have to rest."

Naren nodded again.

The medics did their best to patch everyone up where they were but had to put Victor and Naren on stretchers and carry them to the medical facility in the south end of the city. Nadine, Symon, and Edgar managed to summon the strength to follow on foot, while Sera flew over to where they had slept the night before to grab some food. When she arrived at the facility where everyone was being treated, she was surprised to see Nadine waiting outside, across the street from the building.

"What happened?" Sera asked.

"It was way too crowded, they asked me to wait outside," Nadine replied, frustrated.

"Hold on," Sera replied, as she handed some of the food to Nadine and walked into the building. She came out a few minutes later only carrying enough food for herself. She now had the same frustrated look on her face as Nadine, who had taken a seat on the curb in the interim.

"If you aren't injured, you don't belong here? What an asshole!" Sera said.

"Yeah..." was all Nadine said in reply. She wasn't paying attention. Her eyes were focused on the building in front of her.

"Hey! Relax!" Sera shouted to Nadine, snapping her back into reality.

"I know there's a lot of people in there you care about, but worrying isn't going to help anything. You need to focus on you right now," Sera said as she motioned to Nadine's left hand, which was still holding two untouched ears of corn.

Nadine ripped the husks off and started eating. "Thank you," she managed to say in between huge bites. "I don't know what's wrong with me right now."

"What do you mean?" Sera asked.

"Naren was badly injured. I get that. I get why I'm worried about him and Victor," Nadine replied. "But Edgar, he only had a couple of cuts and scrapes."

"That's true," Sera said.

"So why the hell am I worried about him?"

Sera smiled. "Something happened in Halifax, didn't it?"

"A lot happened in Halifax," Nadine said.

Sera could read between the lines, but she still wanted more details.

"You mean, something happened with the fighting or..." Sera asked.

"With the fighting... and maybe... some other F words too..." Nadine replied with a smirk. Sera's smile grew even more.

"But after the fight in Halifax, you said he has some serious injuries, right?" Sera asked.

"He was pretty banged up, yeah," Nadine replied.

"Worse than he is now?" Sera followed up.

"Oh, definitely!" Nadine said.

"So he was worse off then, and still somehow managed to rock your world," Sera said. "If that's true, then why the fuck are you worried about him now?"

Nadine was stunned. "I... Damnit. You're right."

"Of course I'm right." Sera said. "Why do you think I'm not worried about your brother?"

"Oh, for fuck's sake Sera!" Nadine screamed in reply as Sera fell into a fit of uncontrollable laughter.

Inside the building, everyone besides Victor was patched up

as much as they could be. Naren and Edgar sat up against the window-side wall. Symon was sitting with the still-motionless Victor, who was sprawled in the middle of the room. The battery had been removed.

"You think he'll be ok?" Edgar asked.

"I'm baffled by him," Naren replied. "I can't believe he was able to fully charge that thing. Symon said it took him 2 whole days to charge the battery at his hideout, and that one was older, smaller capacity. That amount of power is scary, and I can't imagine it was good for his health. That being said, Victor is one of the toughest people I've ever met. If anyone can recover, it's him."

"Fair enough," Edgar said, as his eyes wandered over to Symon. "And do you think he'll be ok?"

"That's a much more complicated question," Naren replied. "Guilt can be harder to recover from than the most serious of wounds."

Across the room, Symon continued to look down at Victor.

"You're not allowed to die, you hear me? You're too important, god damn it. Dying is not allowed," Symon whispered. "And you have to be ok, too. You're going to be ok, right? Fucking hell, please be ok."

Chapter 30

"Fucking Christ, Symon. For the last time. I am ok!" Victor shouted in frustration as he walked out of the abandoned building they were calling home. He shouted so loudly that he distracted Naren and Nadine, who were talking by the elcycles across the street, and Sera and Edgar, who were sparring at the end of the block.

"This thing took 28 years to fill up the first time, it's not going to overload again in a week!" he said as he tapped on the microtransformer that now lay just under his shirt.

"You said you felt fine last time! And that's not how microtransformers work!" Symon shouted back. Victor sighed.

"Symon, I know you feel guilty or whatever, but you didn't cause this," Victor said. "You saved me. And now I'm all set up to get treated if it ever happens again," he said, tapping on his microtransformer again. "And now we both know what symptoms to look for if I'm in danger of overloading. So, just. Fucking. Relax."

"Fine," Symon replied. "But I think that it's best I stay behind whenever we decide to attack New York. That way I'll be all prepared and ready if I need to help someone."

"Are you serious?""I was thinking the same thing," Naren interrupted as he walked over.

"Does this mean you figured out a plan?" Symon asked.

"Maybe," Naren replied. "I've been talking about it with Nadine all morning and she says I'm fucking nuts. No matter what plan we have, I just don't see all of us walking out of New York unscathed. I'd rather have you all set up and ready to treat injuries. And we're attacking a building this time, avoiding fights. Not much your bullets can do to bring down that tower."

Symon and Victor nodded.

"Today's the first day you can spar all-out, right?" Nadine asked Victor.

"Yes, yes it is," Victor replied, glancing over at Symon. "The area around the microtransformer is all healed.

"Then come at me, I'm sick of going easy on you," Nadine said with a smirk.

Victor smirked back and charged forward as Edgar and Sera ran over to watch. Victor was a flurry of movement, but his blows were far more calculated and organized than when he fought Naren. Still, he could not land a blow on Nadine, her hands and knees getting in the right place to block just in time, every time. As soon as an opportune blow was deflected, her arm or leg would spring towards Victor. Except her blows refused to land either. Victor was just too quick. They continued their back-and-forth dance until Symon couldn't take it anymore and told them to stop. As soon as he did so, they both fell to their backs, gasping for air. To them, it seemed like the fight had lasted an eternity. In reality, it was about three or four minutes.

"Christ," Edgar exclaimed.

"Yeah," Sera agreed. "We need to step up our game."

"I'll go get them something to eat," Symon said.

"If it's all the same to you, I think we should all head inside, get some food, and discuss the plan," Naren said. "Assuming these two can move."

Victor and Nadine held up one arm and their index finger, indicating they still needed a minute. Everyone else went inside and gathered around an electric pot Symon had set up. Victor and Nadine came inside just as their plates were being prepared.

"So that was kind of terrifying," Sera said as she smiled at the two of them. They smiled back.

"Agreed," Naren said. "Victor, your hand-to-hand skills have improved vastly. That's good, 'cause you're going to need them for this plan."

Everyone shifted to face Naren.

"So this goes without saying, but if we take the Net Tower down, that means Spidre's communication network is crippled. But so is ours," Naren began. "The underground net access points in every city around the world use that same signal. They're going to go dark too when we do this, so we'll need to have them spread the word first."

Everyone nodded.

"Okay," Naren took a deep breath. "The Net Tower is the single largest structure ever constructed in Earth's history. Think of the tallest megaskyscraper you've ever seen. The Net Tower is three times that height."

"Holy shit," Edgar exclaimed.

"Yeah, it's big," Naren continued. "It had to be in order to broadcast a net signal worldwide. Given its importance and the incredible amount of resources needed to construct it, the world government made sure it was next to impossible for it to fall or be damaged. Its defense is fourfold. First, they created and organized the New York forces."

"The World Government moved all those troops there? Not Spidre?" Victor asked.

"That's correct," Naren replied. "That's why New York fell so easily when the war started. The troops were already there and struck the areas with high LO-EC populations before they even had a chance to organize."

"But why?" Victor asked. "Who did they have to protect it from?"

Naren shrugged.

Symon put his head in his hand. "You guys really need to learn your world history," he said.

Everyone looked at Symon with a curious expression.

"I think you guys are under the impression that since there were no wars for centuries before the LO-EC insurrection, that there was only peace. That's not true. The net tower was constructed as part of a worldwide cooperative agreement. That agreement emphasized the needs of the world population as a whole. It not only made net access a worldwide capability but made it free. Most people liked that. Some, those who used to make money by providing net access, did not. And an even smaller subset of those people cared so much about money that they were willing to do anything they could to keep making it. Even violent, illegal things. A few people with substantial amounts of money are capable of quite a lot. So it was those kinds of people that the world government intended to defend the Net Tower from by moving so many troops to defend it."

"No wonder Spidre was so hesitant to move the troops out of there!" Nadine said. "The world government couldn't have been as paranoid as him, and yet even they considered the tower important enough to protect so diligently."

"I guess I never thought about it before, but that does make a lot of sense," Naren said. "Fortunately, we don't have to deal with all of the New York forces, just Brooklyn and Manhattan. Brooklyn will need at least ten to fifteen minutes to organize a counteroffensive on the fly, so if we do this right, we won't have to deal with Brooklyn at all. I don't want any of us getting bogged down in a fight, so if you can run, do it. Especially if Byron finds you. A fight with him would not only take a while to win, but he's strong enough that you may not win at all."

"Yeah, so um, what the hell is Byron anyway?" Edgar asked.

"What do you mean?" Naren replied.

"Well his armor is different, but it's red," Edgar said. "That makes him part of Special Ops, right? So why wasn't he with them in Chicago?"

"Astute observation about the armor," Symon said. "Byron did start out as a Special Ops, but comparing the two is like comparing you all to me. Byron has a higher-than-normal body temperature, so he came into the military through the regiment that became Special Ops. But Byron is fucking huge. Because of his size and strength, he was offered the chance to use special prototype weaponry that was too heavy for a normal person to use effectively. He accepted the offer. I imagine that since he is still the only person with that tech, attempts to make the weaponry lighter failed. I also imagine that during the LO-EC war, the weaponry in his hands proved remarkably effective, and he rose through the ranks to the level he's at now."

"So what kind of tech is it?" Sera asked.

"Oh, I'd have no idea what he has now," Symon said. "The Special Ops suits are customizable. There's no way he kept the same loadout for twenty years. Nadine, did you get a chance to see anything when you fought him?"

"I wouldn't call what we did fighting. More like, I ran until he caught up to me," Nadine said. "I remember his voice being loud, like impossibly loud for it not to be assisted by tech. And his arms and feet had some kind of hydraulic piston system in them. He didn't run so much as bound and leap along. And when he caught me, it was because I ducked behind a concrete wall, which he punched through like it was nothing. As he did that, something on his left forearm rotated, and a shotgun barrel popped out and was aimed straight at me. That's when I gave up."

"Well at least one thing is the same, the shotgun is part of a multi-weapon system that he can choose between with the flick of a wrist," Symon replied. "Only one weapon draws power from the suit at a time, so it doesn't overheat the user much more than the normal loadout. It's just super heavy."

"Yeah, so bottom line, if you see Byron, run." Naren said. "Let's not get too far off topic. We still haven't even covered the other three defenses the tower has."

Victor and Edgar's heads sank in frustration.

"Trust me, these are the important ones. If we handle these correctly, we won't have to worry about Byron or his regiment."

Everyone turned their complete concentration to Naren.

"So, the most resilient part of the tower is its core, a silver electromagnet that stretches the whole way up. The electric field it generates is so strong that no explosion we're capable of generating will bring it down, not even Sera at full power."

"Wait, how is that possible?" Victor asked.

"It's an electromagnet," Nadine said. "Doesn't matter how many little fragments we turn the metal core into, the electrical charge flowing through will keep them stuck to each other."

"So doesn't that derail our plan?" Symon asked.

"No, because we can turn the power off," Sera said.

"Exactly," Naren continued. "With that kind of electromagnetic force involved, there had to be an emergency shutoff console should anything go wrong. Unfortunately, that console was put in the most secure location possible: the very top of the tower. Getting to that switch will be crucial, but it's only one step. Turning it off or damaging it would only bring communications down temporarily. We have to bring the whole tower down, and that'll take two more steps."

"The core is surrounded by a shell the entire length up that splays out at the bottom. The shell is a carbon-fiber composite designed to protect the core from whatever the weather might dish out and also protect the surrounding area from the magnetic forces the core produces. I think it's similar to the material used to make the prison transport that Sera was in when we all met. That means she should be able to destroy it."

"Should?" Edgar asked.

"The transport was different," Sera said. "It was a tiny ball that I was inside, so a relatively small explosion was enough to blow it out. The inside of the net tower is way bigger, maybe too big. So I'll be saving up as much energy as I can beforehand and throwing the biggest explosion ever at that sucker."

"So you're going to fly in, turn off the core, then fly down to the bottom and let loose," Edgar said. "So what's our job going to be?"

"Ugh, I wish it were that simple," Nadine said frustrated.

"It's not?" Victor asked.

"Well," Sera continued, "storing up energy isn't as easy as it sounds. It hurts, a lot, and it takes all of my concentration to not just let it go. Even maintaining flight, staying above the action while you guys set up, is going to be difficult. There's no way I'll be able to operate something like a shutoff console, even if it's a simple one."

"Which means that Naren or I will have to fly in, shut off the core, fly out, then have Sera fly in and blow the thing," Nadine said. "Not only is one task dependent on another's success, but they have to be done in order, not all at once. It's an additional layer of complexity we haven't dealt with before, while dealing with the largest group of soldiers we have ever seen. A lot can go wrong. A lot."

Edgar and Symon lowered and shook their heads, Victor had his eyes closed and was massaging his temples.

"Alright. So what is the other step?" Victor asked.

"There are four enormous steel support beams that keep the tower's shell braced against the high winds it has to deal with," Naren said. "They start at the top of the tower and end in various locations on Manhattan Island. They're plenty sturdy, but Edgar's blade, Victor's air bursts, and a blow from Nadine or I will be able to break them."

"You sure about that last one?" Edgar asked.

"I am the least sure about myself, I'll admit that," Naren replied. "But I was able to knock Tank over, and that's no small feat. And, to be frank, we don't have a choice. There are four of us and four support beams. I'll also be the one who shuts off the core. With no obstacles, Victor could get there faster, but he'll be on the ground, dealing with soldiers in his way. I can fly over everything."

"And what about before all of that?" Edgar asked. "How do we get to the island?"

"We'd first make a run to Pittsburgh and help the rebellion the locals already started. That'll throw Spidre's strategists off, make them think we're trying to hold on to the areas that are contentious rather than take on new objectives. In reality, it'll just get us closer to our real target. Once Pittsburgh is secure, we can put you, Sera, Nadine and Victor on the elcycles while I fly. The area around New York is unsupervised, with only a nomadic population living in the abandoned buildings. So we can get up to a few blocks from the shoreline without being spotted. Then I fly Edgar over while Nadine takes Victor, and Sera just stays in the air out of range of everything and watches for her time to strike."

Everyone stayed silent for several seconds.

"Let me reiterate the plan, just in case anyone got lost on the way," Nadine said. "From here, we leave for Pittsburgh, where there is currently an active rebellion. When we arrive, we help drive Spidre's forces out of the city. Hopefully this is successful. More hopefully, none of us get seriously injured in the process. By taking Pittsburgh, we may throw Spidre off our trail, make him think we're refocusing on holding the cities that are on our side. In reality, the move just brings us much closer to New York. During this time, Sera would start saving up power. Symon stays behind in Pittsburgh and prepares for the very likely event that one of us needs medical attention. We leave for New York with Edgar and Sera on one elcycle, so Sera can focus on saving power rather than flying. Victor rides with me on the other bike. Naren flies along and stays low. When we're among the abandoned buildings across the river from Manhattan, we ditch the bikes, I grab Victor and pray we make it over the river. Naren, being the stronger flyer, grabs Edgar. Sera takes off and waits till we finish our plan. I drop Victor off at the closest support beam and then fly to another one further east. Edgar gets dropped off at the southwest beam, Naren continues to the farthest beam. We take out the beams and then fight our way back to shore through Manhattan's battalion and possibly Brooklyn's, while simultaneously hoping we don't run into Byron. When Naren destroys his support beam, he then heads for the base of the main tower, finds a way in, then flies all the way to the top and turns off the core. When Naren exits the tower, that is Sera's cue to fly in and bring the entire tower down with one massive explosion. In the chaos of the tower's collapse, Sera has to recover her bearings, and then all of us make our escape back to Pittsburgh. Did that about sum it up?"

"Yes, although you added a little bit of pessimism that I wouldn't have," Naren replied.

"But she's right," Symon said, "There is a lot that can go wrong with that plan Naren."

"Look," he replied. "I'm not saying this plan is ideal. I'm saying it's inevitable. Spreading rebellion from city to city only goes so far. Spidre can still respond, he can change strategy. Whatever other plan we might conjure up, in the end Spidre still has the upper hand. We need a big move like this one to turn the tide. If we take down the net tower, it will be a blow from which Spidre cannot recover. There is no strategy he and his men can think of to respond to that. Cities could rebel and Spidre would have no way to know. We could launch any attack we want, and he'd be powerless to stop us. This plan is dangerous, but with three boroughs deployed elsewhere, it's possible. And I think we should jump on this opportunity while it remains that way."

Everyone remained silent for a few seconds, digesting what Naren had just said.

"You're right, Naren. You're right," Edgar said, breaking the silence. "Sooner or later, we're going to need to make moves that cause Spidre to lose control on a worldwide scale. No other plan we might think up will do that as effectively as this one.”

Everyone nodded in agreement.

“So when do we leave?” Victor asked.

“Assuming the locals here don’t need anything else, we can leave tonight, and launch our attack in Pittsburgh tomorrow night while it’s still dark,” Sera replied. “In the meantime, I’d better start saving up power.”

Chapter 31

"You don't look so great," Nadine said.

"I'm Ok, I'm ok," Sera replied, almost as if she was saying it to herself rather than answering Nadine. She was sitting straight up on the back of the elcycle. During the ride, she had gotten so hot that she could no longer hold on to Edgar without burning him. Her skin was no longer visible because her glow was so bright, and her silk Kung Fu uniform almost seemed to be smoldering.

"Look, we're only a couple blocks from the Hudson's shoreline," Nadine said. "If you can't focus on flying, then stay here and I'll come back when it's time to—"

"Not enough… not enough time," Sera interrupted as she rose from the cycle and into the air. The second she lifted off, everyone else sprang into action. Nadine and Naren took off and wrapped their arms under Victor and Edgar's shoulders and around their chests. Naren gained altitude while Victor's dangling feet remained mere inches from the ground.

Got to get higher, got to get higher! Nadine thought as they approached the shoreline. As they passed from land to water, they began to lose altitude.

Shit shit shit shit! Can't pull up, can't pull up! "Cooooooome ooooooon!" she shouted as Victor started lifting his legs to avoid hitting the water.

Fuck fuck fuck fuck we aren't going to make it! God damn—wait, what the fuck? Her thought was interrupted by them gaining altitude again. She glanced down and saw that Victor was spinning his legs across the water's surface as if he was running. It looked silly, but it was keeping them aloft.

We must look ridiculous right now, they thought simultaneously.

Hey, I wonder if he….... Nadine thought.

I wonder if I… Victor thought.

Their second simultaneous thought was interrupted by the sound of a siren blaring as they approached Manhattan Island. When they reached land, Victor grabbed the railing along the shoreline and pulled up, sending the two of them high in the air over a swarm of incoming peacekeepers. They coasted downward while dodging gunfire until they reached the first support beam. Nadine dropped Victor from about 70 feet off the ground and 20 feet above the beam. Victor threw shockwaves in rapid succession downward until he landed. He heard the metal beneath him groan and screech until it buckled and split in half. Victor stood atop the piece connected to the ground as it bent over and crushed the dilapidated buildings and streets below. Machine gun fire around him went silent as a dust cloud kicked up. He glanced up through the cloud as it closed above him and saw Nadine cutting through the air towards the second beam. The dust cloud closed before he could see the hit, but a few seconds later it was all he could hear. Nadine hurdled towards the beam, front flipped through the air, and threw the energy in her feet downward with all her might. The metal roared as vibrations flowed through it, with long winding cracks following right behind. The cracks gave way to enormous chunks of metal falling away until the beam was no more.

Nadine had heard Victor's beam fall a few seconds earlier, and so her gaze went south. Naren was just dropping Edgar off at the intact beam to the west. Edgar landed in the middle of his beam and began to slide down backwards. When he gained enough momentum, he released the blade in his left hand and swung it into the side of the beam. His blade sliced down and to the right as he continued to slide. When his left blade came out from the right side, he plunged his right blade into the center of the beam to bring him to a complete stop. He climbed back up the beam to admire his work. It wasn't as flashy as Nadine or Victor, but he had made a cut clean through the entire length of the beam, good enough to compromise its ability to support the tower. He ducked close to the beam to avoid gunfire below and looked towards the last standing beam. Naren was closing in on it fast while Nadine looked to be diverting gunfire about halfway between her beam and Naren's. Naren came in at full speed and tried to do the same front flip and kick move that Nadine had used. His was sloppier, not as well timed. The metal beam groaned but did not break. He flew forward and turned around to try again and as he did so, he saw a huge blaze where Sera used to be, falling out of the sky.

"Shit!" he yelled as he took off at full speed for her, confusing Nadine and Edgar for a moment before they saw the blaze for themselves.

"Shit!" they both yelled together, though out of range of hearing from each other.

Fuck fuck fuck! Nadine thought. *Now I have to go for the beam and the tower. But the Brooklyn forces are going to be here soon and I'm not fast enough to*—Her thought was cut off by the sight of Edgar leaping from his perch on the broken beam towards the unharmed one.

Okay, he takes the beam, I take the tower, she thought as she took off for the tower's base. *I just hope Sera is still in good enough shape to make the final blow.*Naren was going recklessly fast. Faster than he had ever flown before. Fast enough that his eyes burned and his vision went cloudy from the wind in his face. He could still see the blaze in front of him getting bigger as he approached and lower as it fell. He barreled into the center of the blaze and grabbed Sera. His speed snuffed out the flames, but not before they licked at his already burning eyes. Her entire body was now engulfed in glowing light. He had her pulled close, but she was still so hot to the touch that his reflexes pushed her away. He fought them and at the last second wrapped his hands and forearms around her now bare waist. The pain as she fell against them was excruciating, but he refused to let go.

She seemed conscious but her eyes were closed. "Can you hear me?" Naren asked through gritted teeth.

"Yeah..." she replied weakly. "Something broke my concentration… something was on fire."

"It was your clothes, you're that hot right now."

"My uniform is gone?"

"Don't worry about it."

"What is that smell?"

"Don't worry about that, either."

He didn't want to tell her that what she was smelling was the flesh of his hands and arms burning as he supported her.

"Just get your focus back. In the meantime, I'll move us closer to the action." He also didn't want to tell her that his vision was so blurred, all he could make out was the outline of the Net Tower rising above the city.

"Don't you need to do stuff with the tower?" Sera asked.

"Nadine is handling it," he replied. He had no idea if what he said was correct or not. He hoped and prayed that it was.

Nadine flew around the tower from the north and west to avoid the soldiers coming from Brooklyn. When she had come around far enough that the front entrance of the tower was in view, she dove toward it. Machine-gun fire erupted all around her, but she was too quick. The bullets whizzed behind her as she dove. The 15-foot-tall steel doors marking the tower's main entrance came into view and her eyes trained on nothing else. She didn't see the hulking mass of a human being bounding up the street towards the very same entrance. Only when she arrived at the door and swung around to kick it open did she see a massive fist swinging at her from the right. She was still airborne, with all her momentum heading downward. She leaned back at the last second to dodge but the enormous hand still made contact and sent her tumbling down the street. She gained control of her roll and somersaulted backwards onto her feet, where her eyes met the sight of Captain Byron in full sprint towards her and a circle of hundreds of soldiers surrounding them both.

To the southwest, Edgar stayed low and slid down the beam until he was about twenty feet from the ground. He then flipped off the eastern side of the beam and fell to the street, both blades drawn. The second he touched down, he felt a twinge of pain at his hip.

God damn it I'm shot already! he thought. *Ignore it, it's nothing. Focus on the other beam.* He ran forward as fast as he could. The grid pattern of the streets allowed him to see past the buildings and all the way down to his target. He ran forward, slashing through the endless onslaught of peacekeepers in his way. Bullets whizzed past his feet as troops around him fired low to avoid shooting their fellows. His legs proved a difficult target to hit. Edgar wasn't even paying attention to what he was swinging at. If it was in his way, he was cutting it down. He pushed forward for what seemed like an eternity until, about three blocks from the beam, one bullet didn't whiz by. It hit him in the leg, right above the back of his left knee.

Shit. I don't know if I can ignore that one, he thought, as the agony of the wound started to set in.

Chapter 32

For the first time, Naren heard a bullet whiz by and stopped moving forward. They couldn't get any closer without the possibility of getting shot.

"Can you see what's going on yet?" she asked.

"Not really," he said, choking back screams of pain from his hands and arms still wrapped around Sera's waist. "Just... focus on flying."

"You can let go," she said.

Naren tore his arms away with such force that he gave Sera a jolt. Fortunately, she remained aloft.

Even if Naren could see his hands in front of him, he didn't want to. He could tell from the excruciating pain that the skin on his hands and forearms had been melted away. Tears streamed down his face from the pain and from the burns to his eyes.

"Open your eyes, what can you see?" he asked Sera. She obliged and opened them. She was facing northeast and could see the dust cloud Nadine and Victor had kicked up, with a cut forming in it from something moving south. The added stimulation of opening her eyes compromised her ability to think straight.

"I see… Victor," she replied, having briefly forgotten Victor's name. "He's heading towards the, oh…" her thought was interrupted by the sight of Nadine squaring up to fight Byron at the tower's entrance. Attempting at least, and failing, because every time she stopped moving, a barrage of machine-gun fire would open on her. It was the only time they had a decent shot. The soldiers there were smarter than the ones around Edgar. Rather than crowd in around her, they posted up at the intersections around the tower entrance, creating an open area the width of the four-lane street and 100 feet long. Their tactic prevented her from escaping, but Nadine's agility and Byron getting in the way still made shooting her difficult. Byron himself was making sure to stay between Nadine and the tower entrance.

Not good not good not good, she thought to herself as she darted up and down the street to avoid gunfire. *I can't get out and I can't get to the tower. Wait, fuck fuck fuck…*Her dodging and strafing had brought her close to Byron, who threw an overhand punch that just missed her face as she flew over.

*God damn it this sucks! I gotta get Byron out of my way, but these fucking gunners! I need someone to get them off of me—wait… Victor could still come and help if he was able to see what happened to Sera.*Victor barreled through the peacekeepers at the northwest intersection and threw a barrage of shockwaves all around the clearing, sending some soldiers flying and knocking many more off balance.

"End him!" Victor screamed as he threw another airburst at a gunner taking aim while running towards the following target. With the gunners distracted, Nadine landed, and Byron was immediately on top of her. She threw up a block to stop his right hook and felt something snap in her forearm. It hurt, a lot, but she had to ignore it. She jumped away as Byron extended the electric sword in his left arm, just missing her shoulder. Nadine heard a loud click in his armor and Byron started to raise his arm as if to fire. Nadine rushed in and grabbed his arm as he raised it. She turned and flipped the monstrous Captain over her left shoulder, landing him flat on his back. Before he could recover, she twisted his forearm with all her might till she heard metal breaking. This put her right side dangerously close to Byron's fist. She jumped away just as Byron extended the hydraulics on the arm. She didn't get the full brunt of the hit, but it was enough. She could feel it; her ribs were broken. Byron got up and stared Nadine down. Labored metallic clicks could be heard coming out of his left arm. With every click that did nothing, Byron's face became angrier and angrier.

Got the guns, didn't get the hydraulics, she thought as she tried to stand tall despite the pain in her side. Byron retracted his sword into his armor and prepared for a close-up fight.

I'll never have a better chance to get past him, got to do this, she thought as she ran straight at him. Byron threw a left jab, but he was too big and slow. She ducked under and threw a punch of her own to his gut. It felt like punching a brick wall, but she knew it must not have felt pleasant for him either. She knew a knee was coming next, so she threw another punch at him and pushed off as his leg raised. As his leg came down, so did his right arm for another punch. It was well timed, but still too slow. She ducked under and threw two punches to his side. The punch with her right hand made her forearm hurt like hell, but she had to push through. Byron bent back in pain from the hit, and Nadine kicked him in the back of the leg, knocking him down to one knee. He made a desperate swing backwards at her. Nadine ducked under and unleashed a kick with her right leg to the side of Byron's head. He had no time to dodge, no time to block. The kick landed square on the side of his jaw and Byron fell over.

Nadine had no idea how much damage she'd done, she just knew that now was her chance. She took to the air and went for the tower door. As she did so, she heard the groaning of metal coming from the southeast and reverberating all the way up the tower.

Edgar got the last beam! she thought as she slammed through the front doors. Dim red light and the sound of crackling electricity filled the air as she entered the enormous structure. At the center stood the source of the crackling, the core of the tower. It was a huge coil of wires wrapped around various electronics, all the way to the ceiling. Standing at the door, the core of the tower was about twenty feet away. An aluminum staircase and elevator shaft ran up its left side. She didn't need that, though. She flew upwards, staying as close to the outer wall as possible. Flying while inside a building was an uncomfortable, stifling feeling, made worse by the rising temperature as she flew higher. By the time she made it to the top, she was panting from the heat. Even with her abilities as a LO-EC, the temperature was so high and had increased so much that she glistened with sweat. It was a feeling she had never experienced before, and one she wanted to be rid of as soon as possible. She made it to the top and saw the control panel bathed in white light. She flew over and, with frantic motions, started working the controls to shut it down.

Outside, Sera was having trouble of her own. She was hurting, a lot. Her entire body felt like it was on fire, which it was. Besides the pain, she was also feeling more ill than she ever had before. Something inside her wasn't right anymore, and she knew it. From the pain and nausea, her vision kept fading in and out. Even when she saw something, she was having trouble piecing together what it meant. Her thoughts were scattered; nothing made sense. She hadn't even thought about why Naren couldn't see what was going on. But she did see Byron get levelled by Nadine, the one thing she could focus on was that Nadine was inside the tower and needed to get out before this could all be over. She tried focusing on the door again but couldn't. She tried harder and started feeling her consciousness slipping away from her. So she closed her eyes and focused on staying awake and afloat.

It's almost over, almost over, she thought to herself. *Just... ...got to wait for Nadine to leave... but how will I know when she leaves? Oh, yeah, my eyes are closed.*She opened her eyes and looked downward.

*Well there's the door but... how do I know she hasn't left already? How do I know? Oh wait, Byron's there. He's standing by the door, waiting for her, too. If she was gone, he wouldn't be there... I'm missing something... what am I missing... can't think... something about Byron... Byron's waiting... means she's still inside... she's still inside... I have to wait till she leaves...*She felt her consciousness slipping again and closed her eyes.

Too close... got to hold out... Nadine needs me to hold out... wait, Nadine needs me? I need to blow up the tower... but Nadine needs me? She doesn't need me... she's inside the tower... I know that because Byron is waiting outside, for her, but she doesn't know that.......oh fuck... oh fuck..."Oh fuck, she doesn't know!" Sera screamed.

Nadine was hurdling down the side of the deactivated core as fast as her jets and gravity could take her. Between her injuries and the unbelievable heat that had built up inside the tower, she felt like she was on the verge of passing out. She approached the front door. Her eyes had adjusted to the dim lighting inside, so all she could see out the door was brightness. She couldn't see Byron standing there waiting for her, or the fist that he was throwing in her direction. And in her state of mind, she didn't even think of him being there as a possibility. He hit her with a full-strength uppercut. The last noise she heard was the crunching of her own jaw before her back slammed through the top of the doorway. Her mind went blank as she floated fifteen feet above the ground. She was conscious, but couldn't remember what was happening, what she was doing, what she had to do. Through the ringing in her ears, she heard something, another sound. She listened with more intent.

"Nadine, move now!" Sera roared.

The meaning of the words were lost on Nadine, but the scream was so loud that it scared her into flying straight up. Victor heard the scream over the sounds of machine-gun fire and began to run towards the river in the west. Naren heard it and started backing away from the tower. Byron heard it and turned around just in time to see a ball of light mere feet in front of him. His eyes went wide, and he put up his hands to block, but it was far too late. Sera buried her hands in his chest, piercing right through his red armor and pushing him backwards through the door. The last thing she saw was Byron's fear struck face before he slammed back-first into the core, and she unleashed her explosion.

Chapter 33

Naren's eyesight was still compromised, but it didn't need to be sharp to appreciate the magnitude of what was happening. For five blocks in every direction, the ground was reflecting a pale blue light. Silently, the tower started to lean to the east and topple over. Naren was too far away to hear everything immediately, but the rumbling was getting louder. Then the shockwave of the blast reached him, and he was flung through the air while the sounds of a roaring explosion and twisting metal swirled around him. While he was tumbling, he was able to make out something breaking through the skyline a few feet away, and he boosted over to it for cover. He grabbed the structure and fought his body's reflex to let go from the pain of his burns. The structure was the remains of one of the support beams. It was unstable, but able to protect him well enough. He kept his head down until the shockwave had passed. When it had, he looked up and could barely make out that there was someone up there with him.

"You… ok?" a voice said to Naren weakly.

"Edgar?" Naren replied. "How did you get up here?"

"I climbed… had to get away from the gunners…"

Naren's heart raced, something was wrong. "Edgar, are you ok?"

"I've uh… I've been better…" he replied as he slid down to Naren. Naren reached out and grabbed his ankle. Even with his hands so badly burned, he could feel that Edgar's pant leg was soaked through with blood.

"Jesus Christ," Naren said, panicked. He took off and grabbed Edgar, again fighting the pain in his hands, and threw him over his shoulder. He looked out over the rest of the city and saw the tower had toppled eastward and kicked up a massive dust cloud from its base in middle of Manhattan Island all the way to where its top landed, across the East River in Queens.

Shit, finding everyone in that cloud is going to be impossible with my eyesight shot, he thought. *I'd better head back to the cycles, assuming I can even find those, and hope everyone else does the same.*Floating above where the tower had once stood, Nadine looked down at the ruined city below, trying to organize her thoughts. Her jaw was very obviously broken.

*I got… I got hit hard… can't think… fuck I have a concussion… no, I don't I'll be fine. Wait, am I fine? Or is that the concussion talking? Fuck, why did I have to get hit so hard? Wait… why did I get hit? Fuck, what were we doing!? I should know this… damn it, I'm forgetting stuff… I am concussed… can't rely on my memory… can't think either… fuck, what else is there? Oh, yeah, I can still see… got to just rely on my senses… what the fuck?*The dust cloud was spreading farther and farther. As it passed about ten blocks north from where the tower had once stood, Nadine noticed someone struggling to stand, and about to get enveloped.

That can't be a soldier… the soldiers are all farther south and west right now. Wait, why do I know that? Oh wait, that person doesn't have military armor on, anyway. Oh wait, she doesn't have anything on! Fuck, it's amazing I even saw her… her skin is so dark against the street. Oh, wait it's Sera!

Good, I still remember names. Nadine flew down to Sera as the dust cloud rose over her. A few seconds later, they rose from it, Nadine in only her bra and cargo pants and Sera in Nadine's tattered overshirt. Sera's petite frame was much easier for Nadine to carry than Victor's had been. It was a good thing, too, since the second Sera was wrapped in Nadine's arms she passed out.

What on Earth happened that she isn't glowing anymore? Not important, she looks tired. Actually I'm pretty tired too… or is that the concussion talking again? Is being tired a concussion symptom? Not important, she looks tired. Let's find the others and go home. She looked around and saw Naren and Edgar to the south.

I'd better just follow those two, they seem to know where they're going, she thought. *But where are Victor and Symon?* Nadine couldn't find Victor because he was under the cloak of the dust cloud. He had made it to the western shoreline and was waiting to be picked up by someone, but no one had come before the cloud caught up to him.

Ugh. Something's wrong, and I can't see anything in this shit! he thought. He ran north and broke out into open air again. That was when he saw Nadine carrying Sera.

Fuck. Holding all that energy must have really fucked her up, he thought. It was strange seeing Sera, normally unstoppable, now powerless. He looked farther and saw trucks carrying soldiers speeding across an old bridge to the far north of the island.

That option's no good, he thought, and ran back in to the dust cloud. He came out the south side and saw not only Edgar and Naren overhead, but also a steady stream of soldiers loading into trucks and driving to an old tunnel entrance, all less than a block away from him. The commanding officers didn't even bark orders. The second Victor appeared from the cloud, everyone opened fire. Victor ducked back into the dust but felt a twinge of pain in his side. He had been shot, but the dust was so thick he couldn't tell how bad it was.

Fucking fantastic. Now I'm shot and I have no way out of here. Through the dust, he faintly made out the black railing dividing the river and the shoreline, and remembered what happened when Nadine was carrying him.

Above him, Naren had heard the additional machine-gun fire, and could tell it wasn't directed at him.

They have to be firing at one of us. I doubt Sera or Nadine are flying low enough to be in range. That means Victor's pinned down, hiding in the dust cloud. Naren glanced between the dust cloud and Edgar on his shoulder.

Can I find him in there? Hell can I even carry him if I find him? He stared down at the cloud, trying to figure it out and falling short.

Fuck it, I have to try. He repositioned to descend into the dust when a huge tear opened up through its center, big enough for Naren to see. The tear then proceeded past the cloud and continued onto the river's surface.

Holy shit, he's running on water, Naren thought.

Holy shit, I'm running on water! Victor thought. *Holy shit holy shit holy shit! Stay up stay up stay up!* His bullet wound started hurting, a lot, and was only getting worse with every lightning-fast step he took.

Got to ignore the pain. Fucking ignore it! Just! Stay! Up! He made it to the western shore of the Hudson and reached up to grab the retaining wall over his head with both hands. That hurt even more than the running. He swung himself up over the wall and struggled to his feet. He felt awful. The entire left side of his abdomen pulsed with pain, and he felt nauseated and dizzy. Finally, he looked down at his wound for the first time.

Seriously? That's what's making me feel this shitty? The wound itself was a tiny hole, about five inches to the left of his belly button. It wasn't bleeding much, but with the way he was feeling, he didn't want to think about the damage the bullet was causing inside him.

He saw Naren and Edgar fly overhead and Nadine and Sera to the east.

Are... are Edgar and Sera... He rushed over to where the cycles were parked and saw Naren pass right overhead. *What the fuck?*

"Naren!" he screamed, as loudly as he could in his weakened state. It was a good thing he did, because Naren couldn't see the cycles, and Nadine was following Naren, not remembering where the cycles were. Naren landed first.

"You get lost?" Victor asked.

"I can't see," Naren replied.

"Edgar's ok?"

"He's alive. I don't think he's Ok."

Edgar was now unconscious. Nadine landed, and upon seeing him went to speak, but her jaw was so swollen and in so much pain that she couldn't get it out.

"Relax, he's alive," Victor said to Nadine. "What about her?"

Nadine nodded her head, which Naren couldn't see.

"Why aren't you answering, Nadine!?" he screamed, fearing the worst.

"Stop fucking yelling! Her jaw is broken! Sera is alive!" Victor screamed back.

Nadine had a confused look on her face. "He can't see," Victor replied.

"Are you hurt?" Naren asked.

"I'm shot in the stomach, and it hurts like hell, but we have to move. They're coming from either side of us."

"Shit," Naren said as he thought of what to do. "Can you drive an elcycle?"

"Do we have much of a choice?"

"I guess not. Help me get Edgar on the cycle and get his hand lined up with the transformer."

They both grabbed Edgar under his shoulders and, with Victor's guidance, they hoisted him onto the cycle. The second they put his hand on the handlebar the engine revved to life.

Naren breathed a sigh of relief. "I wasn't sure if that would work. Is Nadine ready to go?"

"She's, uhh, she's just standing there with Sera on her shoulder, staring at the cycle." Victor replied. "Hey! We've got to move!" he shouted to Nadine.

Nadine looked up at him with a dazed expression on her face.

"Something's not right," he said to Naren.

Naren realized what happened. "You said her jaw is broken. Fucking hell, she's concussed.

Naren walked over to where he could vaguely make out Nadine's outline.

"Listen carefully. Put Sera on the cycle."

Nadine did as she was asked.

"Good. Now sit down behind her. Then reach around and grab the handlebars."

Nadine followed her instructions, and the engine revved up.

"Now, keep your eyes on Victor. When his cycle starts moving, twist the handlebar and follow him wherever he goes."

Nadine nodded.

Naren turned to Victor's vague outline.

"You heard that? You're going to have to take lead. I'll follow close so I don't get lost."

As soon as Naren finished talking, the sound of military trucks rang through the air. They were closing in fast.

"That's fine, let's just fucking go!" Victor yelled as he took off. The autonav did most of the work and kept him in line. Nadine took off right behind him, with Naren right behind her. As they made their way away from the city, the sounds of the military trucks faded but never disappeared and were only interrupted by the sounds of machine-gun fire. The soldiers in New York now had nothing to defend and were all trying to take down the five LO-ECs instead. Victor and Nadine fought to keep conscious the entire ride, while Naren fought sheer fatigue. The constant pain in his hands and eyes was exhausting, and he had been flying nonstop for the entire day. The two hours it took to make it back to Pittsburgh felt like an eternity. The roads that had crossed the old railroad tracks at the northern border of the liberated area had all been obliterated, so they had to spend an additional ten exhausting minutes circling around to cross the Ohio River. They made it to Heinz Field, a dilapidated old stadium they had called home the night before, and collapsed at the entrance. Symon and a dozen other people ran out and laid the five of them on their backs.

"There's no way they made it back here alone. Someone tell the defenses to get ready!" Symon yelled, "and so help me they had better hold that line!"

Everyone was put on stretchers and taken inside, where the locals had a medical facility set up. Symon saw Naren was the only one who was conscious and ran alongside him.

"You think the line will hold?" Naren asked weakly.

"I think you don't have to worry about that right now, but yes, they'll hold," Symon said.

"That's… a relief," Naren replied.

"So, did you do it?" Symon asked.

Naren smiled. "Yeah. We fucking did it."

Chapter 34

All at once, the haze in Edgar's head cleared and his vision came back into focus. The last he remembered, he'd been struggling to pull himself up the side of a metal beam in New York. Now, he found himself on a bed in a long concrete room. Victor was sitting up in bed directly across from him. To Victor's left was another bed, where Sera was lying down, Naren standing at her side. Nadine was sat on the edge of Edgar's bed and seemed to be dozing off.

"Christ, how long was I out?" Edgar asked.

"Holy shit, you're finally up!" Victor yelled as Nadine swung around and buried her head in Edgar's shoulder.

"Finally!" Sera exclaimed.

"We made it to Pittsburgh?" Edgar asked.

"Yes, like six days ago," Victor replied. "You've been in and out of consciousness the whole time, but now was the first time you talked clearly."

"I was out for six days?" Edgar exclaimed.

"You lost a lot of blood. The peacekeepers in New York got a good shot to the back of your leg," Naren said.

"Are we all injured?" Edgar asked as he looked down at Nadine.

She looked up at him but didn't say anything.

"Nadine can't talk, her jaw is all messed up," Naren said. "She also has four broken ribs, a fractured ulna, and is recovering from a high-grade concussion."

"Holy shit," Edgar replied, looking down at Nadine in amazement. Nadine simply nodded.

"Honestly, now that you're awake you're probably in the best shape of all of us," Sera said. "I practically cooked my insides holding all that energy in. Symon and the doctors here in Pittsburgh can't even guess how long it will take to recover. I can get out of bed to go let off my blasts, and that's it."

"Holy shit!" Edgar said even more loudly than the first time.

"I got shot in the stomach," Victor said. "My insides have to heal, too, but nothing like what Sera has going on."

"All things considered I got off easy," Naren said. "My arms were burned pretty badly, and my eyes got scorched a little too. But I'm hoping to get back out there soon. The peacekeepers keep trying to break the defenses and…"

"You aren't setting foot anywhere near a battlefield!" Symon exclaimed as he walked in the room.

"Glad you're awake, Edgar. How do you feel?" Symon asked.

"Terrible," Edgar replied.

"Good. One less person I have to worry about corralling." "Look," he continued. "Nadine, Naren, you can walk around because there is no risk of you bleeding out. That's it, that's the only reason you're allowed up and Edgar, Victor, and Sera are not. You still have a lot of recovering to get through. This fight is not up to you, now. Let the locals handle it."

"But today we were extra worried, what with the artillery and the attacks from both sides and…" Sera said.

"It was a new challenge, but nothing these guys can't handle," Symon interrupted. "You might hate to hear this, but your part of this fight is over, at least for now. You did it. Let me say that again. You. Did. It. The net tower is destroyed. Spidre's army is a mess. More cities are rebelling. All you need to focus on right now is getting healthy and planning the next step."

"Did you say more cities are rebelling?" Edgar asked.

"They are!" Symon replied.

"How do we know that?" Edgar said. "We found some way to communicate with the outside world?"

"In a way," Sera replied. "The locals were able to strip the armor off some stolen military vehicles, so they are much faster now. They sent scouting parties in those lighter vehicles south and west five days ago, to find out what was happening in other cities. They just came back today, and apparently there are new rebellions springing up all over the place!"

After that, there was silence for a few moments. Finally, Naren broke it.

"You're right, Symon. As much as I hate to admit it, we've really done all we can," he said.

"So that's it? Are we retired?" Victor asked.

"Let me clarify, we've done all we can for now," Naren said. "We rest, we recover, we let the rebellion spread. Then, when we're healthy, we do what we need to so the rebellion doesn't stop. And then, when the time is right, we bring our fight to Spidre's front door."